The Ark

JONATHAN LOVEJOY

Armageddon Publishing
All rights reserved.

Cover: *The Little Knitter*, 1875
by William Adolphe Bouguereau (1825-1905)

ISBN-10: 0692316647
ISBN-13: 978-0692316641

For every Nela

And the Lord said, I will destroy man whom I have created from the face of the earth; both man, and beast, and the creeping thing, and the fowls of the air; for it repenteth me that I have made them.

Genesis 6:7

Part One

*I*t's a big boat. Bigger than any I've ever seen. The biggest anybody's ever seen, I'll bet. It's taller than the trees.

I guess I can understand why they think Ham's father is crazy, at least, from what I remember. He's been building that… that *thing* since before I was born. They say he's been building it for a hundred years. We all just took it for granted that he and Sara were out of their minds. And we just accepted that this giant boat would be something for us to look at and wonder about. All that time and money and sweat. For nothing.

Mother told me I was crazy for marrying one of their sons, but you can't help who you fall in love with. Ham is silly but I love him. He looks at other women but I love him. He's as good hearted as his brothers, but I

think if it weren't for this family project he would've gotten himself killed by now. That group of boys he hangs around with. The things they've done. They fight. They steal. I know one of them raped my sister but Ham won't do anything about it. If he would just ask around. I know somebody would tell him. They're so scared to death of him they would tell.

They all know about his crazy father. It seems like everybody in the world knows. They think Ham is crazy too. But they don't know him like I do. Mother doesn't know him like I do.

I haven't seen the sun in six weeks. It feels like its never coming out again. Its gray all the time now; it feels like twilight even in the afternoon.

Last night I told Mother I believed Noah. The air is heavy. Sometimes I think it's hard to breathe. Momma said *Nela, I told you not to marry into that family, didn't I? I begged you not to. Now I've got to listen to you talk about that damned flood every time a cloud comes up.*

Not clouds like these, I said. *They cover the whole sky. Have you ever seen clouds this dark? Momma I want you and Nora to come into the Ark with us. I've got a bad feeling about things. Noah said that God is angry. He's going to destroy everybody… everything that doesn't—*

You believe that garbage? Do you? That stupid, idiotic story about a flood that's going to kill everybody in the whole world? Who does Noah think he is? Who is he to say what God is saying? What God is thinking? Who or what is this GOD that Noah's always talking about anyway? Sara thinks he's out of his mind too, you know.

No she doesn't.

I talked to Sara myself about two months back. Around the time your sister was raped. I know it was everything she could do to keep from

breaking down right in front of me. That poor woman. Between that 'ark'
and that wild son of hers I don't know why she hasn't cut her own throat.

I don't know if she heard herself call it that or not. She'd always called it a boat. Or a ship. A *thing.* I hear them all say that word more now. But they don't understand. The same way I don't understand how they still don't believe. Will that change after today? For me, it's not the rumbling noise from the ground, nor the thunder and lightning that's started in the clouds already. As I stand far away from the Ark, and look at the line of animals I've never seen before, walking so calmly in two by two, I know that there is a God, and that my fear is as dark and heavy as these clouds, and stretches as far and wide as this line of animals I see across Creation.

The air smells strongly of dust. The wind dances between warm and cold on my face. It blows a breath of warning.

The trees are burdened with a message I can hear but I cannot understand. They whish and swish around day and night. The chorus of leaves is loud and constant in the breeze.

I stand up from where I sit, all alone, so I can get a look at what I hear. But the wind is invisible on the prairie; there is only the sound of it rising over the grasses, past the people that have begun to gather, and over every strange animal none of us thought we could ever live to see. The birds flying are painted every color I have known, some the color of blood and roses, some the color of lemon fruit. I've seen little grass colored things fly by, some from a far off distance to join the lines and groups overhead. They are called upon, so many the color of the brown earth itself, even a few the color of the cloth I wear, which is the same as the sky used to be. Every

kind and color of bird I have imagined in my dreams, and so many more I have not. The ones I cannot get out of my mind were gold with long necks, and their flight was graceful in this rising wind, and their voices were a honking trumpet like the lowly geese in my mother's yard, but with so much more authority. But how can they possibly be swans, when they are the color of the Sun, when she bids goodbye to another day, and her draperies are caressed in amber? They would be the emperor among swans, if it be so, for their beauty is unparalleled in the light of day.

How is it that these all know, the tiny creatures of the air, how do they know to fly to the Great Ship, and land somewhere on the deck where no man will sail? Then they fly into the open windows—I assume into the place Noah calls an aviary, where I can only imagine what noise grows every hour. I suppose I should go and help. But help do what? The animals move as though they are trained, even going to cages chosen for others, making us understand that it was their space, their new home, preordained from the beginning of time. Noah says that *in the beginning, God created the Heavens and the Earth,* and everything great and small in between.

3

The cool breeze blows warm over the summer prairie, then it turns cool upon my skin. What tiny whirlwinds and currents flow invisible in the wind? I stand up again, alerted by the flashes of light in the clouds; sparks of anger from the pent up Wrath of God. These sparks are hidden from me now, made known by the clouds alone. The Voice of Doom rumbles from behind the cloud veil, but softly, to give solace to the fools and the complacent. I stand up in the warming wind, in the cooling breeze, moved to begin my final walk from down this hill, nearby my favorite grove of trees.

I fear that the grasses and the flowers bow and swirl to a new feeling in the air, one that makes me stop in my tracks and wonder where the warming breeze has gone. The wind is suddenly one color around me, which raises goose pimples on my skin. The air is suddenly cool, though it is the heart of the warmest season. Do the animals feel this cooling breeze, does it hold their voices at bay?

I walk away from the forest grove atop the hill, suddenly stopped again by the loudest whishing through the trees I have ever heard. This place I have known for a year, my refuge from the insanity below, is suddenly cold and uninviting in this daytime dark, and I feel a turning in the world I can see, as though every leaf and every blade of grass trembles and waves in silent screaming, unable to move beyond its appointed place in nature. The white daisies and yellow lilies bloom with foreboding, waving wildly in the cooling summer wind. This breeze is so strong that I feel as though I might be lifted off my feet. I hurry forward, to bypass that crowd that has grown this entire week during the carnival of the animals, during their march to the beat of a drum.

By what mark doth he judge the lowly animal? What evil hath they done! Do they have to pay for the blood they have shed to eat, for their days of sloth and gluttony for survival, for their lives of leisure flight above the trees? What sins have they born, when they do what it is that God hath made them for? This is no longer just Noah's God I ponder for. As I walk towards the crowd of mocking onlookers, I am comforted by what I feel, that Noah's God *is* God.

Would that my mother had allowed this into her heart. Has she been more evil than any other? What of the times when Nora and I had our flesh stripped bare, and our breasts were striped to blood? It is the circle of discipline, transgression and reward. The reward for those transgressions is

punishment, from this comes renewal of nature. Is my mother more evil than most, because she must have her pleasure, that she must derive pleasure from our flesh? It has always been natural to me, when Nora and me are naked in her bed chamber. What abomination is it, truly when she stands behind me close, breathing so hard in my ear? Don't other mothers and daughters share this secret, which begins with a kiss, and ends with a fervent scream? *Hold on to me tight, Nora* she says, while I push her melon sized breasts up with both hands and let them drop back into place, done for so long as to cause her to writhe and shake between us both (my sister and me).

Are these the evils that Noah speaks of, when he says that God is angry? Is he angry with my mother, for having taken our chastity in youth? For nursing at our young breasts, even before they were fully grown? For teaching us how to suckle at her nipples, both my sister and I at the same time? I wonder if her hypocrisy is the same stench in God's nostrils as her corruption—her self-righteous indignation at the rape of Nora, when she herself had already done so? Was it merely the jealousy of possession, that comes when one's territory is breached, and when sold ownership is compromised? I am afraid for her, when I think that though she screams in white anger at such perversity, she screams the anger of blue and black fire in secret.

My mother, whom I so fear and admire, who raised us alone when our father was dead. My mother, who once threw stones at a woman who was only accused of having another man's husband. So bitterly and angrily threw stones at the woman's head. She made me help her rape my sister Nora with a long and smooth stone, when my sister's breasts had begun to grow.

Mother! Where have you gone! Are you less, or more evil than these! These men and women, some of who stink of wine and perfume. I brush past them unafraid, as used to their groping hands now as a tavern girl, perhaps disgusted at them, cursing the smell of them in my nostrils and the noise of their awe and laughter in my ears. Aram, my mother's neighbor, and his wife Bual. The both of them catch my eye. They've always been friendly to Mother, Nora and me. But Bual tucks in her lips, pudgy cheeked, kind faced. Raising her eyes, looking at me in pity while suppressing a laugh she feels I deserve. Aram is too curious to be cruel. Arms crossed, stroking a beard half gray with wisdom. Looking at me with the same awestruck pity laced with laughter. He looks at the small behemoths walking in, with their long necks and tails, so much smaller than they will be a year from now. He joins the others in their fascination—at the great white cats, but these without the long curved sword teeth, coated snow white with thin stripes as black as oil. They have no equal among the cats, even more so than the lions I saw, that walked so calmly to their cages. Every animal known for killing, every claw beast, every razor toothed, bloodthirsty monster is as meek as a lamb, even to fearful uncertainty in their eyes. Even the great dragon, with their huge heads and mouths full of knives, to match the razor claws at their two giant birdlike feet. I have heard of the great dragon hunts, the warriors commissioned as dragon slayers, called to hunt those poor beasts to the ends of the earth. But these surely can cause no trepidation, only fascination, as I touch the rough skin of the juvenile beside me while I walk across the bridge over the stream near the Ark.

I hear a beautiful, whorish woman yell once, standing in this stream, water halfway up her shins. She raises her garment high up her legs and screams *Noah, it's too big!* It gives everyone present an excuse to more

thunderous laughter. Even after a gentle rain, the stream is still barely high enough to touch the knees, but too much of an inconvenience to walk across. The water is good to drink, and is cool to wade in. The fish are easy to catch.

I asked Noah once, *Why did you build this ship by a stream?* He said— *to keep us at a distance.*

I'm sick of the smell of tar. It's in my hair. My clothes. My dreams. I can't seem to get away from it anymore. No matter how far I walk away from the ship, the smell of animals, straw and wood tar dominates every other breath I breathe. It is the spirit of the journey, I know, because there are times when I will bury my face in my blue dress cloth, and will smell nothing but the clean scented cloth itself. It seems that I am being mocked. Haunted by premonition of what is to come. But more often than not, the sights and sounds alone are just memories or fears, while the smells are as real as the hair and clothes they are trapped in. Sometimes, I do smell like the bowels of that ship, even when I am many miles away.

"You stink," mother says with a heavy frown, her nose wrinkled in disgust. *"You smell like a flock of sheep. Your hair is a mess. You don't do your eyes and lips anymore."* Mother is as tall as most men. Her skin is pure and silky smooth, like creme. Her beauty is unmatched. As is the lust that burns inside her. As I watch her bury her strong hands into the bread dough, it reminds me of my own hands buried into her giant breasts standing in front of her, while my sister Nora will hold her tight from behind. When I once asked her if what we did was alright, she said, *what we do is our own business and nobody else's. Two of my friends have told me they do the same things with their own daughters. And a couple more that are denying it even when they tell me how they punish their girls…*

"In this house we don't pretend. Do we Nora?" she says to my sister, who is at the fireplace cutting carrots into the lamb stew. My beautiful sister looks at me and clamps her white, perfect teeth onto the big end of the biggest carrot, then I watch her slide pretty lips down upon it in a sucking motion, still gazing at me, pulling the carrot out of her mouth in a loud kiss, her and mother both bursting out in a laugh, watching me squirm at the table. It is the inside joke they live to torment me with since I got married, Nora having told me already that it is among her favorite things to do, to have the large end of the carrot in motion while Mother lays on her back, one end of the carrot in Mother, and the other end in her own mouth, holding it with her teeth and lips, pushing it in and out slowly, sucking on it, then faster in and out holding it with her hand until Mother squirts water in her face and shakes and screams loud just once, then twists back and forth straining not to scream again, her breast wobbling like two mounds of bread dough. I watch her squeezing the dough with rough, strong hands, her cleavage spilled out in her white blouse open at the top,

her breasts too large for modesty to have any power over them without effort. I am mesmerized by them now, as I have always been, watching the cleavage push bigger and smaller, longer and shorter, shallower and deeper as she kneads the bread dough with both hands.

Oh, how the men have tried! Oh, how they have cried, since the hour when my father died! Adina, Nora and myself, these three, with every man in the village in grieving to provide! But the woman's libido, Dear Sirs, is too deep and wide—her cleavage is too great for any man's wing-a-ling to hide!

A man can't do a damned thing for me anymore, she says. *The touch of a man's cock anywhere near me makes me sick to my stomach.* And this I know is true, when I have watched her and Nora together in our bed chamber. The animal lust they display in roughness and biting, the way Nora holds my mother's hips while standing in back of her, slamming into her without mercy. Two beautiful women, having no more use for what a man can give, turning their lust and love upon one another in secret, their mother-daughter dynamic spilling outward when they are in public, until there is talk of their inseparability, and there is no pretense of it whatsoever. Mother and Nora are known for their beauty, which is their calling, I think, both of them being aware that they were born to be looked at—two tall, strong, bosomy women, much more so than me. And they are the only two that I've seen who are so unafraid to show cleavage in public, Nora's favorite thing being to wear her red or blue scarf about her head and shoulders, tossed back to reveal her big cleavage even to the children out and about. She's been called a whore more times than a few, always by other jealous women, whom I have seen pulling at their husbands, sons and daughters alike when we walk by.

Nora is the likeness of mother. And not just in what others can see—Nora inherited what has got to be one of the biggest female members (she calls it her lady cock) of any woman, anywhere in this whole wide world. Mother's is a least a finger long, yes, and I have felt it penetrate the back of me when we have been alone, first when I was 13 years old. But Nora's can grow to twice the size, which excites my mother from here to beyond the stars, as she has relished many times over the years the feel of it in her mouth, or between her fingers, allowing her spit to fall upon it in abundance. I have watched her on her knees on the floor with her own big breasts pushed together, while Nora stands up in front of her, pushing herself hard against the breasts, as though she is having powerful intercourse with them. And this, I know she is capable of, being two fingers long when she is excited. I have watched her holding up mother's great breasts, her lady member pressed between them, my mother's eyes wide open and staring down, both fascinated and famished for what she sees, looking her daughter up and down with awe and amazement, watching the dreams of her deepest inner self manifest, as her grown daughter of marrying age, both beautiful and smart—watching her channel every inner passion back to her with fire, flames tinted black and blue. Then I watch Nora's body tense and begin to bend forward, where her pumping motion stops, and her body begins to shake violently, while her face is twisted in the agony of it. But the screams I usually hear are dominated by Mother's voice, whimpering and hollering as though the energy is pouring through herself, which oftentimes it most certainly is. It is one of Mother's many talents in secret, that from this wild slamming of her daughter's member between her breasts, the sight of it, the feel of it

stimulates her mind to apocalypse, which then devastates her body to cataclysm.

I have been witness to what is surely unique among mothers and daughters in these last days (latter days, Noah calls them), for how many mothers burn this way for their own daughters? How many daughters share this same fire of forbidden passion for their mothers? And among them that do, how many of them are born with natural parts that grow so big from within, so that they can mount one another with the skill and prowess of a man? For my mother, I think, Nora's raping was a godsend, because it allowed her to complete the foundations of what was already built—that the world beyond these walls is a cold, dark place, filled with evil souls that cannot be trusted, and no man can possibly love Nora the way that her mother can. *Swear off men forever,* her mother had said, standing behind her, both of them fully clothed, Mother's arms tightly round her from behind, whispering loudly in her ear...

Men are weak, she says. *They are disgusting. They have the brains that God gave a mule. They're too stupid to do anything but be led around by their big, ugly cocks—spreading disease and bastard babies, bringing curses down on the lives of every woman they touch. When your worthless father died, I swore I would die before I'd ever let another one of these stupid apes lay a finger on me. I swore I would strap myself to the bottom of a mule before I would touch another man's body. And I've never felt happier, I have never been more free. And now, my dearest Nora, I need to pass this freedom down to you, I need to hear you swear it to me like you mean it...swear it to every god in heaven, swear it to every devil in hell...I need to hear you swear it...*

I swear.

Mother takes Nora by the neck, which seems to squeeze the first tear from Nora's eyes, and from Mother's, though I don't believe she is aware that she is crying. *I need to hear you <u>swear</u> it!* she says with absolute force, still holding Nora's neck, who says *I swear* loudly through tears and the choking at her throat. Mother releases her neck, holding Nora's arms again at the waist. *Swear it to me!* Mother screams. Nora obliges, screaming it with a deep, angry woman's scream, bent over slightly while mother stands behind her, her own head thrown back, her eyes closed, her mouth open in a tortured scream of inner pain and suffering.

I remember that day, soon after Nora was raped, when the two of them swore an undying oath to one another, that come Hell or high water, they would burn and drown before they would separate, or ever consider the stench of a man in their nostrils, or feel his rough, hairy touch on their skin.

A flash of lightning transports me back to the present day, where I sit at the table watching my mother's hands in the dough, my sister stepping up behind her, hugging her around the waist, causing the mountain sized breasts to push forward more than ever. Mother leans back and accepts Nora's lips on her tongue, fully distracted by what it does to her body, which I can clearly see from the raised nipples at the front of the low cut white blouse (the word *"blouse"* keeps coming to my mind but what is that?) A low, booming rumble rolls freely from the clouds, cascading upon itself tenfold, vibrating the air around us, filling the countryside with a warning that only I can hear. As though inspired by the voice of

impending rain, where their bed screams will soon be buried by the storm, they reverse tongues smoothly, with Nora pushing her tongue deep into her mother's mouth. Mother's reaction, that anguish on her face, the brief twitching in her body, is enough to make me wonder if Nora is going to rip my mother's blouse from her body and devour her breasts right in front of me. Would it be the first time? No. It would not.

I think its time, Nora says. Prompting an inquisitive look from Mother. *The bread,* she says, sliding her hand down to Mother's. *Check the stew,* she orders our Mother quietly, as another, softer voice of rumbling fills the air around us.

"What are you doing here anyway," Nora says, shaping the bread for baking. "If you really believed what Noah says, you wouldn't be here."

"I'm here *because* I believe. I had to beg Noah to let me try one more time. I couldn't just stand by and let you two die without trying to help."

A bright flash of lightning. Nora is forced to look at the open window, trying to see what manner of thing makes the sound that blasts into the world thereafter. The three of us are held enraptured by the sudden, rising wind, and the daytime darkness that deepens around us.

"Mother," I say, "Nora. What harm can it do? Even if Noah *is* crazy it won't matter if you two at least come in with us until this storm passes. This is the worst storm I've ever seen, the worst storm I've ever felt. And I know you two can feel it too—there's something in the air, Mother. Something's happening that the world has never seen before. Can't you feel it? What about those two long-necked animals that walked through here a few days ago. Remember that? Where did they come from? Why are those animals all going to the Ark? I begged you to come and watch it happening—so many birds—so many beautiful birds nobody's ever seen

before. Birds of all sizes and colors. The saber-tooths and the dragons were walking in beside cows and chickens. Wolves and lions came in with sheep and deer. And the two goats that turned up missing from our own backyard, where do you think they went?"

"You took those goats to that ark to try and scare us into going with you," Mother says, walking menacingly toward me. "And you've been lying about it ever since—"

"I wasn't lying, Mother, I swear I wasn't. They walked all the way to the Ark by themselves. I swear I didn't take 'em."

"Witches," Nora says, sliding the iron griddle into the small oven. "Warlocks and witches, the whole lot of 'em. I'll bet that ark is some kind of a temple, where they'll worship devils and be given the power to do all kinds of things like cause storms and call strange animals to come from all over the world. How long before you're all sacrificing those animals to Noah's evil god? Does Sara make you and the other wives strip naked before you cut a dove's throat and squeeze the blood into a cup?"

As I open my mouth, appalled by my sister's audacity, the winds of what I know flick the fires of warmth, when my husband opens the door unannounced.

"I thought I told you *never* to come in my house," Mother says, taking the iron fireplace poker into her hand. As it is with my mother, the satisfaction of hatred in my sister's eyes is uncompromising.

"Its time to go, Nela," Ham says.

"You're not taking my daughter into that thing. Get out of my house or I swear I'll bash your skull in!"

But uncharacteristic of the man we once knew, Ham's features are burdened by humility.

"Nela."

I stand up to go over to my husband. Resigned to take his hand, and leave my mother's house for the last time.

"Don't you move," Mother says. Pointing the iron rod in my direction. "You wouldn't have come here if you didn't want me to rescue you from this crazy son of a bitch."

"Ham, you're a pig's ass," Nora says.

"You stand right there," Mother says to me. "I should have done this a year ago. Right after you married this rapist."

"Adina, I told you I didn't rape your daughter."

"But you stood by and watched while four of your disgusting friends took turns raping me!" Nora says. "And you didn't do a *damned* thing to try and stop it."

"Nora, if I hadn't been there. If I hadn't been there they would have killed you."

"And you think that makes it *right?"* Mother says. "The way those animals listen to you. You could have stopped them!"

It is the resurrection of an old phantom. A screaming conversation that lived and died a hundred times already. Brought back to life every so often, by the hatred my mother had always felt for Ham, even before his friends became a rape gang, and made my sister their first victim.

A blinding flash of lightning. A deafening crash of thunder.

"Mother. I have to go."

I watch vulnerability touch my mother's expression. Briefly.

"Even after what his pig friends did? What kind of a man is he, Nela, that he stood by and watched while they raped your sister?"

As I open my mouth to speak, another blinding flash of lightning awakens the thunder, causing me to flinch. Without another word, I walk towards where my husband stands at the open door. Taking his hand.

"You're choosing a man…over your mother?"

I can only look at my mother and sister in pleading. A quiet cry for forgiveness. The fear in my heart is two fold; that of the storm beginning to rage outside, and the one I am witnessing in my mother's heated expression.

"Nela you get over here or I swear you are *dead* to me."

Lips parted to speak. Lightning. Thunder.

As though activated by the blast of thunder from the clouds, my mother runs at me with the fireplace iron raised, her eyes focused at the top of my head covered in the scarf the color of bluebirds. In a noisy, slow motion haze, I see Ham grab my mother's arm as she brings the iron down toward me, my mother grabbing at my scarf and my hair with her other hand.

Somewhere in the chaos, I see Nora's teeth bared like an angry saber tooth, attacking my husband, hitting his face, pulling at his arms while he holds my mother away from me. The fire in my scalp burns this last departure, as my husband struggles to free my scarf and tangle of hair from my mother's iron grip. Their voices fade from lucid sound in my brain, blending with the unearthly sound and daytime darkness in the clouds. Sacrificing himself to the rainfall of hits and punches from Nora, Ham squeezes my mother's wrists to agony, causing her to scream in a rage, loosening her grip just enough, allowing us to break free.

As we stumble beyond the threshold, into the open space of a rising wind, my husband endures a glancing blow off the side of his hand and onto his shoulder, protecting me from what was surely meant for the top of my head. Mother swings a second time, hard onto the top of my husband's

back, measured by the rhythm of my sister's voice saying *kill 'im...kill 'im...* On the third blow, Ham and I are struck once by terror, and the need to run as fast as we can.

Lifted, carried along by the stormy breeze, the two of us run from the jaws of the angry saber tooth, the jaws of wickedness and hatred in battle, braving the sight of the fire iron in the periphery, flown past us with remarkable speed—clanging a dull, metallic thud to the hard and dusty streets of this town, of this bygone place of our future memory.

Carried along these winds of change are the voices I hear—the screaming voices of desperation in rage and inner frustrations too deep to know, screamed in the words "...*you come back here with my daughter you fucking bastard. Nela!*" and "...*she should have hit you on the top of your head and killed you like the filthy pig you are Ham! Ham I hope you die screaming!*"

These voices are a part of the wind around us, forming themselves into icy wraiths of warning, reaching through our garments to our backs, touching our skins with the lightning flashes, gripping our hearts with the thunder.

*N*oah's hair glows silver white. I can see it already from this great distance, in such bright contrast to the dark blue of his clothing, and the wood of the Ark behind him. I had expected to see the usual crowd gathered at the banks of the fishing stream, but remembering that the foolishness of Noah's Ark would have to wait for another day, while people returned to their lives in villages for miles around, while they waited for this terrible storm to pass. And though these blasts of thunder and lightning are clearly unlike anything any of us have ever seen before, not a single soul has heeded Noah's warning, being nowhere near the great ship in this storm.

And suddenly, we are reminded to make haste again on our journey from a former life, when we hear, when we *feel* a booming rumble from

somewhere other than the sky, traveling from the ground through our bodies in strange, unfamiliar waves, making us both stop and look around for the explanation as to why we might fall, seeing no volcanoes exploding, nor thundering herd of horses flowing at us from the horizon. My mind flashes to what two brown ponies there are aboard, as a bolt of lightning arcs from the top of the sky above our Ark, to the ground somewhere directly beyond. We are close enough to see the prophet turn his head to where he saw the lightning in the periphery; then he begins to walk across the bridge over the shallow creek, to the massive door laid open, where I can see Sara and both of her sons, and both of my sister in laws in waiting.

Thunder cracks and falls around us again, in the wake of another shaking of the ground, and a steady flow of wind from across the prairie. Our hurried steps carry us from the path worn into the grassy landscape around us, taking us from this side of time and history, moving us onto the platform of our flight, crossing the bridge to nowhere, in the haze of a motion neither of us have ever known. Holding hands, the two of us inseparable—all traces of separation gathered and dispersed by this wandering wind, which blows with the fury of chaos in heavy restraint, and a torrent of bridled rage never before seen in the history of the world.

The wind whips as a collection of them, joined as a single force of massive devastation pending, nearly plucking me from my husband's hand to toss me into the river, until he grabs me tight with both arms. Then I feel the strength of another around me, as his oldest brother is suddenly there to help anchor us in the storm. Shem helps us gather ourselves against the wind, as the ripples of water are blown over the surface of our stalwart fishing stream.

These droplets of water on my face, I know, are not the icy beginnings that are stored in the clouds, but the last and weeping goodbye I must feel from our homeland, as these waters have reached out to me, to splash this final warning for having tarried, for having looked backward at what once was, trying to draw it forward into what will never be. This fateful trip, these last steps through the air we breathe, reverberate from the wood of the gigantic door laid down, through my spirit to where I cannot resist their revelation, which is the third part of the truth, which is this end-of-the-world cataclysm. In the sound of the wind itself, in the roar of this storm's rising to life, there is the birth of a rage that flows from the beginning of time itself, somewhere in the past when humanity went astray, when the desire to do good left every human soul, and evil became the heart in what comfort he would abide.

This last step, from the vile and violent chaos of wind—to the strange and severe tranquility of the Ark—this last step is as from the grip of certain death, to the welcomed uncertainty of life everlasting.

*I*nside the profound daytime dark, burdened again by the smell of tar and wood, I am gathered with seven souls I have come to know, holding hands not only with my husband, but with the woman I have bonded with in this crisis of insanity, the woman Ada, wife of Japeth, the second son of Noah. The eight of us are gathered as witnesses to what was foretold, to what nary a village nearby the Ark hath witnessed, to what so many of them heard of and refused to believe, of the prophecies that were proclaimed for a century while the Ark was built. There were hardly the quiet rumbles of any voice from the clouds, barely a spark of light from the

sky that was not the sun or the moon or the stars of Heaven (save for the comet that came in the weeks before the skies went gray), barely more than a steady sprinkling and mist of rain to replenish the dry ground and waters of our fishing stream. There was hardly even the echo of what we stand here seeing, our clothes touched and grabbed at by every desperate and intruding gust of wind.

Our eyes blinded, our souls struck by the bolts of lightning from the sky to the ground, our ears deafened by these angry blasts of thunder, our nostrils filled with the dusty scent of the approaching deluge of rain that Noah has called *The Epoch*, that will mark the end of this age of mankind, he says, and the beginning of another one. Seven days after the last animal came into the Ark, seven days after we moved from our homes into Noah's great ship on dry land, we are witness to the darkest clouds in Creation, which begin to swirl over the prairie green nearby—coming alive into something we have never seen before, which swirls downward from the sky like a great finger desiring to find which way to point, clouds twisting and turning into this beautiful shape, the wind suddenly becoming what could not be withstood anymore.

Close the door, Sara says, her mature, beautiful face aflame with fear, but unable to take her eyes from the whirlwind in the clouds. Sara's husband motions to his two oldest sons, who begin to turn the two rope wheels for this gigantic drawbridge, which I have never really imagined as anything but a ramp, being that I have never seen it raised. Infinitely wider than the narrow little bridge it rested upon these many years, I hear the creaking of the wood in the storm, as the door begins to rise high enough to forecast safety from the elements, and an obscured view of the approaching fury from the clouds.

How is it that nature can come to life such as this? To reach down a finger of pure wind from the sky!

From inside a black cloud, spins a white one—a feathery silhouette of pure beauty, reaching down in otherworldly determination, a slow and easy tranquility of foreknowledge. From where this wind hath come, from what earthly wrath this wind is born, surely I do not know, as I look at Ham's brothers on the rope wheel, turning feverishly as if in a race, both hurriedly at a sight which is as new to them as the rest of us. But I notice the face of Noah, his beautiful silver white hair aglow, his eyes fixed in reverent, awestruck gaze of acceptance, as though looking afar off—so far beyond the immediacy of what we see, to the beginnings of what consequences lie along the flow of time, and the fulfillment of the most terrifying promise and prophecy ever made.

As the door is raised higher, the white cloud rope drifts longer and lower down toward the ground, until it is finally covered in part by the great door raised, and suddenly, we all hear a great popping noise, which makes the sweet Ada scream loudly, sparking a fear in me that is physical pain. Then another pop fills the humid air around us, and we all see the door fall back down as if in slow motion, crashing back to the sturdy bridge, raising a cloud of dust in the wind, opening up our view of the whirlwind again, as it touches the ground—blowing up a cloud of prairie dirt amidst the sound of its thunderous voice come to life, sounding as deep and rumbling as the quaking of the earth we felt before, and the lowest booming voice emanated from sky.

The rumble of earthquake and thunder fills the air around us, as the white rope cloud turns as black as the clouds it came from, and begins to slowly move towards the open door of the Ark. Six of us hurry away from

the approach of this sudden death from the clouds, with only Ham running towards the ramp to the upper floors, and then to one of the eight observation windows above the deck, in contrast to the single window built into the upper wall of the Ark itself. What will this cloud wind do to us when it arrives? Is this what the Ark was built for ? To become a field of beams and sticks and dead animals strewn across the countryside? Surely, there is nothing built to survive this great wind, that sucks the very earth up into itself with the noise of thunder. And as it approaches, I see Sara tear away from Noah's grip, running to hide away from the great open space. But I watch Noah stand his ground, in awestruck reticence, having humbled himself to God, and given himself over to His will and purpose.

From behind the inner beams of this greatest barn house ever built, we watch. This darkened gray thing come to us in power and great noise, drifting once from our sight, then approaching again close enough by to make even Noah anchor himself against the outer wall, never taking his eyes from the twisting, whirling cloud rope, already thickened into a cloud column, rising too high for us to see the top now. I see the bridge suddenly begin to break apart slowly, as if by choice rather than coercion, splintering into the individual parts of itself, then flying in condemned groups together into the whirling cloud, as surely the precursor to what will happen to our foolish drawbridge door, and then to the whole of this barnyard ship around us. But the great [twister] stops its motion towards us, hovering the very edge of the door, which begins to raise up on its own, as if lifted by the rushing mighty wind—lifted slow and steady, in the rumbling and creaking of wood hinges, until the whirlwind begins to disappear from our view. I see the last view of the cloud obscured by the wood door, then the glow of daytime dark vanishes in an instant with a loud thud that rumbles the entire Ark, followed by a sudden, rushing hiss of air—and I feel a

pressure upon my very ears, pushing inside them until it seems I am deaf to the screaming whirlwind, and the screaming blasts of lightning and thunder.

The quiet inside the Ark is broken at once, by what sounds like a thousand rocks and pebbles being thrown against the side of the ship, then moving slowly toward the top of where we are, as if these rocks were falling on deck.

" Father!" Ham calls. "You have to see this!"

Shem and Japeth follow hurriedly after Noah, then Shem's wife Seda, then Japeth's wife Ada, then myself. I quickly notice one in our little party of eight left behind.

"I don't want to see it," Sara says, gazing through the profound inner daytime darkness to her husband, who turns and continues up the ramp to the lookout windows above. I go back to Sara, whose beautiful face is distorted by the stresses of our calling. I take her hand, but to no avail, as she says loudly, *"I don't want to see it!"* Snatching her hand back from mine, gazing at me without mercy.

Amidst the sound of the rocks and gravel falling against the Ark, I turn and hurry to the ramp, where Ada is waiting for me, taking her hand and walking quickly with her to where the rest of the family is waiting. From the third floor of the ship, it is a quick climb up to the steps into the observation hall, the light room, long enough to hold many more than the four large windows on each side. This is the most treasured and familiar place on this entire ship to me (this human folly—built on top of God's master plan), having spent many hours over the past year gazing across the prairie east in the morning, and west beyond the afternoon. But what light there is here today is cold and gray, where the sunlight is gathered and hidden behind the clouds, and dispersed as daytime darkness and gray.

On the east side, Noah and his two sons gaze out of the first three windows, followed by Seda and Ada. I slide the fourth window open, feeling the strong wind on my face, seeing the pebbles of ice raining down onto the deck of the great ship. What sorcery indeed, that ice pours down on us from the sky! The noise on the rooftop is deafening in the window room, mixed with the rumble of the nearby twister I can still see, a view striking as it begins to move slowly away, in the backdrop of the open prairie, with sparks of thick lightning striking the very ground near the bottom of the whirling cloud. Even now, I am still struck to flinching from these bright sparks of white fire and light, my own fear echoed with the

sound of fury crackling from the sky. We watch the twister begin to move hurriedly along its preordination, along its predestined path of death and destruction, already so much thicker and darker even than before, being more steadfastly upright, the top of it climbing higher up it seems than even many of the birds that fly.

The hailstones cease to fall all of a sudden, as does the mysterious rumbling of the earth, allowing us to hear the twister's own voice quieter as it moves east, down the same traveling hour I have walked so many times since I was married. I wonder how long it will be, before this preordained message is given; before it will arrive at my mother's village fully grown, shaking the ground with a greater noise even than what we have heard. Already, the air around us is heavier than a moment before, and I think the pressure in my ears is faded. None of us can take our eyes away from this sight, having never seen a whirlwind in our lives, beyond what few grains of dust and dead leaves have whirled harmlessly across the plain.

Then suddenly, I hear Seda laugh.

"Seda!" Shem calls. "Quiet!"

"Noah's Storm," she says. "The end of the world? A whirlwind and a bunch of hailstones?"

Then the wife of Noah's oldest son throws back the prettiest head among us, the broadest, brightest smile among us, and laughs the coldest, heartiest laugh among us. Somewhere inside, the sight and sound of her laughter activates the smallest part of the same fear I have known this entire day. Of all the women I have ever seen, hers alone is the beauty that rivals my own mother's, and I can clearly remember that their connection and comfort around one another was disturbing.

You have my blessing, Mother had said to her once, *to take her behind this 'ark' and beat the skin off her if you have to.* The Sisters, they were. The two of them.

"Seda!" Shem calls again, rushing from Noah's side to where she stands still laughing. Shem whirls her around and grabs her by the shoulders, growling to her in a quiet, controlled rage born of his own fear and stresses of this acquired life. "I told you to shut your mouth!" he says. "I'm tired of your disobedience!"

"You don't know what being tired is," she says, her beautiful, mature face on fire with rage. "How many years did I listen to you and Noah talk about God and rain and judgment—and now look at us. Standing at the top of this *stupid* boat looking at a whirlwind dance off somewhere and disappear!"

"I *told* you to respect Noah and this Ark and I told you to keep your mouth shut!"

"I'm sick of you telling me what to do. You and Noah and can both burn in—"

"Seda!"

The voice of Noah rings loud in my ears, startling poor Ada into such a tragic flinch, as if she was roared at from behind by a wandering raptor. Noah walks over to where Shem stands holding his wife by the window. Touching his son's shoulder, causing him to release his bitter, beautiful wife's arms and step away. Though Seda does not speak, her defiance is as clear as ever, as she watches the handsome, older man move his face toward her—his bright, blue eyes burning a gaze into her soul. We all watch breathlessly, as he looks into her eyes, the rest of his handsome face covered in soft, flowing whiskers of silvery white.

He takes Seda by the hand, firmly but gently, sliding the sleeve of her garment halfway up her arm.

"Make a fist," Noah says, which she does reluctantly, disrespectfully, as if making it to cause brief and violent mischief. "The window," Noah says, "as far out as you can."

"What kind of a sick game is this?" she says. "You're humiliating me because I—"

"Seda, *do* it," Shem says, teeth clenched, face burdened by desperation.

She glances between the two of them, on the edge of resignation, ready to give in to this latest insanity. *So I'll stick my hand out the window*, she says without a word, *what good will it do?*

Noah ushers his daughter-in-law's hand through the window, at the moment that Sara steps quietly up the stairs into our strange space, daring not to speak at the odd sight of her oldest and most beautiful daughter-in-law holding her hand out the window.

"Open your hand," Noah says. Locking eyes mysteriously with Seda, as if in humble, awestruck anticipation for the unseen. But the rest of us soon have to look away from them, leaning forward out of our own windows, two by two, staring at her open hand, waiting for one of the birds to appear and light on the palm of her hand. But we are privy to what is surely the *splash*, the flash of water upon her hand, making her shriek and yank her hand back inside, staring at the palm of her now wet hand as though it were struck by lightning, gauging the droplets of what surely must be the remains of the biggest and coldest drop of rain in the history of the world.

9

*S*hem grabs his wife gently by the arm, staring at the water droplets in the palm of her hand, as Seda watches Noah turn and walk away. Ham runs over and grabs her hand roughly, touching the water, then looking at Seda and Shem for a moment. As we concede the possibilities, not knowing what it really means one way or another, the echo of what it really *does* mean pops onto the roof above our heads. I see my husband turn his head and look up, while Noah stands still at the far window, staring plaintively after the great twister departing in the far off distance.

And soon, the single, tiny thud on the roof is joined by a second and a third. And this third is joined by the instantaneous appearance of three more groups of three, and then I hear each of those groups joined in triplet,

until all counting of the sounds on the roof of the Ark fades into impossibility, becoming the pitter patter of defeat as we have never known. Seda closes her eyes, her beautiful face anguished with sorrow, and the bitter acceptance that no, there will be no axe blade taken to the inside hull of the Ark, and a crawl through the jagged space to life and freedom.

Sara and me, Ada and Seda stand with our husbands in the upper room, all of us having drifted to our respective windows on the east side, watching the whirlwind drift the certainty of its calling, in swirling devastation as tall as the sky. And soon, our view of the twister becomes a dreary haze of sights and sounds, the clamour of noise on the rooftop, the rumble of thunder, the sparking of lightning from the clouds, and the entire landscape covered in a drowning mist of rain.

The storm is unlike anything I have ever seen. Gusts of wind move the rain along in sheets and waves, appearing to have life, coalescing at times into discernible pockets of motion, beings made out of pure water, rushing to and fro across the prairie, carrying messages of doom and devastation; the fulfillment of a century of prophecies given. The lightning sparks and flashes without ceasing, sometimes in silence, but mostly with crackling, booming blasts of thunder. Even above my head, I am blasted unmercifully from the clouds, with sparks of lightning too close for comfort, that split the air so that I hear it at the same time I see it happen. It is the

beginnings of a fury that has no equal, a rage that cannot be contained, one obviously born from He who created all things, who Noah calls the Lord, the God of Creation, the one true and living God. *The Lord is angry*, I heard Noah say more times than a few, and I was never really able to comprehend.

But I do now.

I had heard of people worshipping all kinds of things. Burning sacrifices to every kind of god and power I can imagine. Some even think the cows are sacred—that they might be the souls of the dear departed reborn as a cow, afraid to kill it even to kill their own hunger, lest they kill and eat granny on the supper table. But Noah says the truth is too simple for people to accept unless they humble themselves to it, that there is only one true and living God, and when we die, our souls go to be with Him, or to a place of everlasting torment that Noah calls Hell, which he says is so bad that the human body could not stand the shock of seeing it. And Noah said that huffing yourself against God because you don't like him is like holding your breath underwater. False hope and a waste of time, because it cannot change the Truth, which is Reality. Without Faith, he says, it is impossible to please God, and he requires that we believe in him and trust in him, even though we can't see him. Noah says that God is absolute righteousness and power; that his holiness is purity, and he cannot be corrupted by wickedness of any kind, which is sin. And that when his love, grace and compassion ends, it is because all possible avenues and options have been exhausted, and there is nothing left but Divine Judgment for our transgressions. Noah says that God told him there are no good people left in the entire world, and that mankind is beyond redemption, and the thoughts of man's heart are evil from his youth. No, I was one of the

people who didn't believe, either, that Noah and his God, that Noah and *God* really mattered, because I could not imagine that he even existed.

But I do now.

Oh, God.

Oh, Heavenly Father.

As I hear the sound that rumbles from beneath the earth, that shakes my body, and rocks this great ship as if it is on the waves, as I hear and feel this dark prophecy begin to come to pass, oh yes… *my* God. *My* Heavenly Father.

But O Lord, even in the midst of confirmation, even in the midst of the most terrible storm we have ever seen, even while the earth quakes beneath us, how can I accept what Noah has said—the deepest, darkest part of his prophecy? That these rains I see will not cease to be, that they cover the entire world in this same hour, and that the waters will soon rise, until the breath of life is choked from every man, woman and child?

How can this be, O Lord! Even though I can see the fury of thine hand, though I can see the sheets of rain that whirl and fall to earth, I cannot imagine that even months and years of rain can cover every spot of land over the entire earth itself! Surely, the people will migrate to higher ground, and wait for this Divine Storm of Judgment to pass! But Noah says that God says he is going to destroy all mankind with a *worldwide* flood, and that he has learned over this last century of years, that God not only does not lie, but he is absolutely incapable of it; but he also knows that no matter how hard we try to believe, there is only so far our finite understanding can go. So it doesn't matter that I cannot really believe that this storm of rage is the beginning of the end of all mankind. Noah says all

that matters is that I believe that God *is*. I don't know if I really believed that either until today.

But I do now.

11

Maybe it is the whirling of three separate and distinct shapes from the clouds. Three new whirlwinds a good distance away, one to the far left of our vision, one to the center, and one to the far right, all three very tall and elegant, glowing snow white in the rain and gray surroundings. Their appearance is very tranquil in the stormy setting, very much a part of the wind and rain we see, but separate and deliberate just the same, all three touching the ground at once, in three separate places along the eastern landscape, not darkening at all from the prairie soil, unlike the whirlwind

of destruction that has just come and gone. And these three twisters stand steadfast—neither traveling in any direction, only their elegant, ropelike tips weaving back and forth like slow motion whips lashing.

When God's final plan is set in motion, does it really matter what we believe? Where God is concerned, why do we think we can wish away the truth, simply by choosing not to believe it? Am I like my mother and my sister, who have both gazed out the door and small window of the stone house in quiet disbelief at the fiery lightning in the clouds, and the fervent rain and wind at this storm? No. As I look at the white cloud twister to the far left, the one in the center, and the one to the far right, I know that I can no longer be as they are, who refuse to believe that there is a God. I cannot think and feel as they do anymore, where they hear the otherworldly rumble and crashing coming at them from the distance, perhaps too ignorant to be afraid, wondering what manner of noise and black whirling is this thing coming toward the village, so few of who can even see from inside their houses the source of the noise they hear.

What is that, Mother says, beautiful brow wrinkled with concern.

I told you they were witches, Nora says. *It's a dirt devil.*

But its raining, Nora. This is the worse rain I've ever seen. How can there be a storm of dirt in the rain? It sounds like a thousand chariots are coming. Maybe we should try not to be in this village when it gets here.

I'm not running from Noah's sorcery, Nora says. *Nela probably put a curse on the village. That cloud of dirt is just a bunch of noise, it'll pass right over us, you'll see. They're just trying to scare us, Mother. Well, its not going to work is it?*

Mother opens her mouth to speak.

Is it? Her daughter says sharply. As Mother grabs Nora tight, thanking *God* for her daughter being there, the end-of-the-world rumbling gets loud

enough for them to have to shout to be heard. Mother runs from the bed chamber to the front of the house, opening the door and stepping out into the ice cold rainstorm—blinded by the blowing, icy rainfall, but seeing just enough to perceive the Truth; swirling heavy with black prairie mud from its journey.

As she stands pointing at the end-of-the-world twister, screaming a voiceless call to her daughter in the thunderous sound, Nora goes outside and begins to pull at her mother's arm, struggling to pull her away from the deadly sight in the nearby distance, certainly no more than a minute from the edges of the village. Nora makes one mighty, straining pull against her mother, breaking her free from the spell of the whirlwind, pulling them into the house, closing the thin door and latching it, which hardly changes the volume of noise at all.

The world inside the house is an overwhelming cave of noise and fear, with the mother running to the back of the house near where the fireplace glows with red hot embers and ashes. And it seems that sparks have already begun to fly from under the iron grating over the coals, lifted into the air from the winds stirring about their little space. Mother calls Nora, screaming her name, as her daughter is held enraptured at the window, watching the whirling black cloud overtake the village, amazed as the stone houses have begun to lift into the air and fly apart.

Among the houses blown into pieces are the bodies of men, women and children, huddled hopelessly together inside what was once a collection of homes, now a gathering of pieces that no longer resemble the houses that they were. Mother hears Nora screaming for her, motioning for her to come and gaze out of the window, at the unimaginable devastation she sees. And the roles are suddenly reversed, as Mother begins to pull hard on

her daughter, trying to pull her back to the safety of the fireplace sparks that fly.

But halfway to the back wall of the house, the door flies open and is torn off its hinges, and mother feels the pull of the forces that can neither be resisted nor understood, lifting her daughter up until she is off her feet, dragging the two of them quickly towards the open door. The look of terror on Nora's face is the fear of death, lashing Mother's heart with hopeless longing, and the echo of outer darkness, where there is only weeping and gnashing of teeth.

The two of them are pulled to the open door space, amidst the rushing mighty wind, until Mother is anchored with one hand on the stone wall, and the other holding her daughter who is in the air. The Mother finds the strength to hold on to the wall, but is suddenly zapped by the pain of loss, when she feels her daughter slip from her hand unseen. By instinct she grabs onto the wall at the door with both hands, feeling a miraculous release of the pressure to fly into the air, able now to even look around the corner of the doorway, at the whirling black mass too far away to take her now, having never even moved close enough to cause more than a fatal downdraft blown through the house, plucking a few glowing ashes from the fireplace—tossing every bowl and plate and cloth and knife blade everywhere in the little space, but blowing not as much as a spoon through the window.

The burning ashes of her ordeal glow before her eyes. In the agonizing vision of her daughter's departure. Mother's final scream is held inside by an unseen hand, causing the scream to disperse into her body as poison, making her tremble under the weight of this trauma, swooning her into a step outside, to try and run after the gigantic whirlwind, to be carried off in the pouring rain to whatever black Hell opened a portal into this world, and

took her daughter away. Having so little concept of Faith and hope in an afterlife, that she would choose to die in the same manner as her daughter and go to wherever it is that her beloved daughter could have gone.

But each step plunges her deeper into the abyss; the Chasm of Unknown, the unseen, where her thoughts and motivations are gathered up as prairie grass into a whirl of confusion—where suddenly she feels herself traveling fast toward a wall of solid mud, which is only the wet ground beneath her feet. The woman swoons in the haze of rainfall and a whirling black cloud, and falls unconscious into the mud, dreaming that she is buried in a tomb, with water slowly creeping through the cracks around her grave stone.

here are no cracks around the windows of the Ark when they are shut, so that the effect is pitch blackness throughout. None of the thousands of animals I have seen tucked away in their cages is visible by more than the faint glow of torchlight, so that the beauty of the long-necked [giraffes] is subdued day and night. Already, these animals have displayed the limits of their calling, which is to near total silence, with hardly a sound over a moan or a low growl, so many of them having already gone to sleep for the many days they have been here. As they were all guided to their cage rooms, there was not a single incident of chaos or discord from among them, not even from the stubborn asses themselves, whom I can distinctly remember moving so calmly and obediently together into their cage. And the female had always been stubborn and noisy, and Ham and I were ready to have to push, pull and pound that ass into submission if that's what it

took. But she had simply glanced at the two of us briefly, knowingly, and walked into the cage by her own will and satisfaction—sharing the same spirit of refuge with every other animal on this ship, that they would rather be here than anywhere else in the world. I haven't seen them since the latch slid closed on them, but I imagine that like most every other animal aboard, they are asleep. The unnatural tranquility of these animals is but one of the many signs, I think, that this entire journey is guided by an unseen hand, an uncompromising hand of purpose, that has moved upon every part of its own creation, to see that it bows to a specific will and purpose. The spirits of *"sit down and shut up"* and *"lay down and go to sleep"* have settled a hush over our little animal kingdom, to where I wonder when it will be a time for them to wake up and be fed. I have rarely seen any one of them take a drink, and the piles of hay that were already in some of their cages is no more than half eaten. Even the baby behemoths, already the biggest animals on board, have hardly touched a bite of straw. And while these animals all rest in the tranquility of their calling, around the rest of the world—every fowl of the air, every beast of the field, and every small and creeping thing hides and trembles in fear for what is coming upon the earth, even for the rumbling from the ground and the sky that has already been, and for what they feel in their hearts and minds will soon be. Unable to understand much of anything beyond the instinct of hiding—burdened by the fear and terror of premonition, and the hellish feeling of impending doom.

Across the landscape of the entire earth, the rain falls in weeping, in grieving for what mankind is condemned to see, for what warnings he chose not to heed. These are the rainfalls of revelation, that spread across the face of the world as we know it. Falling in solemn, steady assurances over the castles and courtyards, while queens stand at the windows of their balconies in amazement over this rain's steady power, and the energy rumbling constantly from the clouds. From the palaces and pristine lawns of prairie green, over the walls of privilege and beyond, that flows only the sheets of pouring rain—with not a pittance of charity or pity for the masses of the poor, those born under the same gray clouds of poverty, and the bloom of ashen gray regret.

And inside the walls of these palaces looms the burden of human instinct and depravity, with every form of decadence that the world hath imagined rising and falling with the ocean tides, and the traveling of the Sun and the Moon. But the sunlight of these last days is darkened, as the full Moon behind the grieving clouds was turned to rust and blood. These moons had risen above the great palaces of discontent, wherein the queens were privileged by their daughter's nakedness, whether in pain or pleasure, under the shelter of discipline or perversion. And these same queens, having tasted the elixir of their maidservant's lips, were turned from the natural use of their husbands, to obey the burning of their bodies in the bedchambers of night, under the rising Moon of rust and blood. These same queens, spending many waking moments overwhelmed with thought, on how to capture the maidservants in the tiniest infractions; so that they may see them undressed in the queen's chambers, to see their white skin striped to blood. The Sun is darkened by the clouds of grieving, over the naked queens atop the unresisting princesses, as the perversion burns royal blood to chaos and screaming.

The rains of revelation fall. Unconcerned with the lowly man and his eternal lust and diversion, but obsessed now with what is hidden behind the walls of secret, even to be hidden from the understanding of the mind, of these mothers in the high places, who burn in such a lust as was never imagined, even to see their young daughters in the nude—holding the long, yellow fruit between their naked legs in naivite and shock, while their mothers, queens and countesses and high ladies of every court are on their knees, behind the walls of secret, their mouths wrapped around the yellow fruit; their smooth, white hands up at their daughter's undeveloped breasts, infusing the girls with the burning of blue and black fire—that which they

will nurture somewhere deep inside, beyond their ability to comprehend, or even to resist what instinct they cause. These fine ladies of the court, bent over behind the walls of secret, as the beautiful young daughter stands behind her mother who is bent over, leaning her hands on the bed. The mother is all too glad for the bright flashes of lightning throughout the palace, as they tell of the blasts of thunder to follow, telling her daughter to place the tip of the yellow fruit into her backside, but to hold the pushing until she nods her head.

O, what daughter of what queen is this I see, when I close my eyes in the bowels of the dark! Who is this heavy breasted queen of silken black hair pinned to her head, that is bent over her Queen's Bed in the storm! And she sees the fateful flash of this lightning storm, and the cracking of the sky begins to hide her voice from the rest of Creation as she nods and yells push it in! The sound of her last word morphing into a death scream of pain and pleasure as one. Who is this beautiful queen I see, whose breasts hang and swing gigantic in the storm, as her daughter stands behind her, her fruit pushed so deep into her mother's bowels in grieving! Holding onto the woman for dear life, her own head thrown back in surrender to her mother's perversion!

And this violent scream lifts from the walls of secret, flowing across the rainsoaked forests and fields to the "Houses of Want and Need"—the houses of poverty—where these vile motivations explode behind these same Walls of Secret, powered by lifetimes of broken dreams, bitterness and oppression. Mothers and fathers raping their daughters, brothers raping sisters, sisters raping younger sisters, children abused under the shelter of discipline, where all love is lost, and only hatred and pain for pleasure's sake remains. Women abusing their husband's pride and manhood; itchy, witchy and bitchy attitudes pitched and spit at their men for no good reason

to be found—words flung through the air in the hiss of a feral cat, in the sting of that from the mouth of a spitting cobra, splashing the eyes of their husband's love over and over again, until they are blinded to feelings they once felt, feelings of affection poisoned and transformed to disaffection, where the spirit of chaos and family discord may live and prosper.

Husbands stripping their wives down to bare skin and beating them with the mule stick or the horse leather, until their white skin is cut to blood. This selfsame burden is then laid from mother to daughter, the mother's top completely off—breasts swinging as she burns the bitterness, the rancor and rage of her life onto her daughter's naked breasts and skin, with the same punishment stick or piece of horse bridle, or sacrificing at times the skin of her own palms, enduring the fire as she bruises the bottom of her full grown daughter who has been married and widowed, or her daughter of marrying age having never even left home. Mothers who whisper secrets to their daughter's husbands in the night, until the husband knows that it is alright to beat the woman he loves and force her to bed against her will.

Across the landscape of the entire earth, the women have turned their lust upon one another in violence and shrieking in cold, catlike cruelty to friends and enemies alike, until the husbands and sons are no longer their focus and concern, but only how to outdo and undo one another; gathering together as one at times to bring fear even to the men of the village, one husband having been stabbed through the veil of sleep, and his body drug away in the middle of the night to parts unknown, and reported as missing to everyone in the village.

Across the landscape of the entire earth, these rains fall in weeping for what they know, turning the corrupted dust of the ground into mud, to

wash away the covering of secrets buried beneath the soil. And these too are the bodies of children that once lay dying—infants and small children smothered to death by their mothers, by women whose hearts were broken down to nothing in weeping, some having taken their dead children up in their arms, while they run to the neighbors, crying tears of fear rather than regret. Or some having stolen away in the quiet of a starry night, and buried their child underneath the waiting soil, returning to the village in pure relief, and no remorse for what they have done. These rains fall in mourning, in rage and grief for the sons and daughters of men, for what tragedies have befallen them, and for what great and terrible tragedy there is to come.

Across the landscape of the entire earth, every part of Creation wonders already what to do—some even wondering where to go, to escape the flashing of tiny floodwaters on their muddy streets, soil ill-equipped for such a deadly downpour such as this, rancor already flooding through the streets as a small river, or lining the stone tiles of the open courts, so that many of those at the palace windows have marveled already at the waves of wind blown across the surface of these waters. From behind the Walls of Prosperity, across the grieving, drowning landscape to the Walls of Poverty, all continue to eat and drink and be merry, planning to marry and be given in marriage, to return to work to their herds and planting fields, fending off the lions and wolves that lurk in the shadows, and the antelope and deer that come to devour the young crops at dawn and sunset. Many turn to the gods they worship in praise and thanksgiving for the blessed rainfall; [Baal], the god of rain and storms, standing on the hilltops and the high places with outstretched arms to the stormy heavens, wailing thanks to [Baal] and his wife [Ashera], the goddess of fertility, some giving thanks and praise to [Moloch], believing the rains to be his blessing, in return for

the sacrifice of a child stolen from a nearby field of play. And these are ordinary farmers and their wives, having allowed the desperation and lust for plenty to cloud and devour their judgment that they may enjoy further increase and riches, with the accumulation of land, and the harvesting of greater and greater yields, until they must acquire workers and labour, and they no longer have to do the work themselves, but only have the job of supervision, and the gathering of treasures created and earned by the blood, sweat and tears of others, who work endlessly from sun up to sundown—to be paid less than a living wage, so that the farmer and his wife may accumulate a mountain of gold, with silver and sparkling jewels scattered about. *For the love of money is the root of all evil,* I have heard the rain prophet preach, causing men to lose touch with righteousness, and carry a heart frozen cold, where the warmth of compassion can no longer live and prosper.

Across the face of the entire earth, all eyes witness the falling of a fervent rain, one that splashes violently in the fountains and lakes and fishing streams and puddles in the streets. And in every part of the world, all who breathe the breath of life look to the heavens in blessings or curses, all grieving in their hearts after a single day for this storm to end, so that they may breathe the air in resurrection of who they are—the mistresses and masters of what palace or stone hutch they survey. Around the world, in the splashing of rain across every square [inch] of dry land, there is a collective apprehension unknown, with no real knowledge of what to do or where to go, except for this tiny part of the grieving earth, where the people have a century of knowledge about the ark that was built, a refuge from what was called the Great Flood, and the coming judgment of God over all mankind.

The sound of a woman's voice penetrates the torchlit darkness, muffled by its journey through the pitched wood from outside. This voice is joined by the voice of a man, muffled by this selfsame journey. The woman's voice calls to Sara, and the man's voice calls to both Sara and Noah alike. I can hear something about "water" and "our homes", then a fervent and bitter knocking at the bottom of the Ark. Curious, since I know the bridge is gone. I hurry down the long hall of cages to the wall of wooden stairs, being a quicker climb than the trip up the long shallow ramps would be. I climb the stairs up to the second floor, then to the third floor. It's a long walk to the center of the third floor of cages, where the stairs are narrower and much steeper.

I climb the stairs to the Hall of Light, the window room which is a world past four windows long (four on each side), but still miniscule compared to the length of the Ark itself. These windows are so much wider than the one window inside the ark, down on the third floor. These Windows of Man's Wisdom were built, Noah said, *so we can keep watch,* and *to help the birds get in*; but strangely enough, the birds all flew into the big door and the single third floor window. Not one bird came in through these big, long windows. One of the many signs, I suppose, that this trip is divinely ordered from top to bottom. At the top of the Ark I climb, seeing that I am alone in my curiosity so far, driven to the heights by the sound of the first cry for redemption.

But these are they which are beyond Redemption. The souls at the edge of the abyss, ready to be tossed in by the Holy Angel, charged to carry them to their eternal and just reward. *It grieves the Lord that he made mankind,* Noah says, a decision that we all must pay for, until the final sacrifice for sin is made, and mankind can be redeemed through the shedding of this blood. But things are so bad, so irrevocably beyond repair that Creation itself must be destroyed and washed clean and made anew. And every soul on the face of the earth is condemned.

I hear the first cry of condemnation outside in the pouring rain, when I slide the window open and see the fishing stream turned into a small river. The deck is just too big for me to see the family at the bottom of the Ark. Oh, how desperately I wish I could climb out of this window and go foolishly to the edge, but these windows may as well not even exist, because even the clean air inside them is as the iron bars of a prison. As I look out over the prairie, I can still see the three tall whirlwinds standing guard over the plans of God here on earth, to provide warning to any

wayward thinking, or any ill advised plan to the contrary. Even this long and strange window room which I could not imagine us being without, is here only out of *"our basic necessity"*, Noah said, so we can all breathe some fresh air every now and then, only existing here at the top of the Ark because God didn't tell Noah *not* to build it—being the natural progression at the top on any ship, I suppose. It is a long and dreamy corridor of loneliness, an uneasy refuge from the bowels of darkness and animal scent below.

I gaze through an opening in the upper room, hardly surprised by the people I see flowing toward us from the distance. Of the many souls I see, who among them is my mother! Having awakened in the pouring rain, her other daughter taken, Mother climbs to her feet, soaking wet and muddy from her ordeal. Scattered before her, in the impossible rain, in a space greater than the village itself had been, are the remains of houses and the sparse lives within. Among the stone slabs and pieces of cloth and wood are the bodies of men, women and children twisted and strewn about, some half buried under curious and conspicuous piles of stone slab walls everywhere else except from the houses they lived in. And strangely enough, the houses on her side of the village still stand undamaged, while every house on the other side is gone. Surely, anyone who may have seen her lying in the rain thought that she was dead. It seems that what is left of the village is deserted, with nary a living soul left to lend comfort, and to remind her of what is normal.

Mother splashes over the muddy street and into the house, inside of which bears no resemblance to order. But even though the door itself is gone, everything she owns, every insignificant piece of iron, cloth and wood is gathered and fallen by the whim of Chaos, scattered and thrown in unbelievable fashion, as if the house had been raided by angry soldiers out

for blood. While she is inside, wondering how best to proceed, the rains fall over the poverty field with steady assurance, to where it appears to pour down in streams, with heavy flashes of lightning and angry blasts of thunder overhead. And besides this, the moment she reaches down to pick up one of her daughter's garments is met by a wave of thunderous motion all around her—more intense, and with greater purpose than the times it happened before, knocking her off her feet, dusting her wet, red dress linen with fine powder from a crack in the stone rooftop above. The roof above her cracks and falls nearby her in a huge chunk, making her stand up in the quaking noise, going back out into the rain.

The earth continues to rumble, causing the roof of her house to turn to powder and rock, crashing inside as if it had been crushed. The rumbling of the earth ceases, with Mother resigned to her place in the drowning rainfall. She walks slowly to a neighbor's home, an old woman she had always been friendly enough with, opening the door and going inside the dank, dim, daytime darkness and desolation—calling old Rosanna by name but finding no one. What she does find is a house whose inside is gutted like her own had been, with the table leaning up against the wall as if it had been placed, with pieces of clay pots all over the room, with one still resting on a shelf in back of the house over the fireplace unbroken.

Looking out the window, Mother wonders whether Rosanna was taken by the whirlwind as her daughter had been. Or if she was taken up by another wind, this one of concession and inevitability. As Mother stands in Rosanna's house, surveying the field of mud and clay, she is drawn away from the uneasy shelter, with no strength left to hide from the Truth of Premonition. Truth is a gigantic swath of earth painted black—a line of churned up ground from her devastated village to the rainsoaked horizon in

the far distance. A Truth that tells of Rosanna's whereabouts, along with every other terrified soul that survived, and has travelled through the rain West across the prairie towards the Ark.

$\mathcal{I}$n my mind's eye, in these waking visions I have suddenly been burdened to suffer, I can see my Mother's rainy trip from the mouth of devastation and despair, drowning in the darkened rain. She is joined by scattered groups of people from villages all over the plain, many of who seem drawn to the beautiful woman in the bright red garment. *My daughter is married to one of Noah's sons,* she says to one of the women. Trying to maintain the false hope for herself, and to the few who seem gathered around this same energy, many of their homes having been destroyed by small, powerful whirlwinds themselves, some villages hit by floods of rivers forming within the hour—the hard, dry ground having no hope of absorbing the rain quickly enough to prevent it. These many hours of hard,

heavy rainfall have sent many hundreds of people in these low lying valleys away from their homes in terror, some of the homes already flooded to the ankles with water from the small, powerful flash floods crashing through. The ones that have not sought higher ground are fewest in number, and have fled the safety of a former life, gathering with others from over a dozen nearby villages and towns flowing into traveling bands of people all over this rainy prairie—all driven forward by some irresistible instinct and premonition, the irrepressible urge to survive.

But survive what? Some questions cannot be asked, serving as an iron rod to clay pot sensibilities, as fragile and feeble as a lamb's neck in a lion's mouth, grieving to be free from the crushing blow, the crashing force of revelation and truth. Sadly, oh, so tragically, all are primarily motivated by fear, and underneath the bravado of sin, everyone is hardly more than just plain scared to die. *We hear that there might be a very bad flood,* is the prevailing energy here, gathered around the beautiful woman in red, and many small groups approaching us from every horizon across the prairie.

And these groups of people approach steadfastly in the rain, despite the rumbling of the earth beneath their feet, the rising breath of wind all around them, and the three towering whirlwinds stretched out over the plain. They pass the threshold marked by these swirling clouds of death, trying not to hear the answer to unspoken questions asked, and premonitions fulfilled in ashen gray regret.

The great ship rests across the plain, beyond these towering signs of the times, and the winds of grief and warning they blow. But the sight of these dozens, untold scores of people filing towards us, against the backdrop of the three twisters seems to be my curiosity alone, as I am the only one up here in the Hall of Windows, watching the people gather like nomads on the other side of the little river I can see. This stream comes from a large

river many days walk from here which I have never seen, but which my husband has fished and swam in. And as the people gather nearby the Ark in the rain, some already raising up tents against the storm, the spirit of chaos and fear begins to move slowly through the crowd of refugees looking for a place to hide, as the wind billows every attempt at tent making and flies them off to nowhere, and the Earth continues to move and quake beneath their feet.

The number five hundred settles in my mind, about the mass of hopeless longing and desperation below, as some of them begin to splash into the river and out of my sight below. And among those who are hopeless and desperate enough to navigate the rushing waist high water, is the woman in the red garment soaked to the bone, who even from this great height I can easily recognize as my mother Adina, with my sister Nora nowhere in sight. When my mother vanishes below (to where I cannot see her beyond the edge of the deck), there is a rumble and quaking unlike any we have heard and felt before, making me have to grab onto the side of the window to keep from falling. Then suddenly in the distance, I see a tower of steam blast from the earth, spewing high into the air, followed by a burst of water like a fountain—billowing up, upward as high into the air as the column of steam, beginning to widen at the bottom, as more steam blows out of the ground in violence unheard of from left to right where I can see, which is north to south, building a towering wall of water from north to south along the horizon, blocking my view of the three twisters who guard the door of this realm from doubt and unbelief.

What shock and disbelief there is on my face, I can feel, as I rush from my view in the upper room down to the east window, the third floor window built into the Ark itself. Not even Noah himself is at this window

when I arrive, as I slide it quickly open, calling Noah as loudly as I can. In the eternity it takes for him to arrive, I can now observe the chaotic mass of humanity just below. Now I can see everything. Including the wave of fear that rises to terror, as the people are pushed into the waters of the river by pure instinct, including one man much taller and meaner than the rest, a look of rage on his bearded face, an axe blade held with purpose in his hand. This man wades through the waters of discontent, believing in his heart that he has a calling to answer.

Noah himself joins me at the window on this high platform, where there is hardly room for us both. *"My Lord,"* he says, but more for the towering wall of water from the ground, *"and the fountains of the deep were opened,"* he says, looking down at the man with the axe blade in his hand.

"We can't stop him."

"We won't have to," he says.

Then suddenly, apocalyptically, a whirlwind moves smoothly through the towering wall of water, flowing fast toward the people down below, seeming to arrive in but an instant, and those who did not go into the river are lifted from the ground like fallen leaves and whirled into the cloud, their screams covered by that of the screaming wind, rain and thunder. Then the outer edges of this same violent wind lifts the axe spinning from the big man's hand, spinning it back towards him and plunging it into his back, making his eyes go wide with shock as he falls mightily forward as if grabbed and dunked, splashing into the river and floating away like a piece of wood. Of them that remain, the river can no longer keep us at a distance, as the rest of five hundred splash toward us screaming, the air inside of the Ark already alive with the muffled scream of a crowd of hundreds of people left, and the eerie pounding of their fists along the side of the Ark.

And smoothly, as quickly as it came, the twister moves away from the Ark and flows back toward the gigantic wall of water, sliding effortlessly through it, so that the top of it is nearly obscured from our view by the mist at the top of the upside down waterfall spraying up from the underground.

I now know that without a doubt, this is the beginning of these Days of Noah, so much bigger than even his own life and family. Who are we, that we have been chosen to watch this destruction from a safe distance, sheltered inside from an infinity of wind and a steady, pouring rain. Since the wall of water exploded upward, the crowd below has been made frantic, every scream and pleading layered on top of the other until they are one, so that no individual voice can be pinpointed in the storm. Including the one that belongs to my mother, which I cannot hear coming from the woman in red, whose beautiful face is twisted in a scream of agony, where my name is screamed as loud as she can, but to no avail. *Nothing can save them now,* Noah says, answered by the continuous sparking of heat and light from the clouds, and the noise of cataclysm cascading.

"Noah," Sara says. "Please come away from that window."

Noah only turns to her and holds up his hand, nodding slightly in agreement. Then suddenly I see the beginning of the end of this age, coming at us from the southern horizon in the form of a wave of water at least twice as high as the Ark itself, having not yet touched the southernmost twister, but already devouring the great wall of water spewed forth from the crack in the earth.

Unable to speak, I grab Noah's arm and point out the window. Quickly, he closes the shutter to the east window and seals it tight, escorting me quickly from our place at the high window, amidst the noise of the pounding against the ship, and a sudden thumping and clamoring in the

roof house above our head, the sound of men's voices yelling furiously, and many footsteps, then a sudden pounding at the roof of the Ark just above our heads. I suppose in madness, some of them had climbed to the top of the nearest tree and jumped onto the deck, and the ones who didn't slide off made it to the window room and climbed inside.

The sound of epic ambition thumps the rooftop above us as we all go quickly to our holding stations on this floor, four of the tall beams of wood where a leather strap is tied. Noah, Shem, Ham and Japeth all tie the wives to each of the four beams where we stand, then tie themselves to the same beams on the other side from us. From the front of the Ark to the back, there is Noah tied to Sara, strong and loyal—Shem tied to Seda, beautiful and bitter, Japeth tied to quiet and kindhearted Ada, and Ham tied to his own shy, fearful wife. And in the din of chaos above and all around us, we hear a blood curdling scream emanate throughout the Ark, born from the mouth of the lovely Seda, to call forth the spirit of Fear, and to echo every prickling of nerve that torments our bodies to the bone.

Then on the far end of this great scream comes the sound louder and greater than what Creation can endure, a splashing and rumbling together magnified to infinity, like the approach of mankind's past, present and future coalesced into a single wave of sound. And suddenly, every sound in Creation vanishes. Swallowing us in a pocket of lifelessness. An irreversible concave. A pressing down of Death itself, breaking this silence with a great and powerful groaning throughout the ship, which flows from one end to the other, around and through our hearts, minds and bodies— holding us breathless, with only Noah and myself knowing fully what has happened to the world outside the walls of the ship.

And as this groaning and creaking begins to die, we feel a suddenly lifting that brings a scream from the mouths of every woman on the ark

except for myself, as I am too afraid to scream, as we all feel such a powerful and unfamiliar force in the pit of our stomachs, as if being tossed high over the top of a great hill, followed by the distinct sensation of falling, which pulls a scream this time even from myself, amidst the echo in my soul of these very words, *and the Ark rose higher than the branches of every tree.*

Coastlines around the world are the beginning of the end, as waves taller than every tower of man begin to come ashore, lifted by the hand of the Lord from the waters of the deep, sent rising higher and higher toward the shoreline, as those in the towns and cities by the sea begin to flee in terror, the bonds of their denial broken by the sight of impending death. The women grab the children from their homes and begin to run for the borders of the towns and cities, the men gather the wives and children alike, running for a phantom higher ground in the pouring rain and lightning, those that can stand on the rumbling ground without falling. Men and woman of privilege leave their fine homes, the storehouses of silver and gold behind, running through the streets from the approaching wall of water that stretches from one side of Creation to the other.

A waking nightmare, many of their bleak horizons blighted with billowing ash and smoke from the ground, some awestruck by the gigantic spewing of liquid fire from the exploding hilltops, and the rivers of fire that flow down to the bottom. Many are quick enough to have run beyond the city limits, into the surrounding fields of the grassy plain, believing they have escaped the impending destruction of the approaching waves, only to be swallowed up by the wall of moving water, where there is no scream without the breath of life, some put instantly to sleep by the heavy weight of the water knocking them senseless—some living to fight in full strength under the crushing sea, struggling to swim to a surface they can never reach, their bodies on fire with the craving for air, their lungs betraying them, opening their mouths against their will, drawing the water in past their resolve to live and return to their lives, to care for their husbands and wives, to care for their children, to see their loving mothers and fathers smiling faces once again. To love , to hate, to work, to play, to conquer, to rebel, to lend their swords and blood to the seeds of battle that grow and blossom into war.

To return to their lives of killing or being killed, of survival of the fittest, where there are divisions of labor, and classes of those who earn their bread, from those who work in the slaving fields for what roof and meals there be, to those whose storehouses of riches overflow with abundance, so that every waking hour is only joy, and the fulfillment of every lust of the flesh, every lust of the eyes, and every pride of their life come and gone. From the innocent children cursed by the wickedness of the first man and woman who sinned against the Lord, to the eldest mouth now choked with the irony of Creation itself, that these same waters of life are transformed into waters of pain, suffering and Death.

These mothers and daughters of poverty have been exalted up, the mothers and daughters of privilege laid low, those that walked the straight paths of man's law have been made crooked, and those that were crooked have been made straight, and the glory of the Lord is revealed to all in the power of his might. The Spirit of the Lord is not mocked, and the day of the Lord is reserved for the judgment of the wicked and the unrighteousness. In the palaces and the spiritual high places, men and women of earthly renown, the sons and daughters of fallen angels who took their part of the daughters of God, these great men and women of power, privilege and prosperity now float lifelessly in the chambers and great halls, above their palace beds and thrones, the kings and queens and rulers of the masses of underprivileged, made an equal part with them at the end of this age. Queens buried with their princess brides, beautiful mothers and daughters of the high courts entombed, buried underneath the Waters of Discontent, the waters of outer darkness, the waters of wrath and divine judgment.

Across the water laden plain, through the forests covered under this cloak of sea brought inward, where the leaves and branches wave in their own slow desperation of dying life, their leaves choked from the life giving light of the sun hidden away, and the air that every leaf must surely breathe to grow. Past the waving forests where the creatures of the deep must now float and swim according to their calling, from the forests of the deep, across the rolling fields now buried beneath the rolling sea, to the farmhouses of poverty where those who stayed in their homes now rest, floating dreamlessly in their homes across the poverty field, their hovels of want and need now the tombs of misdeed—the burial places where they were already dead, having died to the spirits of love and peace, given over to the spirits of hatred and chaos, and every form of family discord and

private wickedness known. There is the mother who choked upon the nakedness of her son, there is the daughter who choked upon her father's nakedness, there is the mother who uncovered her daughter, then sat upon her daughter's nakedness, her hand pressed at her daughter's throat to choking. These are the bodies of them who have corrupted themselves, the water having risen to push away the air that they breathed, so that they must surrender their secret lives to choking. These bodies that were the vessels for every perversion and corruption imagined.

$\mathcal{I}$ see beyond where the ocean wave can reach, to the inland villages and surrounding dirt farms, where the rains were once so blessedly welcome, burdened now by the unbridled outpouring, by the deluge of water that pours from the sky. Hidden inside their stony houses of fear and dread, amazed at the ferocity of what they see outside the window, of the rain that often falls sideways at them inside. I see the man and his young new wife, huddled together at the window of their home, gazing at the water bubbling from the stone well, water gushing and overflowing like nothing they have ever seen or imagined. These two now burdened by the same fear and dread suffered by the child kept locked away in a tiny storehouse made of wood, forced to eat pieces of raw grain to kill the bouts

of epic hunger, but having been given too little water to drink. This child, this little girl that was held still by the young, bitter wife and beaten to tears and blood by the husband, this child who was raped over and over again by them both, until the lower parts of her body were damaged unrecognizable, in accordance with what impossible perversion there must be. These two, this man and this woman, stand fearfully at the window of their isolated house, unconcerned now for the goats and sheep of livelihood, nor for the body of the child who died of thirst on the sunrise of a new day, at the dawn of this great and terrible day of the Lord.

These two, staring at the stone well overflowing, feeling the mighty rumble from the beneath the earth, watching the stone well crumble and give way, then suddenly explode from the powerful burst of water broken through, which rises into the sky too high for them to see at the window, rushing to open the door in the rain, seeing the water tower rise into the air like an upside down waterfall, splashing a plume of white water from the top toward the ground below…

And these two are unprivileged, to see the wind gather itself around this tower of water, swirling a great portion of it away, until they see a whirlwind of pure water begin to form, fed by the water pouring forth from the ground and the sky. These two, bearing witness to a *water devil*, a whirlwind of water risen up from the ground in the rain, moving toward the house where they live and breathe, evoking a scream from the bitter young wife, even a fearful yell from the husband as they slam the thin, flimsy wooden door shut, suddenly blasted with water pouring into the house from the whirling water devil, held immobile over where they live, seeming to take their breath away even before the house is filled with water spraying in, bursting in through the window and the door blown off its

hinges into the house, striking the man at the neck, to sever his head from his body. The young, bitter woman is captured by the slowing of time itself, as she sees the blood pour like a fountain from the headless body, coloring the water rising at her feet the color of rage and sin. As the water rises, she will not be comforted, struggling to breathe what air there is left, until it rises to the top of the isolated house, to cover every part within with water.

And the bitter young wife breathes her last breath of air, sinking from the top of the house to the middle, feeling the fire in her lungs sparked by the waters of burning agony, seeing the body of the man she knew, blood drifting forth from it in her fading vision, imagining the head that she cannot see, in the underwater light of dying life. As the pain flows from her lungs to the rest of her body, she slips and fades from this life, into the outer darkness of eternity, where there is a river that flows by the souls of epic thirst, and where there worm dieth not, and where there is weeping and gnashing of teeth, before they are judged by the Almighty God, and cast into a lake that burns with fire everlasting.

These two, who died a sinner's death of fire and blood, drift lifelessly in the isolated house filled with the icy waters of discontent, as the water devil begins to die in desperation and fury to live, unable to hold the water it has gathered into the house. The water devil dissipates into the surrounding storm, as the water risen into the isolated house flows out, carrying with it the head and body of the man inside, and the body of the young and bitter woman that was his wife.

From the remains of humanity's rise and fall, through the blinding sheets of rain, billowing black smoke rises from the fiery mountains unseen, as the fire spewing and pouring from within dies hard—the black smoke being rapidly converted to gray by the steam shooting upward, high into the sky, the cloud from the burning mountains filled with lightning and blasts of thunder, as the fire in the mountains is put out from the inside, while the smoke rising to the heavens is billowed and rained away, banished by the clouds of mist and snowy white. Of the untold numbers who remain, there stands a woman of wealth and means

at the window of her palace, safe from the clouds of billowing smoke and vapor from water burst forth, adrift in the tranquility of sorrow and deep though, of the sight of her seven year old daughter in her husband's arms, his voice echoing deeply through the palace, calling for servants and palace guards, giving his daughter's cold, lifeless body to the mother in wailing, whose mouth is frozen open in shock and disbelief. Oh, how violently her husband did protest and scream, grabbing servants and maidservants by their garments to ask and demand what they know, sending for soldiers and men who guard palaces to come for hire, to set up guard at this palace now, where before there was none, and to spread out over the countryside and offer ransom for any word about who may have snuck into the unguarded palace, and killed the seven year old little girl, whose body was found fully unclothed, and whose neck was bruised from the rope twisted around her neck by her wealthy father, and whose private nakedness is stained from the dried streams and droplets of blood.

This mother stands at the window of the rainy palace of wealth, un-noble, unforgiven for what secret she had endured for years, unable to accept or believe that the skin burns between her daughter's thighs—the princess—the swelling and pain in her daughter's bottom and privacy could possibly mean what the flood of revelation in her body tells her it means, but inexplicably keeping a sharper and closer attention on the girl, alerted only because of the attending lady's concern, who noticed her garment with a spot of blood from where the girl had sat to play. This, from the age of four, recurring every so often for the next three years, until whatever energy is born hath spilled over, to see the mother at the rainy palace window, days from having buried the secret into the waiting soil, to remind the lady of wealth and leisure—un-noble, unforgiven for what she has known and allowed, for the rope she knows was fashioned

about the little stick once used about her own neck in the bed chamber for his purest pleasure, this same tiny rope fashioned to the little stick put about her daughter's neck and twisted until the choking little girl lay dead.

What nightmare has it been, that awoke the fine and beautiful woman in one single blast of vision, that saw her little girl unclothed on her stomach, underneath a man whose face she could not see, whose strong hand lay clamped without mercy around her neck in choking. And when she woke up that night in the dark, oh what flash of fear it is, when thy husband is not laid beside of thee! Go back to sleep, woman of privilege! Thy fear is not required of thee! Stand at the window of thine discontent, Dear Woman, see the rainfall of thy tears and reckoning! For what can the rumbling earth, what can the driving, drowning rainfall do to thee! In thine heart, hast thou not already taken thine own life? Oh, what a blessed deluge of fear and devastation this is, Dear Woman! Why can you not feel the sting of terror, as the earth cracks nearby the palace where you can see, and the earth begins to open up towards the very window where you stand, splitting the wall before you, but with precision, forcing you to back up from the window whose shutters are laid open to the storm.

This crack in the earth now divides the room where you are knocked to the ground, where you are left alive to see the water explode into the palatial room itself, as the walls come tumbling down around you. Feel yourself falling, falling, falling free, Dear Woman, to the bottom floor of your fine palace in a shower of rock and water, un-noble, unblessedly alive to feel the water on fire in your nostrils, and the cracking of your leg from the fall, from the second floor to the bottom, and the crushing of your lower body from the heavy wall of rock that crushes thee. But still, you are kept alive on the grand palace floor that remains, Dear Woman, in the storm of noise and water that remains, Dear Woman, in the storm blasting into your house, splashing against the ceiling and

falling around you while you lie there on your back, unable to move, unable to feel the pain in your lower body and legs anymore, as the fear of Death begins to rise inside you, as you struggle to draw a breath in the cold water splashing in your face, obscuring your vision now so that you can hardly see as you lay dying, but kept alive to endure every moment of it, while the water begins to raise itself to substance on the cracked and broken palace floor around you. Raise your head, Dear Woman, as the fountain splashes into your face. Turn your head away, Dear Woman, hear the power of it in agony upon thy ear! In pain, you must hold your face to the fountain splashing down from the fountain of the deep, water which tastes nothing of the dirt and metal that it should, uncorrupted, the pure waters of Judgment and conviction. And now, Dear Woman, the panic must set in, while you realize that your arms are pinned beneath this wall fallen down upon thee!

Look through the hole broken and torn into your world, Dear Woman; look up, through the broken wall at the top of this floor, where you can glimpse the terrible lightning, where you can hear the sky proclaim the coming of mankind's ultimate Redemption, where you can see the Cross of Lightning spark, so that you may know in your soul what evil you have done. Now cough, Dear Woman, spit and cough the water rising up from the floor into your mouth, when the fountain of splashing has ceased in thy face, so that you may be free to breathe your last, just as the water rising overtakes the air just above thee, to obscure thy remaining vision to its shimmering and crystal clear demise. Open thy mouth wide, Dear Woman, laid helplessly on your back, unable to keep your mouth closed any longer, as your body pulls this water into thy lungs, to cause you to try and scream through the agony and the Fear of Death.. But there is only the noise of a woman's muffled, gurgling underwater cry, a tragic twitching and jerking in wide-eyed resistance to thy fate, then a sudden and fervent

stillness that overtakes thee, as you drift away from this watery grave, to where there is weeping and gnashing of teeth.

Then suddenly, the rumbling of the earth grows again beneath the woman's body, and her house explodes from the force of the water, grown to many times its former strength—blasting the house and dead body away, into a towering plume of water that arcs in every direction like a gigantic water blossom, every petal made by the flowering sheets of water, underneath the cross of lightning returned to split the air by four, with the greatest pop and crackle of thunder since before the earth itself was formed, as the water flower rises high and wide over the surrounding countryside, spreading outward, splashing giant drowning petals hard to the rainsoaked earth below, replaced by the shapeless fountain of water spewed from the cracked earth underneath the palace blown out of existence, and the bodies of every manservant, every womanservant, and the woman of wealth and privilege are carried into cataclysm and oblivion.

And it repented the Lord that he had made man on the earth, and it grieved him at his heart.

Genesis 6:6

Jonathan Lovejoy

Part Two

19

The end of this rainy day fades far into the night, as the crashing of water and sound attacks our journey without ceasing, causing us to have to stay tied to the beams for many hours on the first part of this journey, as the great ship dives beneath the violent waves continuously, climbing back up to the surface and splashing hard upright, with nary a drop of water so much as leaking through the ark window, closed shut, or the door to the long hall of windows on the roof. I have imagined many times what became of the bodies that I know were drowned when the water came pouring through those windows left open there, when the men had tried so desperately to get inside. But there has been no trace of sound from anyone above us, and I wonder, are there a lucky few who survived the wave's

passing, and are just so grateful to be aboard that they are hiding as quiet as the mice that are tucked away in their tiny spaces somewhere inside?

I am burdened by visions of calamity outside the ark, where I see that far into our darkest night, the skies are lit up by bolts and rivers of lightning above the ocean deep, where a thunderous rage that rattles Creation from the clouds every moment—of this new timeline marked by the alternating loudness of one blast of thunder to the other. The courses of every river on earth have been buried to nothing, as the flow of every river and stream is gone. What people there are who are alive and remain have abandoned all lower ground in time to see it disappear behind them, many men, women and children unlucky enough to see the truth glowing from beneath the water in the night, as the valleys glow from the melted rock pouring up from the flooded ground, cooling off, entombing all traces of human life in layers of solid rock, as the water pours from the sky in something greater than pain, and spews from the ground in something greater than a flood.

This deluge of water covers the valleys that have been exalted, climbing the nighttime mountains and hills laid low, gathering together with the quaking of the earth itself, to cover the cities that have crumbled to the ground in these earthquakes, and those covered by the fiery liquid rock from below. These earthquakes have appeared in diverse places, different places around the world even before the floodwaters came, carving grand canyons in the great plains of the earth, and laying waste to entire mountains, or crumbling away parts of the tallest in the world, to create sharp, high places that seem to stretch to the heavens, or rising up chains of high, rocky mountains that stretch beyond the horizon, where before was only the soil of an open prairie. To the base of these new mountain chains, the waters have already arrived, past the new valleys and canyons already

filled in. The waters soar and rage through the night, from the ark that rises and falls upon the waves, to the untold masses of humanity foolish enough to have taken higher ground, to witness the last of this present age of man, to hear the wrath of God blasted around them from the stormy sky, and to see the sign of his coming shine as lightning in the clouds.

And the earth is ravaged once again, by a quaking from somewhere deep within, all dreams of earthquakes brought together as one, to send rock slides tumbling onto the heads and backs of fools, who hath said in their heart that there is no God, to join the blasts of hill and mountain winds in the dark, and great splashes of rain poured into the sky and blown, to wash the remnants of the breath of life into the waters risen around them, to be swallowed by the crashing waves, and pulled into the briny depths of the worldwide ocean sea. And behind this final thundering of water-covered lands that proclaim, in this proclamation is the final explosion of wrath that begins, in the icy waters of the Great Northern Sea, where the earth itself cracks in a blinding flash of light from underneath the nighttime waters, this flash of undersea light traveling forward across the leagues of nighttime ocean waters, followed by a fountain such as never was, blown from the cracked earth underneath the sea, rising from the ocean waters as a Great Wall of Water, to dwarf any seen from land on mankind's final day, a wall of water exploding upward from the very ocean into the night, traveling from these icy waters unseen, following the lighted flashes from below the waters of the open earth—from the northernmost parts of the earth and downward, through the warm waters of Paradise Lost, and down beyond where any boat or ship hath dared to set sail, to where the leviathans lurk the unseen waters of bitter and icy cold, where hellish cold lies beyond the southern waters of Paradise, down to the

southernmost waters of the earth itself. Across the leagues of nighttime ocean, this Great Wall of Water stretches from north to south, as a barrier between east and west, lit up by the bright flashes of lightning above and beside it, from the storm that covers every square cubit of land and sea.

Every part of the waters beneath the earth are gathered and pushed up through this great rift at the bottom of the sea, rising high into the air as a great wall of water across the entire nighttime earth.

Throughout the night, some who have been washed into the sea, bear witness to the end of this age in water, lit up by the lightning, before they are dragged beneath the roaring waves for the watery agony that must burn, that must purify the earth through a cleansing, and the fiery deaths by lungs filled with water, and the choking away of the life and air they breathe. Through the night, and into the dawn of morning, this day after the first drop of rain fell into the palm of the woman's hand. In the stormy light of day, in the gray of this daytime darkness, the fury of this storm hath not ceased, and the Great Wall of Water is clearly visible by a few stalwart and stubborn souls, clinging to life and hope on driftwood from the wrecked pieces of so-called boats and ships, or the trunks and branches of trees cast aside as driftwood, a few of these souls survive for a final moment in the storm, where the sun is darkened by the dreary clouds, and the Moon can no longer give her light. These wayward souls are set adrift upon hopelessness, some witnessing the exploding water barrier, stretched from one horizon to the other, out of which are born great twisters of the open sea, that drift rapidly along with purpose, to find them who cling to these last branches of false hope and wicked dreams—these are twisted and carried into these great water whirlwinds, some carried aloft into the clouds of fury, where they see and hear the wrath of God in thunder, lightning,

wind and icy rain, before they are tossed without mercy into the stormy ocean waters of the deep.

And in the light of this new day, somewhere above the waters of the Great Flood, there are the final two souls that must be, huddled together in the highest mountain cave that was found by man. This widow and her young girl, huddled together at the mouth of the small cave, sheltered from the downpour but still touched by the rain blowing inside, in awe of the waters of the great flood that splash and roar outside the small cave, having risen so dramatically fast since yesterday, when the tops of trees were still visible just above the valley floor, as the base of this same mountain hill. Through the forest she had traveled that first day, when the floodwaters came into the village, lagged behind the others in weakness, having to pull her little daughter along but so fast, shocked when the tiny caves and crevices were only big enough for two or three people at a time, as many of the groups pushed her and her daughter away from the tiny spaces, forcing her to climb higher, higher, and higher still, up the mountain hillside in the wind and rain to save her daughter, at last finding a small cave for her and her little girl to hide in. They are at the mouth of Hell, these two, their space lit up by the flashes of lightning, the mother unable to fathom what she sees upon the waters in the far off distance, unable to conceive an answer to her daughter's question, as to what the thing is that they see, and whether or not it is a boat, or whether or not there are people inside.

Deep inside the roaming ship, inside the darkness of our journey, we stand tethered to the four beams, each man with his wife, all of us weary from the splashing of the waves, the crashing of thunder booming, the thrashing we have taken in the pitch blackness hardly touched by the raised torches and flames. Outside the ark, in the gray of the second day's

passing, the flood waters rise higher and higher over the land, until the breath of life is extinguished from all mankind, from every beast of the field, every bird of the air, and every creeping thing. Every good and evil deed, every thought and dream of man, and every work he had wrought with his hands, every work of mankind is destroyed and buried beneath the waves, as the water rises to the very top of the highest mountain peak on earth, until every part of dry land is come and gone.

Since our third day aboard the ark, the ties that bind are unraveled, our straps having been long undone, hanging unused on the four beams we were tied to. For three days, our ride was so filled with twists and turns, the ark rocking and leaning so far as to slam animals about in their cages, and so that anyone untethered or untied would have been rolled and knocked like a stone—our ride was so violent with motion that we could not leave the emergency beams to get to our benches, for fear of being slammed to the top of the ship when it tipped over. But through the wrath of the storm we persevered, unprepared for the knowledge of the truth. But on the third day, we noticed that the voice of the storm calmed to a steady rolling of deep thunder, and the rise and fall of the ark no longer threatened

to turn us upside down. Seven days after the ark was lifted from the earth, I take my place at the third floor window, where I can look upon the storm that blows now with a steady assurance and protracted, end of the world longevity.

Far into the distance, I see the three whirlwinds set afar off, to the far left, to the center, and the far right of my vision. What terrible and violent winds these must have been, to toss us about at such a fevered pitch for three days and nights. How completely irrelevant and unimportant were we, having only survived their closeness to us, having survived their proximity by the Hand of God! They travel with us over these stormy seas, to guide us from one millennium to the next, from one part of the timeline to another, where there will be no people, no places, no things upon the Earth as we knew it, where what survival there is for humanity will come from us. I am unable to look at the three whirlwinds without my mind being set adrift, back to the days before the floodwaters came, in the days when the sky was blue.

21

*N*ora is twelve years old at my mother's bedside. Four years younger than I. A whirlwind of tranquility rises high into the stormy sky, towering as mother Adina once did over us, where my sister Nora was twelve. It is one of the legion of days burned into the Heart of Memory, burned so deeply into my soul. This is the day of my sister's twelfth birthday, when my mother whispers to me, concerning what I am already four years acquainted with. *Nela, I need to talk to you*, she says, *come with me to the well. Nora, stay here and watch the bread. And don't let it burn this time.* The wind from the storm blows hard into my face, to remind me of the cooling late afternoon breeze of a summer's day, when a single cloud passes over the sun as we walk.

At the well as we fill the pots with water, *I need to watch you nurse your sister's breasts.*

I am unable to pretend. Unable to keep looking at the water going into the clay pot. Raising up from the stone well in our village, where we are blessedly alone. If we were not, could she have possible spoken those words aloud. *After dinner tonight,* she says. Her pot is filled with water, as she turns without looking at me again. And I am transported from the well backward, to four years before, on the day I saw my twelfth birthday. I was twelve, when the spirit came unto me. I was twelve, when the Spirit hath come.

I can remember clearly, as I have always been so inclined, the terrible anguish on her face four years ago, and the power I felt coursing from every part of my body, through my breasts, and into her mouth that day. Oh, but how can I rescue Nora from this agony, from the burning of blue and black fire! I should tell her, and confront our mother with the knowledge of this truth, of what devastation we are burdened to feel. But what pure foolishness is this thing I imagine, to confront this tall, strong, beautiful woman with such insolence, such profound disobedience as to be epic. Do I wish to have my legs tied together, with her knee in my back, with the bottom of her sandal turning my white skin to blood? Then why don't I just grab my little sister by the hand, and run with her into the wilderness, like two clouds of prairie dust in the wind, blown up from nowhere, blowing down to nowhere still? Why does the dove seek to flutter away from the she-wolf's mouth, when there is no escape, when there is no relief from suffering?

In this lady's den, when dinner has been eaten, when the earth turns toward the evening, I am sixteen at my mother's fine, comfortable featherbed, when my sister Nora is twelve. *Take her dress down,* Mother

says to me, *but don't take it off yet. Now, put your tongue to her nipples for me.* And this, I do. Glancing once pitifully into her eyes, then touching the tip of my tongue to her nipple. Young Nela twitches hard once, as if to pull away, until mother's voice soothes her to calm. *It's alright Nora*, she says, in understanding and compassion, taking the top of her own garment away from the mountainous breasts, her eyes fixed on the sight of what must surely be forbidden.

Lick it good, she says. *Now suck it. Suck it good. Suck it deep into your mouth.*

And mother stands there in awe of what she sees, of what she feels in her own body from just this visual alone. *Take each other's clothes off,* she says, *one at a time. Nela, take hers off first.* We obey quickly, as my mother slowly takes off the rest of her garment, her fingers at both of her nipples. Holding them still. She makes us leave our headdresses on, Nora's bright red, mine as blue as the petals of a cornflower, the cloth contrasting with our white skin, as mother tells little Nora to put her hands behind her back.

Now put your teeth at her nipples, she says, but gently. *Bite down softly. Harder. A little harder. Hold still, Nora. A little harder, Nela.*

The sight of my little sister's cringing, the sight of her innocence corrupted, the grimace of this pain upon her beautiful young face, causes Mother to twitch once ever so slightly, pinching the front of her breasts in slow and continuous motion, her face burdened now by shock and disbelief.

Stand beside her, Nela. Take your headdresses off. Wet your finger, Nela. Spit on your sister's finger, Nora. Her middle finger. Get it good and wet. Now Nela, put it in your sister's bottom.

I watch my mother lick and kiss my sister's young lips with power. With purpose and conviction of the soul. Her tongue leading first in each kiss followed by a powerful pressing and sucking of each of Nora's lips separate, then together, then separately again. Then she moves this forbidden kiss to me, and the mere touch of her lips, the feel of her tongue in my mouth goes straight to my groin.

I want you to both kiss my breasts. Don't suck the nipple yet. Kiss around the nipple.

This, we do. As she looks down at both her daughters, at the daughter who is sixteen, and the daughter who has crossed over from innocence, her beautiful young face in the aftermath of trauma, kissing her mother's breasts nearby the nipple, causing it to grow in preparation to this new craving.

Nela, watch your sister, she says. *Put your nipple against mine. Rub your nipple against mine while you watch your sister.*

This, I do. Savoring the feel of my nipple against my mother's. Mother's desire is such that she shakes both of her breasts free, telling Nora and me not to touch them with our hands, while one bounces freely against her young daughter's face, and the other against my breasts hung free. My own breasts are twice the size of most, but still so much smaller than my mother's, who has the largest bosom I have ever seen or imagined, with a deeply curved waist and full, rounded hips. These breasts, and the beauty of her face combine as oil and flame, to strike fire in the soul of both men and women, fires of lust or jealousy, many in our village having drifted to sleep on a pillow of desire, to be where I am now, to see what depths of sensual depravity is done in secret.

And mother leans over with purpose, and violently licks her twelve year old daughter's breasts, sucking each one so loudly, each wet from the spit of her mouth, then moving to my heavy, wobbling breasts, pulling the nipple deep into this same violent licking and sucking, her voice bellowing like the oxen pulling a cart, holding both mine and Nora's smaller, undeveloped young breasts with both her hands, endeavoring to lick and suck dry every drop of the energy she has brought forth, soon licking my sister's neck, then running her tongue to Nora's chin and her cheeks, even kissing both her eyes, with even one good sucking kiss to her daughter's perfect little nose, then to her moth and tongue again.

Stand beside me, she says. *Both of you. Now work my breasts with your hand. Please. Pinch the nipples hard. Pinch them harder. Squeeze my whole breast. Lift them up. And squeeze. Lift and squeeze. And lift and squeeze. Lift, pinch and squeeze. Lift and squeeze.*

She must put her head back, shaking it 'no' in denial, in near resistance to what heights of pleasure that can be achieved, looking down again at her young daughter's small, white hand buried into the breast flesh, moaning again in that same expression of mysterious, inner suffering I have heard before.

Get behind me, Nela. Keep your hand on my breast. Pinch the nipple. Put your other hand between my legs.

This, I do. Holding it there, at where I have been accustomed to do. Holding onto her tight and strong, to lend support for the crashing that must be.

Stand in front of me Nora, she says. *Take one breast up. Hold it with both hands. Please. Put the nipple in your mouth, Nora. Suck it good. Keep it in your mouth. Suck it like you want the milk...*

And upon this word, I feel my mother's body tremble and shake of its own accord, taking her breath as she struggles to breathe, and then she doubles over in a mighty lunge backward, with a single, unearthly shriek— while I feel a small fountain of water gush into my hand from somewhere deep inside her. In the manner I am accustomed to, I hold onto her in full strength, aware of the strong spasms at my hand down below, holding it still at her swollen self gushed free, holding onto her as she screams through the second wave of energy bursting into her body, a cry traveling through time and history, far into the bleak and hopeless future of mankind.

*N*oah may be the kindest, most understanding person I've ever met. Which is why I was so shocked and disturbed by the incident with Seda, even though she clearly was on the edge of going too far. Which is

what she often does from time to time, tending to work her husband Shem into a rage, then crying foul when he grabs her and tries to shake the life out of her. One might think that my relationship would be the most chaotic, since Ham is the wildest of Noah's three sons. But the truth is , we have hardly had a cross word between us, while Shem and Seda argue almost all the time. It's because I mostly just keep my mouth shut, and I don't [push Ham's buttons], and I don't look for opportunities to attack him, or antagonize him into a rage. Of the three wives, I think that Seda is the most resentful of her fate, the sorriest that she had anything to do with this ark

business, the sorriest that she's had to spend all those years in poverty and ridicule because her husband, who they said was too old for her anyway, was a dirt poor nothing with a crazy mother and father. And I have noticed that among the four of us women, Seda is by far the meanest, sometimes with a serpent-like personality, where she will wait until any one of us is at our weakest and most vulnerable, then she will strike with the lowest blow she can. Seda would have to be beaten into submission like a mule, which Noah will not allow, telling Shem *love your wife, and don't be bitter against her.* This, even though she has spoken out against the ark many times, calling it a "stupid waste of time," and telling Shem during an argument I heart once, *you can take this ugly piece of shit and cram it!* Seda's beauty and strength, her regal presence does put me so much in mind of Mother, that I am often afraid of her, and sometimes I still worry that she has a beating stored up for me that is long overdue.

Japeth refuses to argue with her, being the most like his father, but with an even greater soft spokenness and humbleness about him, so that he and Ada together are the center of our tranquility. But Seda and my husband used to argue and rage at each other all the time, getting in each other's faces like two angry sabertooths, often having to be pulled apart as if they were on the edge of a physical fight.

So there is no wonder that Noah had finally had enough, on the day the floodwaters came, when she was probably the edge of bringing a curse down upon herself. She had fought even to the last, until she was chosen to be the one to receive the first drop of truth that fell from the sky just one week ago.

Truth falls at the window of the ark, across the rolling seascape of wind and waves, to beyond every horizon on earth. Our seventh day in this great ship brings the calm of uneasy acceptance, the realization in our souls that everyone, every *thing* we ever knew and took for granted is gone forever. But the spirit of that world is carried with us all on this journey, and the memories of the condemned souls we knew.

My mother dominates my heart and mind. From the time I was a little girl, til the day I married into this family. Until the day she cursed me to my face and spit on me, and the day my sister called me a stupid bitch for what I had done. It's impossible for me to remember mother now without the flashes of aggression and secret craving that burned her up like no other. Why is it that when I close my eyes, I can see mother and Shem's

wife Seda together, though it surely could not have happened—I see them in Shem's house when he is away at the ark. I see Seda and my mother in private wrestling, holding hands, pushing their breasts together, teeth blared in two angry, lustful grimaces, like what Mother often has done with my sister Nora in times of their greatest need. A powerful and profound outlet for Seda's burning frustration it would have been, to take out this inner rage and secret feeling on another with like understanding. These many months I have known Seda, I have been unable to separate her from my mother in my mind—two beautiful, angry women—kindred spirits, forever linked in my fearful imagination, where I have been awakened at night in a scream, pulled from the world of dreams, where Mother and Seda were on top of me together, holding me down, with my arms pinned so tight, pressing on me so heavy that my breath is taken, causing me to panic and scream violently. My dreams are flooded this past year, with images of this flood in which we travel, and of Seda and my mother's phantom connection across time.

Adina! Seda! Push thy breasts together in combat! Blare thy lovely teeth in violence! This, I cannot cease to imagine, maybe because I have seen Mother and Nora engaged in this so often when they wrestled in the nude, or when Mother stood close by while Nora and I were forced to wrestle when we were older, the loser having to be whipped by Mother. This made for such feverishly violent wrestling between us, where there was much grunting and loud breathing, with Nora getting the best of me most of the time, which I know Mother enjoyed the most, being that my curves are the softest and the heaviest, the most reminiscent of her own.

Nora is taller than me. Slimmer and more athletic. Features so exquisitely perfect as to be painful to look upon—to cause intense

concentration, intense contemplation as to how such beauty of the eyes, nose and mouth are possible, whose body bears smaller but more beautiful examples of the nude female forms, of the kind that men tend to carve statues to. Big, firm breasts above a tiny, slightly muscular waist—a powerful, feminine athleticism put to brave use behind the walls of secret—many times when our wrestling had found its victor (usually Nora), whose beautiful mouth would clamp down upon my breasts in hard, painful sucking, before she would hold me down and insert herself into me, her great anomaly that so few women have ever known or possessed, the ability to penetrate another woman with the enlarged member she possesses. Slamming herself into me with the fever and prowess of a man, but with the benefit of a woman's softness and beauty besides. She would do this until she had to give in to the power of it through a pitiful, wailing cry, followed by a quick and violent shaking of her body, as she would struggle to continue to thrust and drive her body through. I have seen my mother defeat Nora in these powerful wrestling matches, then sit upon her unclothed, bouncing herself upon her daughter's enlarged member until her entire body was alive with trembling, her curves rippling like the waters across a pond in a summer breeze.

Their energy from these heavy memories will often reach out, and pull me into them, where their violent wrestling will ensue, mother eventually winning by getting behind her, reaching up under Nora's arms, then clamping her hands hard together behind Nora's neck—lying on top of her on the bed, and slamming herself hard into her, hard enough to rattle her insides. Mother possesses what surely must be a masculine strength, a strength I have felt myself, when I have lost private wrestling matches with Nora, and mother performed this same move on me even after I had been striped to red welts and a touch of blood.

"You're thinking about your mother," Ada says. Shocking me awake from my stormy daydream. Ada had climbed the stairs up to this window platform without me ever realizing it, as if she just appeared beside me. Like a ghost.

She stands beside me, pressing her soft body up against me, both of us looking out of the stormy window, still able to see the three whirlwinds in the far off distance. With her arm tightly around my waist behind my back, her other hand gripped firmly in mine across the front of me, Ada whispers something in my ear of such great comfort as I have not known in many months, making me close my eyes and hold my head back to breathe in, while she kisses me hard on the cheek, causing me to swoon, as though I might be lifted from my body, and be drifted as a spirit out into the storm.

"What are you two doing up here?" Seda says, walking up the stairs toward us.

"Nothing."

"I wouldn't call kissing Ham's wife nothing. If you two think I don't know what—"

"I only kissed her on the cheek."

I watch Seda relax her beautiful expression, her lips parting in contempt and inner frustration.

"How long before you're kissing her on the mouth?"

In their silence lays the seed of bitterness and discord, born from Ada's quiet strength, and Seda's inability to make her afraid. Since I came into this family, Ada has protected me from the Wrath of Seda, and what harm it is she intends to do with either a stick or a leather strap.

"Maybe you want me to kiss *you* on the mouth," Ada says.

"You do and I will slap you silly."

Between the two of them, there are pressures I have seen, stresses I have felt, that have threatened to snap and unravel their civility. Though Ada is the center of tranquility and peacefulness, she has endured many years of incessant bullying from her older sister in law, which has built up pressure over time, made worse by the stresses of our calling, our moving into the Ark, the arrival of tens of thousands of animals, the life and death of the entire world, and our entombment inside the worst storm the earth has ever known.

"I was only joking," Ada says.

"You goddamned right you were joking. Now you and Nela get your asses down from here and help us with these torches. The ones that are out have to be soaked and relit. They're going out all over the ship."

"We'll be down shortly," Ada says. With a disdainful, contemptuous glare, Seda turns and walks hatefully away, descending the stairs from our high place at the top of the third floor, descending somewhere into the bowels of the great ship. What few torches there are still burning on this floor are low, and threaten to soon plunge us into near total darkness.

$\mathcal{I}$n near total darkness. When the evening day has turned to night. I am a lonely figure, abiding in the fields, a long walk from the village. Drawn here every night by the appearance of a new star in the heavens, in the weeks before the floodwaters were upon the earth. Others have been unable to accept this as the last and greatest sign, having already refused to look at it with more than a passing glance, as if not looking at it will make it go away. *There is room in the Ark for all who believe and repent*, Noah says, even though he already knows that none will be saved. In these few weeks before I must go with my husband into the Ark, I stand in total awe of this night sky, understanding what Noah means when he says that the heavens declare the glory of God. And this new star I see, on this long

walk from my mother's village, is the brightest and most beautiful traveler in the sky, with a tail of wispy white and blue light trailing behind it, as it plunges down toward the Western horizon every night after sunset. Noah says it is the return of the sign he was given a century ago, when the building of the Ark was but a voice in the night.

I married Ham under one condition. That he *never* deny me access to my mother. Brief visits. Long visits. It didn't matter. A day. A week. Two weeks, if it should come to that. I could never have married anyone who would have come between my mother, my sister and me. There is a closeness that we have, an unbreakable bond, a connection that goes deeper than anything he could ever understand, nor could he believe it, I imagine. Is it because my mother is beautiful? My sister? Is it because they are prettier than all other women that I am so impossibly drawn to them? There is so much failure and mediocrity in the world, so many failed attempts at everything, including beauty itself, that is it not a natural thing to be inextricably bound to excellence and greatness, to be drawn to it like a honeybee to a spring flower, especially when it is members of your own family? When the natural love between family members is enhanced by beauty, or money, or extreme kindness, the allure is irresistible, creating a bond as solid as a wall of rock. My mother has no money, nor is she particularly kind or respectful to me. But from the time I was a little girl, I noticed that the beauty of her face renews itself, so that upon second viewing, and on to infinity, one is reminded that hardly a woman like her hath ever been seen from far and wide—a face to delight the soul and spirit—to allow one to explore the possibilities of hope, and the pursuit of happiness itself. And this woman who made everyone in our village smile and wave and stare continuously, (then eventually turn in a tide of fear and jealousy), this statue goddess come to life is my mother Adina, as well as

my sister Nora, and from their appearances alone is a power, an unbelievable attraction, as is the eyesight to the silver light of the crescent moon, and the brightest star above the Western Gate.

And does it matter, that my earliest memory is of a whipping? I don't know if it matters, that the love I have for my mother is bonded with pain and suffering. Does that strengthen the power of what I feel? It is true, that as long as I can remember, my mother has taken every opportunity allowed and then some, to deliver her frustrations through the leather and onto my skin. Not sparing my sister either, who made it so much easier for Mother to deliver this message, being more willful and stubborn than I. There were times when Nora would refuse to move, as stubborn as Ham's mule, until Mother would suddenly come down onto her shoulders or her back with the mule strap, grabbing Nora's arm and commencing the task at hand, which was to deliver a message of unquestionable obedience, which the two of us had burned into us early on, through many hundreds of mild and severe whippings, until we both regarded my mother with fear and dread. And I can remember that her approach to Nora was more feverishly violent than it had been with me, but coupled with an even greater affection and comfort on the other end, as she would gently wipe her eyes and kiss her young tears away as she stood nude in front of Mother.

These hard and harsh whippings continued throughout our young years and into our adulthood, me having received my last whipping only the night before my wedding, so that my husband was even inclined to ask about the welts and fresh scars on my body. *My mother gets angry sometimes,* I told him, which was the only part of the truth he was truly interested in, I suppose. Yes, my whippings did not end until after I was married, and even then, there were veiled threats of it happening when her

mood was wrong. A long time ago, when I was sixteen, and when my sister was twelve, my mother began to pull off the cloak of pretense from around our punishments, until there remained the nakedness of pure truth, that she was going to whip us because she *had* to, whether or not it was anything particular we had said or done to deserve it. And she mostly, but not always, had us strip down to our bare skin, and either wait for her to come into the room, or she would begin immediately. And those were not the playtime whippings or spankings, but always done with a serious tone, as though to have done otherwise would have breached a barrier of energy she always built, which brought extreme pleasure to her body every time.

There have been times when I would come upon my sister sitting alone outside, her refusing to talk to me, causing me to go inside and ask my mother what was wrong with her. *She's going to get a whipping,* Mother would say.

What did she do?

Its just her time, Mother says. *And she's angry. Well, good. The angrier, the better. She'll scream louder.* And she would go on about her cooking affairs as if nary a wayward breeze had blown, though Nora had clearly not misbehaved, nor given her disrespect of any kind.

I can remember going back out to her one of those times, trying to comfort her, telling her *it will all be over soon,* and to *just pretend it doesn't hurt.* In the heart of memory, sixteen year old Nora lowers her head in the cooling summer wind, allowing the tears to fall.

I'm tired of it, she says. *It hurts so bad, and I want it to stop.*

Its not going to stop, I say. *You're miserable because that's what you want.*

But why does she have to hurt us all the time? She hits, she whips, she pinches, she bites. My body is sore from it all.

It's a part of who she is. If you want to live here, you'll just have to accept it.

The beautiful Nora leans over and rests her head on my shoulder to try and draw comfort from where there is none. Because this afternoon, or tonight, one or two, or three, or four hours away, it does not matter to Mother, Nora is going to receive the whipping of her young life.

From the darkness of the Great Ship, to torch lights dipped in oil and lit, the flames serve to light the halls of my memory as well. From the center of thought along the timeline, which is my walk under the sign of the new star—I am carried to the depth of my life as I knew it, the burden of these things which are done in secret, which are too implausible to be believed, understanding too imperceptible to be achieved. I am cursed to carry the oppressiveness of a past life in torment, behind the walls of secret, where these things are common to mothers and daughters through time and history, lying as the greatest and most well kept secret known and unknown. That women are heavy laden with sin, she-beasts a burdened by depravities hardly imagined, covered in a veil of beauty and fine cloth linen, jewelry and faces painted to mask a soul of debauchery.

This wild and wanton need lies inside my mother, who hath gladly buried her husband when my sister was a little child. This woman of such towering need, whose desire rises from the East, burning blue and black fire. This woman moves about the house in near total silence, when the evening day has turned to night. Enjoying the first part of the truth, which is the telling of the punishment to come. I know that her greatest pleasure, aside from our nakedness together, is to watch the disillusionment come over our faces, to watch it transform itself into fear. All afternoon, through the twilight, and into the early part of night, she has enjoyed the tension in the house, knowing every part of it was caused by her. When Nora and I are outside under the stars, both our necks sore from counting and discussing every other star in the heavens, we hear Mother call Nora's name, a song sung in the pain of acceptance, causing my sister and I to look at each other, even hugging one another briefly, again trying to find comfort where there is none.

The song of the lark calls again, from behind the walls of her nighttime prison. Nora turns away from me, and I must not go inside tonight, lest I be called inside to watch. But I know that what pleasure she derives from tonight's whipping is pure pain, which is the second part of this devastating truth. It begins when Nora arrives in the bedroom, dimly lit by many candles on the small tables, where Nora sees the woman unclothed in the candle light, her great breasts hung down as she places her linen cloth on the floor against the stone wall. She rises up, her beautiful face heavy burdened with suppressed desire built up, to where the holding in of it is the cause for a frustration unendurable.

Take off your clothes, she says. *And I don't want to hear a word. Just keep your mouth shut and take all of your clothes off.* This is truly the

underside of the two parts of who she is, which is lightness and darkness. This is the dark side of motherhood. That which occurs behind the walls of secret, which cannot be discussed, or even acknowledged as truth, or that it has ever existed at any time in history. It is this touch of the forbidden, the release of it as an explosion from the deep, it is this which races my mother's heart in the dark, as she watches her beautiful sixteen year old daughter take off her clothes, while her fearful expression becomes burdened with shame. In the fog of this epic humiliation, my mother calls Nora to her, to watch her walk ashamed and afraid toward her, in the sorrow of this type of fear unleashed, which is the Fear of Pain.

Mother grabs Nora's arm and begins to whip her—to deliver the third part of the Truth—which is: *I need to feel you suffer, daughter, every pitiful sob and scream you make rises me up inside—rising me higher and higher with each blow, until I feel as if I may float off the floor and beat you from above. As I whip you, Dear Nora, learn the third part of the Truth, which is that I am bound by this craving, that my body requires it as a [drug], that you were born to me as part of my struggle to find happiness, as those who seek it through wine or strong drink, the sound of this strap across your skin, the sound of your screaming in my ears, the sight of your breasts shaking and swinging about, the jiggle of your thighs and hips, your beautiful face of fire with fear, these have all worked themselves into me by candle light, Dear Nora, until my body has begun to spasm from deep within, making me wish to piss myself in front of thee, but it is only the dampness of suppression unleashed, the waters of instinct fulfilled...*

Mother delivers the third and deepest part of the truth in leather and lashing, her arm stretched far back, her great breasts swinging mightily with each blow, as she begins her daughter's full conversion to her

required state of mind, where there is no resistance to her will, and there is only obedience and submission. By the light of candles that still burn, in the aftermath of traumas so rarely understood, Mother shoves her daughter hard away from her toward the bed, where Nora sits in sobbing, her arms crossed over her breasts in the modesty of humiliation. *Lie down,* Mother says, her face made impossible by the unique gathering of candlelight, unwrapping the end of the strap from her hand and tossing it to the floor. She climbs on the bed with slow, solemn determination, climbing on top of her daughter in the candlelit dark, placing the front of herself down upon the front of her daughter, feeling her daughter's great anomaly pressing firm against her, aching her body into a gyrating motion, which morphs into a rhythmic slamming of herself between her daughter's legs—in slow, hard thrusts, that do not deviate from this pattern, as Nora lies underneath her in tears, holding on through the violence, as Mother's lower body slams itself in this powerful rhythm of its own accord, every part of her thighs and buttocks shaken from this motion, until her body ceases to move on its own, and her bottom begins to shake violently, coursing through to her legs and to the rest of her, as the weeks of pent up energy begin to slowly release itself into her body.

I am 20 years old this night, when I hear the sobs of my 16 year old sister, drowned out by the wailing cries of a woman condemned. The wailing cries of an accursed woman.

I was twelve, when her spirit came to me. I was twelve, when her spirit hath come. I am but a girl of twelve, having not yet known my mother's kiss, playing tag with my sister and several other neighborhood girls, on a warm, breezy summer's day. The sky is a deeper shade of itself, intensely blue, with fluffy white clouds in the far off distance. I run squealing in delight from whoever it is we have touched, while she chases us with an outstretched hand, with fingers surely on fire with some unknown witchcraft ready to burn our skin. I am hardly aware of wherever it is my beloved mother could have gone, as to whether she is in the house alone or whether she is in the company of women. Somewhere in the space of Creation itself, I am vaguely attuned to her presence, sitting on the low, rock hewn benches with the woman who is likely her best friend, the

mother of the oldest girl in our little group, who is only fifteen, but hardly the fastest or the most aggressive girl we see. Though my little sister is only eight, she is the prettiest among us, appearing older than herself, running the fastest to catch any one of us that she pleases.

"Have you ever kissed your daughter?"

"I kiss them both all the time," Mother says.

"What about Nela?"

"What about her?"

"I mean… have you *really* kissed your daughter?"

Mother is a stone's throw from naïveté. If that stone is hurled from a slingshot.

"Why do you ask?"

"About a year ago, I met this wealthy woman in a town market, about three days ride from here. Another one of Nathan's failed schemes. But it keeps things interesting. There's no telling when we'll just pick up and go somewhere. Well, in this market, I met a lady who had to have been rich. All the jewelry, the make up—the clothes. She walked right up to my daughter and me, and started asking all these questions about who my husband is and where we were from. And of course, I started talking to her about how beautiful she was and admiring that gold jewelry. And she gave me the strangest look, and she said *"I have a daughter about your age."* But she wasn't smiling anymore. It was the strangest thing I've ever seen. And she said, *"My husband travels a lot. My daughter and I are always looking for good company. Would you mind visiting our home for a short time today? I'd like for our daughters to meet, and maybe our husbands can discuss business."* Well, the way the woman carried herself, confident, beautiful, I couldn't say no. So, my husband met her husband, they hit it

off beautifully, and so we all went to this woman's house. They had a big farm, fields full of workers and the house was like a palace. Well, we all had the best dinner I've ever eaten, and the man invited us to stay a few days, even took Nathan away with him on a business trip. People we had never even seen before. Rich people, Dina, and here we were in their big, beautiful house, with not a single care in the world. I'll never forget this because I can remember it was raining that day, and I was alone at the balcony window, just sort of lost in the feeling. It was like a dream. Well, she comes up behind me, deep sultry voice, holding me by the arms. She says, *"Your daughter is so exquisitely beautiful."* And I thought she was just being nice because it was *her* daughter that was the pretty one."

"Your daughter's beautiful too," Mother says.

"Nadia is… cute. And very sweet. Very innocent. Even though she looks like a grown woman, you can tell she's only 15 by the way she acts. But she was only 14 at this woman's house. The woman's name was Diana. They remind me so much of you and your daughters. The beauty, I mean. Well, this woman Diana, she kisses me on the cheek while standing behind me."

"What did you do?"

"What could I do? I knew that something weird was happening the day she asked me to her house. You could sense the loneliness, the desperation. It was like she was clawing at me to save her from drowning. And besides, she was so beautiful. So sensual. I still can't see what it was about me and Nadia she found so special."

"Because of your innocence," Mother says. "Unspoiled. Uncorrupted by riches. Plus, it was like you said. She was just lonely."

"It was more then that. She said to me—*"What do you think of my daughter?* I told her, she's the most beautiful little girl I've ever seen. And

then she said her daughter wanted to spend time alone with me. And she wanted to spend time alone with *my* daughter. Her daughter Anya came to me later that same day, told me she wanted to sleep in my bed, and that her mother wanted Nadia to sleep with her."

"Didn't you know what they were up to?"

"You would think I would, right? But my mind just didn't allow me to see that. I kept thinking—this is a nice, beautiful visit, these are nice, beautiful people."

"What happened?"

"Well, it seemed kind of fun, Diana and me exchanging daughters for the night. I enjoyed lying in the bed, listening to that beautiful little girl go on and on, chattering about everything and nothing."

"What did she talk about?"

"She never stopped talking about her mother. How beautiful she was, how nice she was. How lucky she was that such a beautiful, nice woman was hers. Then, just out of the blue, she says *"Mother even taught me how to kiss."* I acted shocked of course, but to tell you the truth, I think I was just plain turned on by it."

"Her mother kissed her?"

"That's what she told me. And I believed her."

"What else did she say?"

"Its not what she *said*. Its what she *did.* She rolled over close to me and leaned in like it was nothing, and laid a kiss on me better than anything I ever felt from my husband. Always touching my lips with her tongue first. This little fourteen year old girl was kissing me like a lover. Touching me all over with her hands. Telling me to relax. It happened about a year ago. But I remember it like it was yesterday. Because I remember that the best

feeling I ever had was when she put her pretty little mouth on my nipple. It sent a wave through me. Like a bolt of lightning. I've never felt anything like it before or since, than when she sucked my nipple. It was like I suddenly couldn't see. Like I couldn't breathe. Then she took her nightgown off, and she helped me take off mine. Then she gave me what she called a tongue bath. And she kissed and licked every inch of me from my face and neck, my shoulders and my arms. My breasts and nipples again. My stomach. My thighs, my legs. My feet. Then the beautiful young girl with this tight little body, she straddled my between my legs. That same lightning bolt was building up in my mind again, watching this girl snake her little hips, grinding her little self on top of me. Then she started to hop up and down."

Mother feels her friend reach over and grab her on the knee, watching her close her eyes, then lower and shake her head.

"The lightning bolt," Mother says.

"The more she hopped, the stronger I felt it. And eventually, I had to grab onto her and strain to keep from screaming at the top of my lungs. But her beautiful little voice. She let it go. And there was nothing I could do but lay there straining and breathing and shaking while her voice echoed all over their house. She sounded like I was killing her. Which is exactly what she was doing to me. And when she was finished grinding and hopping, she laid down and opened my legs. I had no idea what this girl was doing. But she went to work with that mouth of hers again. Right on it. Lips. Tongue. Everything. And this time, I screamed."

Sharon is unaware of the drained and tormented look on my mother's face. With her hand on top of her best friend's at her knee, Mother looks across the brief distance, down the dusty streets of the village, where the little girls squeal in delight at play.

other allows these days of summer to pass, where she pushes

the Sharon Revelation to the back of her mind, until it fades somewhere

into her grieving soul and spirit. Here, it takes firm root in the soil of

desire, where it begins to grow and blossom. And these new and powerful

frustrations have taken hold of her unbeknownst to eight year old Nora and

me, causing her to find more excuses to punish us, to keep us crying,

depressed and disillusioned as she. All summer long, she has resisted the

urge to go to Sharon and confess that she understands every part of that

rich woman's need, having felt it even from when she bathed me as a little

girl, having to punish us frequently as an outlet for these impossible urges.

Mother and her best friend Sharon have found a new inseparability, born from the need for one to tell of what churns beneath cultured civility, the other with the need to listen. At least once a week these last two months or so, Mother has listened attentively to the stories of this wealthy woman Diana, even turning down an invitation from Sharon to travel with them to the rich woman's house.

"I told them about you," Sharon had said. *"I told her about you and your daughters. I told her that you were the most beautiful woman she'll ever see, and that your breasts were like those of a goddess. It was the first time that it happened between us that I told her. She had become just as interested in me as she was in my daughter. What she really likes to do is to tie my hands behind my back and nurse my breasts hard enough to make them sore, or to spank them until I have to cry from the pain..."*

These things you have heard, Mother, listening intently, hearing the focus and center of your fantasy life laid out in reality—Mothers and Daughters, women loving women, without regard to boundaries or pretense, nor any delusions of morality in secret. These are the same things you have imagined, thought about, lusted and craved your entire life, burying and repressing these desires in marriage and motherhood, so glad now that your husband is six years in his grave, since Nora was only two years old. Of course, Sharon was there to pick up the pieces of your shattered life, and help you put them back together. And how is it that the forces that guide us seem to know all things, knowing that in these thoughts and perversions, you and Sharon are kindred spirits? But you have told her already that you cannot let her have me, and that you cannot see her daughter as anything other than a sweet girl. And she is relieved and appreciative of this, is she not? Because you are a refuge of purity for

her, Mother. A confessional place, a lady priest to take upon yourself her sins, and cleanse her from the unrighteousness of perversion.

But what of you, Mother? Who do you tell, of the things you want to do to me? The things you want to do to little eight year old Nora? When the two of you sip the fruit juices from the little wooden cups, why do you ask her: *What's your favorite thing to do with your daughter?* What does it do to you, Mother, to learn that she is obsessed with lying on her back underneath her, watching her bounce and grind herself to oblivion? Sharon always has to strain when this happens, does she not? Holding her head back in that angry gnashing of teeth, to endure the height of suffering that courses through her body. And already, you are learning, Mother, that your obsession will be the opposite when it happens, that you well be on top of me before I see my thirteenth birthday, writhing yourself into an end of the world quaking and trembling.

But Mother lets these weeks pass, uneventful, except for the frustrated increase in violence, Nora and I being the victims, learning this summer that we are going to be whipped with the strap or the cane when she feels like it, whether or not we've done anything to deserve it. If the bread is burned, if the cooking fire is not properly tended, if the water pot gets too low, if Nora and I are talking and laughing too loud, if we are outside and do not come immediately when she calls—anything now seems appropriate grounds for a whipping or a beating. And I made the profound mistake yesterday, of not tending to the cooking fires as I should, until they went out. Mother had inexplicably not said a word about it, except for me to bring her the oil and wood so she could light the fire again. Nora and I had both watched closely, fascinated by the striking of the rocks together, that seem to spit sparks into the oil soaked pieces of straw until they light,

in turn lighting the pieces of kindling wood. But though she was clearly frustrated, she gave us no clue, lighting the fire as our caregiver in good spirits, then cooking us a lamb stew such as we had never tasted, a meal she said was from Miss Sharon, with seasonings and spices borrowed from her. I had gone to bed last night remembering that lamb stew, even waking up this morning hungry for more, eating it hungrily again at our noonday meal. Somehow, it tasted even better today, though it was the same stew left over, being a warm and homey refuge from the new chill in the air, as the first echoes of Autumn flow in to take over the Summer heat. There is a gray and foreboding to this day, the sun having been hidden behind a veil of clouds, that seem to cover the sky all over Creation.

Nela, Mother calls, in the hours past the noonday, when the sun seems to have said goodbye forever. I get up from my little project with Nora, helping her build dolls to add to our little collection. I stand up and skip from our room to Mother's room, who is sitting on the edge of the bed with the strangest look on her face, one the flows and flashes a mixture of serenity and sorrow.

What did I tell you about that fire?

What fire?

She stares at me without a word. Waiting.

I didn't let the fire go out, I finally say. Suddenly in remembrance of our dynamic, the force of her beckon call.

I promise I won't ever do it again, Mother. Nora and me were playing outside and I just forgot. The stew was delicious.

More so than the stew ever was, the fear in my voice nourishes her body and beyond, into the core of her mind, in places deeper than even she had been willing to go—feelings risen up as ghosts from the night woods, reaching inside her to bestow their calling, forces passed down through the

generations, through the mother line, from Mother to Daughter in tragedy and secret.

Besides that, Mother says, *I had a dream last night that you were becoming rebellious and disobedient.*

But I'm not, Momma. I'm really not.

Get undressed, she says calmly. Savoring the Spirit of Fear.

Momma—

I said take off your clothes. Her voice is low. Almost whispery.

Like so many times before, I have no choice but to begin the pathetic, pleading motion of disrobing, baring my developing young breasts to her, which are mostly areola and nipple now, jutting outward in new growth, so sensitive to touch, even to the very air around them. I am so afraid that Nora is going to come through the bedroom opening and see me standing naked in front of Mother.

Put your hands behind your back, Mother says. This, I do. Standing there with my lips tucked, already on the edge of tears for whatever reason, standing here, fully exposed in front of her, watching her stare at every inch of my body from my neck to my ankles. Come closer, she says. And this, I do. Looking her in the eye, seeing none of the shyness, none of the nervousness and discomfort I feel. And from the center of this boldness, emerges the energy of her calling, which moves her head forward towards me, until her mouth is at my breasts, which twitches my entire body as if it were stuck with a sewing needle, as she pulls my entire breast into her mouth, her cheeks sunken in from the strong sucking motion. Several times, I feel her tongue in a nursing pull at my breast, every drink of hers causing my body to come alive and making my groin ache inside. She releases this, staring me in the eye, saying quietly *I told you never to let*

that fire go out, didn't I, to which I can only nod my head, my lips still tucked in, eyes welled up with tears I pray will not fall. But when she leans in to my other breast, when I feel the nursing deep in her mouth, the feel that courses through my body is an epic weeping, to finish the cycle of pleasures I have never imagined or thought about before, and to overflow the well of tears at my eyes. I know that somehow, this is a level of discipline, a level of punishment bestowed as s sign, that the world itself has gone awry, and that it is a shame to speak of those things which are done of them in secret.

Mother releases this nursing in a loud kissing sound, and I am aware of a single, quiet twitch of her own body, fully clothed, which she ignores, through the deepening of despair on her features. She takes the front of my breasts with her fingers, one in each hand, and she begins to pull and twist the agony of a wasp sting through them. *Put your hands behind your back!* she yells, holding the twist at the edge of pain while I comply, twisting them again hard enough to haze my vision, and make me bend over against her hands, while I hear the sound of my own screams in the room around me. But these are quickly hushed by her, until there is only the quiet, plaintive wail of disillusionment, defeat and despair. She releases them in the hardest, most biting pull possible, evoking a quick shriek, by which she responds with a hard slap to my face, and an admonishing point to my nose, without a word as to how bad my punishment certainly could have been.

But even with her quiet, stern warning, I cannot stop the tears, the sniffing, the quiet sobbing. She stands up from the bed and smoothly, quickly disrobes in front of me, exposing the fullness of herself, the largeness of the gigantic breasts unhidden. She sits back down on her bed, a bed lifted higher up than any other I have seen, built by her husband

before he died. A bed with a finely crafted wooden headboard (normally seen in homes of privilege), her refuge and transport from her failed, miserable excuse of a life. On this finely crafted bed, the woolen stuffed cushions supported on a wooden frame—this finely crafted bed she sits comfortably upon, unclothed, pulling me forward, my hands no longer behind my back, but clasped together at my sniveling little mouth, staring at this beautiful older woman, both of us grieving to be free. Mother takes my little face into her hands, pressing gently the sides of my head. Staring at me mysteriously in the eye, until my sobbing is soothed away. Then she leans closer to me, until I feel her lips touch mine in a softness I can barely endure. As to the feeling that travels through my body from the kiss, this I cannot tell. This hearty and forever kiss, that lingers at my mouth so that I cannot breathe—gripping my lips and gently pulling them, then pressing around them in a deep, sucking kiss that I think will make the room spin around me.

And then I feel my lips being parted, as her tongue slips into my mouth without mercy, causing my mouth to tremble, as I instinctively press my lips around her tongue in sucking. She holds my head, slipping forward on the bed, moving her tongue in and out of my mouth as I struggle to catch a life giving breath through my nose, unable to release her tongue from my mouth. She pulls it free, then continues to kiss me deeply, firmly telling me *put your tongue in my mouth*. This, I do. In awkwardness and fumbling, I push my tongue deep into my mother's mouth, which causes her to moan and stiffen, pressing hard on the sides of my head, nursing onto my tongue hard enough to cause pain. But she quickly eases the pressure, gliding her lips up and down the length of it, her breathing louder through her nose, her concentration grown ever so wide and deep. She releases my tongue,

pressing hers again to my breast in profound and fervent licking and kissing, her face anguished to the point of frustration and sorrow.

Without looking at me, she stands and tells me to climb on the bed, telling me to stay on all fours. This, I do. Hearing the wood creak as she climbs onto the bed behind me. Feeling like live wolf bait—staked and tied out in the open, knowing that not even a single bleat is worth the trouble. In an instant through time, the woman is on her knees behind me, leaning over top of me, her breasts laid down heavy on my back. I feel her hands on my thigh. Sliding up to my sides, then around to my stomach, her body twitching ever so slightly, inching forward, to press the front of herself against the back of me. Her hand slides underneath me, down my stomach to between my legs, which causes my entire body to jerk just once, and my breathing to escape my control. *Hold still,* she says. *Let it out through your voice.* And she rubs me gently at the unfamiliar place I have not really known until today, when the clouds have devoured the sunlight, and there is ashen gray regret. She rubs me ever so skillfully, breasts laid heavy on my back, as the pressures of a thousand years begin to bear down, until I am no longer a creature of free will, but bound by the curse of Destiny, by the force and will of what is meant to be. Each rub bears agonizing pleasure at my swollen self, beginning to flow into my back and my arms, at my backside where she is pressed hard against—and now to my breasts where her hand hath begun the skilled touch, until I have to remember that I am not supposed to move, nor can I push away the force arisen suddenly into every part of my body, making it impossible for me to breathe, impossible for me to think, impossible to stay still, impossible to move. There is only the feeling risen at my breasts and my groin, connecting as one place throughout the space of my body, pushing a pleasure outward to every inch of me that is frightening, causing me to yell aloud in something

close to fear, while I struggle hard not to pull away from my mother's hold on my mind and body.

But she has mercy. Ceasing the tug at my nipples and the rubbing at my groin—kissing me hard on the shoulders, then resting on all fours, pushing herself hard against the back of me, grinding herself against me as a woman in heat, driven by something beyond desire, which is instinct, where there is no freedom from the bondage of the body's craving. Upon this hunger, she pushes herself slowly, a rhythm uniquely bestowed, as each slow push against me brings her higher without effort, until she knows that she need go no further, but only to hold herself still, to cease the pushing of the rolling stone, cease the whipping of the horses, and let the force of power roll and glide her to the end of this journey, which forms a center of feeling in her body that makes her wonder as to the nature of pleasure in a body, and how it can possibly be endured, as her hips jerk mightily forward on their own against the back of me, and her voice makes a sound I have heard before in my dreams… the sound of a trumpet blared across the countryside, as a lifetime of repressed energy begins to erupt into her body.

I was twelve, when her spirit came to me. I was twelve, when her spirit hath come.

Even in the dark, the striped horses are two of the most beautiful animals in God's Creation. They look like mules, I think, with the prettiest black and white stripes all over. None of us knows what they are called. They are on the first floor with the lions, tigers and bears. Oh my, how lovely is God's Creation!

There are many different kinds of cat like animals great and small, some too beautiful to be imagined—spots and stripes aplenty, with one pair as black as midnight shadows moving in the absence of light. One pair of bears is as black as those two cats, and one pair is snow white like two owls I have seen, and the other pair is big and brown, like two small trees

when they stand up, pawing at the air with such an amazing awareness on their faces, as if they would like to speak but cannot, with five giant, curved raptor claws on each big paw. These killing claws, these paws of death belong to animals with the gentlest disposition, with looks of kindness about the eyes, and an air of friendliness upon their expression. They seem friendlier than many of the dogs we caged up, and even the small, cantankerous herds of goats and sheep in their pens, who seem more likely to bite then these giant bears ever would.

Two weeks into this journey, while the thunderstorm still rages outside, while we are still tossed and turned about in the wind and waves, I've noticed that these stupid goats and sheep have to constantly be tended and fed as if this were just another rainy day, while those two giant brown bears have done hardly more than sleep and take in a little water every so often. And it seems that this pattern is taking over the entire ship, from the greatest animals downward—a pattern of sleep that seems to last for days on end, with only a few hours awake, where they hardly move or make a sound, their glowing eyes sometimes visible in the firelight when we walk by their cages.

"I think every animal knows," Ada says, matching what I too have felt all along, that they all know that these darkened corridors and cages are the only safe places on earth. The spirit of refuge permeates the hellish cold and dark, to at least give us all the comfort of shelter and safety, and soon maybe even the comfort of home itself.

The sights and sounds of this animal sanctuary on the ocean are quickly becoming a part of us, despite Seda's bitter, caustic complaining and *"spit on these damned animals, I despise everything on this boat like a sickness!"* She has become impossible to deal with, even by her own

husband, who understands that his threats of violence against her are as dead as the world outside this ark.

"It would've been better for us all," Ada says, "if Shem had just let her leave."

"She's too pretty," I say. "She's almost as beautiful as my sister and my mother were."

"Looks aren't everything," Ada says. "Seda is just mean. If she looked anything like she acted…"

Seda moves the torch off the cage with the river dragons, eyes glowing wide awake with hunger unsatisfied, one of their voices rumbling with malevolence deeply suppressed. The river monsters were the only two animals (except for a few ducks and geese), of the tens of thousands that came aboard, that detoured away from the path leading to the bridge to go into the water, and they swam beneath the clear water for a brief time, before they slowly climbed back out of the fishing stream and returned to the beaten path. These are like the two-legged dragons that walked so timidly aboard, only their bodies are flat and low to the ground, walking on four legs like two great, scaly lizards, with snouts full of long, sharp teeth. By instinct alone, one of them had lunged out of the fishing stream at a flock of white ducks with a great roar, and a loud snapping of its huge jaws shut, to deliver its empty promise of death. The other animals nearby, the few birds that had wandered to the river to drink, even the timid antelope had hardly twitched a muscle in fear, blessed with this end of the world instinct that no non-human creature aboard this vessel would be allowed to draw a single drop of blood. This privilege is reserved for us, as we have killed and eaten two of the ducks already. Shem was smart enough, I guess, to insist that we take a separate flock of ducks and geese and chickens, to include as the foods that we are allowed to eat, that we may satisfy our

bloodlust every now and then. But the meat eating animals, I do pity, having to make do with the dried chunks of sheep and goat's meat in their feeders, short on taste, I'm sure, but long on keeping them alive and healthy.

29

The smell of wood tar is strong in my nostrils. It haunts my dreams when I drift to sleep, so that I wonder why my mother's stone house smells so strongly of wood, before I am awakened into the blackness again. This moment sees the burning of my mother's belt across my skin in my dreams, colored by the wood tar scent in my nostrils, as mother's angry face and swinging, heavy breasts begin to fade, transformed into the darkness around me in reality, with Seda waking me up to the voice of a strap across my thighs, shocking Ada and me awake from our accidental nap in one of the hay stalls. Seda had followed us this time, and is now bringing the leather strap down on my body full force as I try to roll away helplessly on the floor, with Ada standing by off to the side in something close to fear.

I want to get up and run, but I'm afraid that if I uncover my face, she will hit me in the eyes, nose and mouth.

"Seda, stop it!"

Ada's voice only angers Seda, who begins to bring the strap down harder on me, even across my arms covering my face, causing me to finally start to whimper the world please, as if it could possibly do any good. Then suddenly, the blows stop, and I look up in time to see Ada grabbing Seda's wrists, a pained expression on her face. Seda tries to pull her arms away, but cannot.

"Let go of my arm!"

Quiet Ada holds on in full strength, staring the angry, beautiful Seda in the eye. In the next instant, Seda brings her other hand down across poor Ada's lovely face, saying *"Who the Hell do you think you are,"* wrenching the strap away from her, then doing to her face what was reserved for me, making Ada cover her face with both hands, while Seda brings the strap down over her head and her back. Ada trips and falls backwards into a pile of hay grass, bringing herself up to endure the storm of Seda. Oh, Ada, what have you done! Drawing this she lion from her meal! Now, you too will be killed, and devoured even before her first meal is done!

Seda slams down onto Ada's back, putting the strap around her neck, holding it secure with one hand, then pulling Ada's arm up behind her back with the other. Sitting on Ada's back, Seda holds her there, while I stand with both hands over my mouth, still having not grown accustomed to fear.

"Titty loving bitches," Seda hisses. "I know you. I know you've been planning to suck titties for months. You've been planning to get between her legs since Ham first brought her home, haven't you?"

Ada does not answer, if she can even talk at all from the choking strap around her neck. Then I watch beautiful, angry Seda push Ada's arm up further, causing Ada to howl a pitiful, choked voice from the pain.

"Please stop," I say. Rushing over to them, grabbing Seda by the arm, causing her to release Ada and push me away. She leans forward and grabs the strap tighter, with both hands, hissing vile promises of future pain, filthy accusations of Ada and me doing every manner of thing, fingers and tongues and lips everywhere. Even while I get to my knees, terrified to say another word, knowing that there is no one on the ship to go to, not even Sara, who is devoted only to Noah, and does not interfere with the foolishness of her son's wives. Even while I am on my knees in quiet begging, in quiet waiting for Seda to release this frustration, I can remember my time in my mother's bed, with her leather strap pulled tightly around my neck, when I was only 13, slamming herself down onto me until the motion was involuntary, and I would hear the bellowing as a wailing cattle in my ears.

After several long moments, when the three of us are quiet, the sound of the waves and the thunder still raging outside, Seda stands up calmly.

"Get up," she says, unmoved by Ada's hopeless expression, the devastation and despair. "The next time I catch you two nasty bitches hiding and grinding in the dark so help me I'm going to strip you both naked and beat the blood out of you."

"Seda, why do you have to treat us like this? What did we ever do to you?"

Seda slaps Ada hard across the face, hitting her on the head and shoulders with her hands, unsatisfied that the quiet, humble Ada has learned her lesson. She quickly brings the strap down again over the top of

her head, making her cover her head as I stand there dim wittedly, frozen dumb with fear.

"Now go and find your husbands, *both* of you," she says, grabbing each of us one by one and shoving us hard from the hay stall into the corridor, where we both begin the lonely, confused walk into the torch lit darkness, looking for wherever it is that our husbands could have gone.

30

In the summer of my twelfth year, Mother has taken to her bed. She sleeps for most of the day, and is sometimes up late at night burning candles and weeping loud enough to be heard. And though she has not said anything to either of us, Nora and I both know that she is devastated because her best friend has moved away. Hired from her failed life here in the village, to work as a servant at the wealthy woman's house, her husband now a part of the wealthy man's small farming empire. Luck has no morality. It is an uncompromising, uncaring spirit of fortune or misfortune, usually sent down the path of a person's bloodline, to bring good or evil into a person's life—either the blessing, or the curse of God. My mother's friend Sharon is the beneficiary of a blessing passed down through the generations of her husband's family, having always been lucky

at finding good work, even though their own business success had always eluded them. And finally, at the far end of this part of their timeline, when her husband's business failures are complete, his family's line of luck kicks in, and his wife captures the attention of a wealthy woman. His wife Sharon. My mother's best friend.

And this luck is indeed no respecter of persons, having lifted Sharon up into these latter day winds, to carry her away to Heaven on Earth, to the paradise that exists on the other side of Hell. This, the Hell of mediocrity, the Hell of want and need, the Hell of unrequited and unfulfilled desire. And what is the double edged sword of this, what is the swing of iron and steel that cuts both ways? Is it the fact that a woman who had never considered such things in the first place, the perversions, the diversions of wealth and leisure—is it a double edged blade that this woman was approached by a wealthy woman of leisure she didn't even know, and be invited to a strange and beautiful home far away, to work these things which are a shame to speak of in secret? Is this double edged blade swung through my mother's grieving soul, that though she is a devastating beauty, with deep, secret lusts that none could easily believe, that she would be given no outlet for these feelings, that she would meet no one that could sweep her away from this life of struggle and sacrifice and suppression, to a life of ease and erotic expression unleashed? *She* is the beauty, not Sharon. *She* is the one whose heart hath already been burned to a glowing cinder with the raging fires, this cinder glowing bright red, lit in fires of dark tinted blue.

Luck has no morality, Mother. You have been the faithful widow, deserving of this powerful good fortune that your friend hath achieved. What is the hot iron of this backward truth Mother, that your plain-pretty

friend and her plain-pretty daughter should stumble onto this mother lode, and that you, a goddess, should be denied? To stumble upon one dead, rock filled endeavor after another, and be left with nothing but shovelfuls of dirt, dust and stone? Oh, how you have longed for this thing that Sharon has been given Mother—how you have rocked your own self to sleep at night imagining that you had someone to share in this burning you have inside for other women, and even for the innocence of young girls displayed before you. How is it that your best friend hath achieved this valley of flowers and green, while you are left behind in the Valley of the Shadow of Death?

Lay in your bed of depression, Mother. Lay in your bed of despair and pray Mother, pray to the God you do not believe in! You would have given in to your best friend's idea of behind closed doors pleasure, wouldn't you? You were going to give in to it, weren't you? But you were not ready yet. You know if my chastity had to be taken, if my innocence were to be burned up, then it would have to be you that would light these fires first! The first fruits of this increase, Mother, these fruits of longing must first be devoured by thee! But you were not ready. So you could not offer me to your friend—nor could you take her offer of young Nadia, though she grieved and ached within herself to watch her daughter upon both your breasts like a starving calf at its mother's milk! But you pleasantly rejected and refused, until it was too late, Mother. Now, your friend is swept up by the impossible, by the cool winds of renewal and prosperity—oh, what secrets she will have to tell, if she ever sees you again!

But you are left to dry in the hot, desert wind, Mother. To roll as the tumbleweed bush unnourished, in the dusty winds of poverty—with only Nora and me as your oasis of possibility, your only sip of brief nourishment and relief. But what form will this so called relief take, Dear

Mother? Will it be the joy and laughter of some, the pleasant and peaceful days enjoyed by so many mothers and daughters we see, even those in our village, who we see constantly on the streets and at the well—some of them bold enough to come knocking at your plywood door, to roll in on wheels of plainness, without the allure of sensuality, always so glad to be in your company, so glad to be in your presence, you and your two little girls, whom they say that as mothers and daughters go, that you and your two daughters are unmatched. And they say that little eight year old Nora is the most beautiful child they have ever seen, with an angelic little face, with big, beautiful eyes of pale brown and piercing, that bewitch one upon the looking, so that many wish to have her meet and play with their own little girls, to which you so often refuse, instead inviting them over to your house, rather than let Nora too far out of your sight.

How can you allow your only source of hope and life to drift too far away? *Don't leave sight of this house,* you always say, though every other time you look out the window, or out through the rickety plywood door swung upon, you have wondered where it is that your beloved daughters could have gone. And you have sometimes walked up and down the dusty streets of this town, this little collection of houses and families, calling Nora's name and mine, but seeing only the little faces unfamiliar, descending you into a simmering, quiet rage, Mother, which will rumble and boil underneath the surface of who you are the rest of the day and into the night, angry with both Nora and me for our disobedience.

Lay there, Mother. In the pain of this depression. Knowing in your heart what form of relief your time with us will take. You wait now, you pray, for the next time we drift away from the house, so that we are beyond where it is that you can see. Oh, why, Mother, can some children not be

made to understand? Why, oh Mother, do we choose not to obey? As you lay here, Dear Mother, you can already see the sunrise of your next horizon, the hope that you have been given, the lighted path from the darkest part of the wilderness, that will lead you to this oasis of hope. It is the vision you see in half sleep, that shows you yourself and your two daughters in the nude, both the twelve year old and the eight year old, enduring the swing and lash of the belt, while your long, black hair and your low, mountain sized breasts swing free.

And though you swore it would never happen to thee, Mother, that you would not allow this spirit to pass from your mother to your daughters—that is the very problem, is it not? That we wrestle not against flesh and blood, Mother, but against principalities, powers, rulers of the darkness of this world—so that your motivations and desires are to none affect, and will come under the power and control of these selfsame spirits. These are they which coursed through your Mother's body, by whose breasts you received this right and power, a woman widowed such as thee—but whose perverted attentions had already turned in her heart, and the heart of her lover taken the day after her husband's body was returned to the dust of the ground. And through these two women, your mother and her *sister*, you were soon acquainted with what it means to suffer.

31

*Y*our mother's sister. Already being jealous of your 15 year old beauty, infecting your mother with desires that had laid dormant, latent urges repressed and ignored long enough—two women born of the same parents, who had rejoined themselves from their own childhoods, to wreak havoc on what is seen as normal behind closed doors, many times in front of you, Mother—not hesitant at all to kiss deeply when you were around, though they were full blood sisters themselves.

And it was not long before you were awakened in the night by a nightmare, where you saw your mother and her sister standing nude, engaged in fevered whispers and talk as if they are discussing business, with your mother's sister turning suddenly to stare you in the eye, sending

a spark of fear through you great enough to wake you up in a breathless panic, wherein lies a scream unreleased. And those dreams, Mother, tormented your 15 year old self—these are not speculations and fears about what *could* happen—but they are revelations and prophecies about what is *going* to happen. Not even rising to the level of warnings, Mother, because that would suggest that you could take another course of action. No, Mother. You are going to be raped, Mother. And whipped. And beaten to within an inch of your life.

And this first raping, as you remember, carried with it leather stripes to blood, where they took turns whipping you to exhaustion, as well as punching you in the face and the stomach and your back and your head with their fists, until your little world spun around you, and you could barely remember your name, Adina. And somewhere in this memory lives the feel of your mother laid strong and heavy on top of you, with your mouth gagged, her sister underneath you holding you tight by the neck. Somewhere in this memory, is the weight of your mother's heavy breast laid on your face, covering your nose so you cannot breathe, until she has mercy, and lifts it away.

You are strong, Mother. Which is why they had to beat you so badly. And what is that new agony you feel, Dear Mother, that is pushed into your bottom from behind, from the member that is strapped to your mother's sister? She holds you strong and tight, while your mother prepares herself to enter you from on top, with the smooth piece of wood 2 fingers long that her sister carved for her—not strapped on, but held tightly between her legs so that it protrudes her desire into the space between your chastity and she. This memory is yours to carry, Dear Mother, the feel of your mother's hands, fumbling at herself down below, guiding the smooth wood into the front of thee, until you must cry out from the agony that grows, until it

bursts into your body, to cause tears and fervent weeping through the cloth tied around your mouth. You notice that she is out of her mind, Mother. Acting as through you are but a receptacle for what must be, where her wickedness abounds, and what love she had for thee is waxed cold.

All you can do is hold on to the small, fleshy waist of hers, then the flesh of her great buttocks, feeling them squeeze together mightily once, and then once again, pushing herself hard downward, to feel the energy of the wood, that flows between her sister, her daughter and herself. One final squeeze she makes, and then you see the anguish in her face deepen as she lowers her head away, while the depravity expands into her body beyond endurance, and flows out of her voice in wailing trumpet song.

As you rise from your death sleep, Mother, to gather yourself up for our whipping, the scent of your mother's sweat is strong in your nostrils, and the pain in her voice is eternal in your aching spirit.

The tragedy of human existence is our separation from God. The tragedy of human existence is sin.

But what is that to you, Mother, as you call Nora and me into the house. *You two are going to get a whipping*, you say, not even sure as to why, but just knowing it is something you have to do. The pitiful looks on our faces serve only to deepen your resentment—our attempts at sympathy only make you angrier.

I told you two not to leave sight of this house, didn't I? I open my mouth to speak, but can only glance at my little sister pitifully. Tucking my lips in fearful respect, gazing wide eyed at Mother again. *One of you had better speak up before it gets worse for you than it already is.*

I told Elsa that we couldn't leave sight of the house. But she wouldn't believe us, and she got all the other girls to go with her. She told them not

to be our friends anymore if we didn't go with her. Didn't she say that Nora?

Yes.

So you chose to deliberately disobey me.

We couldn't help it, Mother. We didn't have time to come and ask you. We didn't think it would matter because it was just Elsa's house.

What was it that I told you?

What person can speak destruction to their own body? Who can speak damnation to his only soul?

Answer me!

Nora and me both jump from the force of her voice in our bodies. The types of fear are many, and uniquely distinguished, I think. Among these is the Fear of Pain. And this is the power which courses through our bodies—created by Mother by necessity, so that she may feed upon it as milk for nourishment—having the deepest depression of the spirit heaped upon her as a sickness, with our fear being her only hope, to transform us into what can nourish her body—my little sister being Pain, and me being Suffering and Despair.

As to her command, we remove every stitch of our clothing, glancing at each other often, trying to understand that this is not a dream, that we are both awake in this nightmare, and are about to endure the burning pain of another whipping on our bare skin.

33

The storm outside the Ark rages on, until three weeks of our journey is come and gone. I avoid Seda now like I would one of the coiled snakes I hear rattling and hissing in the dark. A warning noise very loud, reminding us that evil is still in our midst, and will be carried to the other side of this trip through our flooded wilderness, to wreak havoc someday in a new world. Noah has no idea when this storm is going to end, as it seems as though it may rage forever.

And the winds have suddenly begun to blow harder than they have in many days, brushing by the Ark in a great noise, a sound of wailing and howling such as I have never heard since we were lifted onto these waters, a wailing, whistling wind, a high pitched moaning of ghostly voices unseen, voices of great weeping and lamentation, grieving to speak of

those things that have come upon the earth. And I find that I am unable to stay away from the window, always looking to see if the three whirlwinds are still there. And I am shocked to see that the three of them have persisted through the full three weeks of this journey, through the rising and falling of the wind and the waves, moving forward with us through time. As I stand awestruck at the open window, I notice that the three twisters have begun to move from their stormy positions left, center and right, moving slowly towards the ship itself, likely the source of the great, howling wind we have heard for the past three days and nights, making the seas rougher on this part of the journey, to where there is a great rising and falling of the ship, to which we have all grown accustomed by now, no longer strapping ourselves to the safety beams or benches, but just grabbing on to whatever beam or cage is nearest us, to steady ourselves against a fall. I have learned to enjoy the epic ride, such as it is, feeling sometimes as a bird in flight, loving the feel of the Ark's forward push, the steady climb to the top of the next wave, and the steep and steady fall on the other side of it. It is a trip that I was meant to take, having had my life spared with the other seven, out of the many billions of souls that were drowned.

I have been awakened out of sleep in a full laugh of insane fear at least twice already, having seen the men of sailing knowledge at the head of their little boats and ships, screaming orders to their crews pointlessly, while the last great wave of their trip slams into their boats and turns them upside down from the front, flipping them over and disappearing them far beneath the waves. And then there's the devoted family man in the fishing boat, huddled with his terrified wife and children in the storm, hardly able to believe that such fury is possible outside of a nightmare, having braved

and resisted all premonitions of death, and memories of every thought against the spirit of God, which visited all of the billions of souls, and was rejected by the collective masses of them. This poor man, devoted in kindness to his family, in desperation to look ridiculous in this little boat, striving to resist the judgment of the Almighty on his own, hearing the screams of his wife and children as the tiny boat rises to the top of one of Creation's most mountainous waves, as they are tossed high and far into the air through the blinding rainfall, the tiny silhouette of their death barely visible in the flashes of lightning from the clouds.

34

I see the rising of a new wind, these three. The whirling of end time catastrophe. The three faces of God, Noah says, these whirlwinds are—sent to guide us and protect us in the storm. At the single window we have access to, I see them every day, also on this, the twenty first day of our journey. Sometimes they are a great distance away from the Ark, to where it seems that they will never return to where we are, to where the great wind and waves they cause cannot be seen and felt, as if they have been carried away to some greater or lesser unknown purpose than ourselves. But on the rising of this morning tide, upon the rushing of this new and

mighty wind, I can feel the strength of their death and destruction, as the three of them have begun to flow nearby the Ark with purpose, going around us one at a time, seeming to cut a groove into the water itself around us, pulling us along in the wake of their mighty passing. Oh, what force above and beneath the hidden sun there must be, that guides the path of these mighty twisters around us, that keeps them from crossing our doomed path, and flaking every piece of our safety into splinter and flotsam wood.

Ham and Noah don't bother to call me from the window much anymore, knowing it is the same as calling a child away from the rising of the flaming blue white star that appeared over the horizon in the weeks before the Great Flood came. I drift back up these steps at every spare waking moment, mesmerized by the bands of whirling death nearby. As they pass quickly around the Ark one by one, I see the three of them as the three faces of Eve, that of mother, daughter, and sister—whirled into private, unspeakable corruption and sin.

35

When the Rose of Sharon left my mother Adina to her own grief and misery, the spirits of what is meant to be took their tragic hold—settling into my mother as this apt and appropriate spirit—reaching through her grief out to Nora and me. Yes, I was twelve years old when the Spirit came unto me. I was twelve—when the spirit hath come. I think it was the first time I truly understood the iciness, the cold energy of fear itself, when my mother said to us—*I want you two to take off all of your clothes*. And this was said in the wake of a trembling sigh from her, as if she had finally surrendered to what had tormented her for so long as it is, which was activated by what Sharon had told her already before she moved away. Oh, what lusts and secrets flow the blood through the motherline, what things are there which burn in the body too hot to bear!

And the burden of this I feel as I disrobe, the burden of this I see upon Adina's lovely countenance, the burden of extreme beauty corrupted by the severest grief and depression—which simmers as the dormant volcano awakened—threatening to boil over in the stages between anger, rage and fury. This beginning I see as a darkening upon her lovely features as she begins to remove the top of her garment—to expose for the first time to us her naked breasts gigantic and smooth, hung and wobbled down so low and heavy, where the front of them gaze at me in knowing, and a natural instinct beyond the unspeakable. The sensitivity of them, the power they have always possessed is apt to be unleashed upon the two of us in the name of discipline, until the pain she feels, the blame of her friend's departure is burned into our skin.

Even now, at the window of the Ark, I can feel the memory of my mother and sister rising high in the three whirlwinds, as they move dangerously close to the Ark and away again, beginning to move in a steady and gigantic circle around where we are, until the Ark begins to pick up speed, giving us all the distinct feeling of being pulled along, perhaps to finally be grabbed by the hand of God, and judged for our audacity to think we can escape, but from the rest of the world's destruction we have been spared, made to live and regret what we have seen, and to feel what remains of the undiluted power and wrath of the Almighty God. In my mind's eye, and in the light of the jagged rivers of fire in the clouds, I see what the three whirlwinds have begun to do to the waters nearby the Ark, as a small fountain whirlpool appears when we dip the pots in the water—this whirlpool having appeared in a size and dimension unknowable, as the Ark begins to move around the middle of this great whirlpool, faster and faster downward into the Hell of the watery

chaos around us, until I know that the Ark will soon be swallowed up, and buried beneath the waters of the deep blue sea.

And in the heart of memory, as I watch the Ark circle the middle of the great whirlpool, I circle the whirlpool of perversion in my spirit, the whirlpool that is my mother Adina—the sickness that has her knee in my sister's back, as she beats Nora's eight year old buttocks to bruises and dark red, undeterred by Nora's constant kicking and flailing, her full weight pressed through her knee into Nora's little back, focusing the burn of the palm of her hand onto a single spot, until Nora's little voice is hoarse from the screaming, and her skin is on fire from the pain. In the awe of fear and revelation, I watch Adina's great breasts swing and wobble free with the flurry of passing blows, watching the angry and merciless cloud overtake her lovely features, perverting them into a frown of controlled pain and fury.

Lovely and calloused fair-skinned hands, I see, burning her eight year old's skin alive with one hand, while the other hand is pressed firmly against the middle of her tiny buttocks, where her middle finger is pressed and pushed so completely up inside. And when she is done, she tells me with the breathless anger within, to get over to the bed and lie on my stomach, which I do in tuck-lipped, breathless disbelief, feeling the full weight of my mother's knee on my back, and the pressure of her lifeline pushed so far and deep up inside me.

36

These are the memories of the three faces of Eve. Mother, daughter and sister—these three—formed in the mist of the storm that remains, in the unseen shadow of the three Great Whirlwinds, plunging us into our watery abyss. Every animal on the Ark is silent at this moment, and the eight souls rest breathless where we are, all of us waiting nervously for the cracking and crackling of wet and splintered wood. But the walls of the Ark are steadfast and strong, to carry us from one end of the timeline to the other. To rise us up from the depth of the world we came from, and plunge us deep into the storm and watery world we are in. And in the mist of this new world, as the whirlpool swirls and begins to pull us down, I am pulled downward into the heart of memory, where I see Adina's breasts still

unclothed, standing over the two of us with the leather strap of her heart's desire—both of us weeping and unclothed on our stomachs—our hands underneath ourselves, tucked tightly between our legs as she hath deemed and desired.

And as the lightning sparks above the whirlpool rising, above the smooth and churning, turning waters of our Great Demise, I jump as if hit by a spark from a fireplace cinder popped, as my skin remembers the popping of her belt strap to our backs as we lay tied, our legs bound together at the ankles, our wrists now bound together underneath us in front. To the tune of Nora's wailing started first, a wail of her eight year old defeat and confusion unbridled, the straps live and die upon the snapping sound, where the goddess breasted woman swings a slow, determined rhythm upon our scarred little backs, buttocks and thighs, until even I have to open my mouth in acknowledgement of what new fever this is, and the heat by which it brings fire to our skin. And this , she does until something is satisfied, until an aching is alleved beyond where any of us know, until she is able to stop swinging the leather strap upward and downward.

She unties the cut cloth from our wrists and our ankles, when the world outside is dressed in amber, in the bright orange light of a setting sun. It is a sunset I have not known before, where I can feel the world plunge toward the era of mankind's darkest night, towards the nighttime of my own soul's tragic awakening. As I hear, as I feel Seda and Sara's weeping aboard the Ark, my soul's memory turns toward the evening day, where I see the rising star that rules the world past sunset, where the light of my Redemption draweth nigh.

The Ark

It seems that the eight of us have given all hope over to the sea, to let it devour us in the drowning waves, to swallow the Ark with the same anger of watery judgment as the rest of mankind. I stay locked at my rest at the window, no one remembering to gather me up and away from it, believing that this miraculous turning, this monumental downward spiral is our end anyway, as we were saved by God for his mysterious purpose to bring us to destruction later down this path, beneath the waters of the Judgment Sea. I can only peer through the cooling, darkening air, lit up by the shards of lightning speared and broken, the rivers of light sparked and thrown at the walls of the Great Whirlpool, the largest such of its kind since the dawn of time and history, with us so lost and alone within, while the three waterspouts turn and drift at the surface around it, high above our heads. I am held enraptured, captured in disbelief at the depth of our descent as we turn upon this ride, flowing smoothly forward and around this vast and endless curve until at last, my vision is enveloped by the briny deep, by the waters of the deep and darkened sea.

And this darkness is a doorway to my soul's past, to the world that was not yet drowned in judgment, to the quiet calling of my mother to me in the dark of night, where I hear her voice in apology for what she must do, when she gathers me up from my sleeping bed in the night, by the light of but one single candle, to cast a glow of foreboding over me. I was twelve, when the spirit came unto me—I was twelve, when my mother's spirit hath come.

I am plunged beneath the waters of this memory, as the Ark is mysteriously plunged beneath the waters of the ocean, where only the memory of the rain is present around us, within the violent creaking and straining of every inch of the wooden ship, and the muffled sound of the thunder rumbling and blasting above us. And only I am aware of this

marvel, watching it first hand in the awe of revelation, as I see the sparks of light blow the waters brilliantly and dimly before my eyes, to the flash of the shadow of a great silhouette before me, as it swims in mountainous glory, in the manner of a fish too great to have come aboard where we are, the shape and likeness of a great whale beneath the surface of the water I see, even while I notice that the waters of the deep and dark'ned sea do not pour, trickle or splash through the open window upon me.

And upon this brightest flash of light, to where this mountain of an animal swims above us in grace and beauty, my spirit flashes the memory of my mother's great breasts which she exposes to me in surrender and defeat, giving herself over to the reprobate mind, having heeded every seducing spirit of her bloodline, both her mountainous bosoms hanging free for me to see, as my body is sparked alive by the feel of her tongue at my twelve year old breast for the first time, which runs a feeling to the center of who I am and back, until I have to shudder as if from the cold, though there is only the warmth of this summer evening around us, and the heat of a phantom burning on my skin. She releases the nipple in such a loud kissing noise, then puts her lips and tongue to mine, until I understand that there is no shyness with this kiss, but only the tilting and moving of the head, the closing of the eyes, the parting of my lips to receive the fullness of her tongue, until it is all that I crave, while her fingers touch and fondle the front of my breasts, to devastate my body in feeling once again. And when she can endure no more, she lays me on my stomach on the bed, and removes the rest of her garment until her curves are fully exposed—the gargantuan breasts above the small and fleshy curved waist, that flows outward to the hips of fertility, feminine strength and beauty.

I lay still on my stomach, placing my hands between my legs as she whispers me to. I feel the weight of her climb on the bed to me, the weight of Predestiny, the motion of what is preordained, the movement of what was sent down by Eve through the timeline, the torment of this motherline through the generations passed down from mother to daughter, behind the darkened and candlelit walls of secret. The hardened nipples of her Great Breasts brush against my back, which twitches her body once as a bolt of lightning strikes, to reaffirm her calling to announce her arrival upon the timeline, that her and her daughter's time has come.

Then I feel the warmth and swollen part of this gift which she hath become, this great gift of depravity she possesses, as her expression descends to awe and defeat, shaking her head no while she presses her swollen self to my twelve year old bottom, and begins a slow but immediate power, a forceful and deliberate humping rhythm that seems to gather strength on his own, as if powered by an unseen lift, by the invisible hand of Perversion itself, when it takes hold of the body, to caress the muscles with lusts impossible to fathom and endure. And even before the crashing of this first wave, her weeping hath already begun, as if she knows what end of the world torment awaits her body, and what violent and agonizing awareness every part of her spirit must endure. As to what punishment pain, as to what unbearable pleasure this must be, she does not know. She only knows that it is what must be done, what she must open her body too, what game must be laid aside, to allow the flower of these spirits to come and go.

And I hear the arrival of this first spirit to her voice, as she feels it caress her at the nipples first touched against my back, then flow to her own buttocks and her groin, then back through her body to her hardened nipples again. Across the timeline, beneath the judgment sea, I hear the

pitiful wailing, as this first orgasm passes through her in waves and trembling, shaking her body to a violent and continuous quaking that never ceases, but only subsides until it vanishes away. Above me, and in my body I can hear the Agony of Souls in her weeping, and can feel the quaking of the condemned earth flowed from her body and soul. And this, followed by a period of heavy rest and deep breathing laid upon my back, raising up again before long, as I feel the Ark ascend itself upward, my spirit, my spirit intertwined with the doom of the present and the past, feeling her slamming herself against me again, but this time with a hard and fast determination covered by anger, which rises to a calling she hath answered, a rising upward of the hunter rage she hath repressed, until I feel her body tense and shake violently again, as the Ark emerges like a catapult slung forth from the depths, to the sound of my mother's fervent screams in my soul's memory, and the fury of the screaming thunder, and lightning that threatens to tear the sky in two.

Part Three

Jonathan Lovejoy

And every living substance was destroyed which was upon the face of the ground, both man, and cattle, and the creeping things, and the fowl of the heaven; and they were destroyed from the earth: and Noah only remained alive, and they that were with him in the ark.

Genesis 7:23

37

*I*t is by the Spirit of the Almighty God that I fly on wings of eagles—these majestic birds in whose nostrils was the breath of life, but among the unseen carcasses of every living thing they are now hidden, whose feathers and bone are now wet and scattered to the wind, somewhere in one of the far corners of the Earth. As the waters continue to rise up, up and upward, until I know that the islands I see in the gray light of these rainy days are the tops of mountains. But unlike in the early days of the flood—these are quiet and quintessential—majestic mountain peaks of calm and contemplation, mountains which do rumble and smoke and spit fire as did their lower counterparts, as a sign to those unlucky travelers and tragic souls who were left alive to see the liquid fire pour outward into the rain. These are the mountains of tragedy. In the tragic calm of uneasy

acceptance—the icy peaks of splendor we pass—that tower high above the roof of the Ark, as did the lower mountains tower above the ground many weeks ago, these highland precipices, these points at the top of the world itself now serve as the lowland markers—the places where the footsteps of those past—the ghostly footsteps of the present approach on the invisible plain, to look briefly upward to their jagged majesty, to marvel at how it is that they once stretched from Earth to Heaven itself, but are now made lower than the carcasses of the dogs themselves, when the last days of God's wrath shall be spent, and the bones of the lowly valley dogs will bump against their heavenly heights and glory.

By the power of the Almighty himself—I am burdened by the scent of the dead dogs that splash and float in the former skies uncurled—the skies undrenched of that which they held, as the bodies of those wet dogs are a stench in my nostrils as they brush past the rocky mountain peaks, unaware in death as to the great and powerful height and distance they have gone. Up past the lower mountain trees they were flown, on the wind and the waves of God's perfect judgment—until the forests themselves were a long and distant memory left behind far away below—the bodies of these dogs lifted and carried along, one by one, so that it is as through they were the only life that had ever breathed in the space big enough to separate all life to their singular parts. To be tossed on every thunderous wind and wave, to fall against the echo of their lonely destination.

And somewhere far away from the hair of the dog that bit me—there is the same smell and scent in my nostrils, but from a higher form of life— whom I know was somehow created only a little lower than the angels themselves—among this form of life being the body of the woman who gave me life—but then took it from me so abundantly. In the swirling

winds, in the curl of lightning flashes that remain of the Almighty's pain and paradise of mercy lost—I see the flash of my mother's living beauty, as her youngest daughter Nora pours the water of her bath over her head, wetting her head and her beautiful face over and over again, my sister with the top of her garment down as she pours the water over my mother standing nude in our private stone bath, a very heavy and beautiful thing just large enough for two of us to sit in at a time, one of the only baths of its kind found beneath the hallowed halls of luxury—my mother having insisted upon it long before she was widowed. As part of our chores every day, Nora and me, is to empty it of her bathwater from the night before with much walking and dipping and pouring—then to travel back and forth to the well for many stone pots of clean water until it is filled. This is the labour of our youth and younger years, to drain and prepare our mother's bath, unless the cold autumn and winter breezes visit for too many days hence, which are not many where we live—where the sun burns hot through even the winter months, and there is no echo of the winter chill and snow.

I bear witness to one of these warm, winter baths, when Mother is inspired to stand fully nude and upright, her gargantuan breasts hung so heavy and wet down against her body—breasts grown too big in mountainous dimension—so unique, so unusual as to flash a picture in the mind and in the soul, so powerful as a grand and overblown echo of the mother of all living, who wandered the garden herself in breasts hung to impossible size and length of stature. These majestic bosoms of my mother, whose size and shape hath touched my own through my bloodline—I see the size and shape of them wobbling free as Nora stands up behind her, her clothes tied up at her waist gleefully wet, while Mother's fair skin languishes in the nude, on this warm winter's day of my

memory, before the skies were dreary and gray. Nora locks herself tightly, calmly around my Mother, hugging her about the waist tightly, to let her breasts hang free—and I watch them in this position for several long moments of time, her breasts still hung exposed and untouched, until I watch her eyes close permanently, with her leaning back against my sister in total relaxation, with Nora fully pressed against my mother in a tight hug that embraces her, that wraps her up, that envelops and smothers her in the lust of her days and ways combined. The busty, encrusted lust that must be, that so many mothers and daughters and sisters around the world have known behind these walls of secret, and have kept hidden from the hearts that stare. It is the profoundest of feelings, that runs as wide and deep as a river that flows—whose price is a moral degradation of the spirit—but one they are willing to pay, to achieve a pleasure beyond rapture, an ecstasy beyond endurance to their bodies.

These are the songs that sing glorious melodies in the night, when the stars of heaven twinkle by firelight, above the breezes of the open countryside, to whisper of these private beliefs coalesced into secret action, like raindrops that are formed when the clouds of weeping are gathered, but then have given again to the beauty of the night, and the glory that sings to every light that shines across the eons, that twinkle as the stars of heaven. I see the weight of this heavy burden of pleasure flash over my mother's face, as the lightning flashes from the clouds of judgment I see and feel—I see the end of the world pleasure wash down from the top of her head to the bottom of her feet, as she begins to moan in an anticipation without coherence, to moan a song without words, but knowing not to say what it is she feels, but only to send with her mind and her voice to the mind of her daughter what must be done.

The Ark

And to my mother's glory, to Adina's epic satisfaction and luck, according to this private gift bestowed—her youngest and most beautiful daughter, her daughter whose lust is of equal power and stature—her youngest daughter knows instinctively to gently caress her mother's long and beautiful neck with her teeth, which brings a deep and breathy grunt from Adina, acting as the signal to make Nora slide her hand around to the front of Mother, gently, firmly secured down between Mother's legs, where Mother does not dare move, save a profound and slow lowering and shaking of her head, as if to glance at what is the precursor for what must be, as if to glimpse the wave approaching from so far off shore which was only sensed before, but now is no longer among the unseen. And I notice a firm and powerful staring she does at her own breasts, whose nipples have hardened to ripeness, and where the tiniest drop of what trickle of milk they contain hath appeared.

Throughout our childhood and teenage years, Adina has given milk at various times, depending on her arousal, and how long and hard our sucking hath been given. But the miracle of this sign of hers, I see today, when the waters of her bath drip no further from her breasts, replaced by the tiniest echo of nourishment and sweet. And though Nora hardly moves her hand at all, but merely pressing her hand firmly against Mother down below, Mother opens her eyes fully to contemplate what rumbling has already begun, which I hear in approach through the breath in her lungs escaping—like the distant, quiet thunderous roars of the beasts I once heard approaching the Ark, or the booming apocalypse that came forth from the ground horizon to wake us up in the night when we slept on the Great Ship, in the weeks before cataclysm hath occurred. I see, I hear the quiet and quintessential rumbling, the slow and distant approach of this warning in Mother's voice, while Nora knows to readjust her grip slowly

and to remain still, while Mother opens her eyes again to stare in awe, as though she can see this great lumbering leviathan, this force of nature which threatens to bear down upon her, as if the awe in her expression threatens to transform to a place of fear and dread.

And as though it can be held back no longer—as the crashing of the wave comes ashore, as she is taken up into the mouth of the leviathan, as the rumbling of the earth at her feet hath begun—and the voice which emanates from her deepens, as her eyes roll back as she closes them, trying to look upward to an unseen God of history, to an unknown God of her body's coming devastation—and as her eyes flutter closed over the white I see in them, her mouth hangs open in deep, guttural voice, as a phantom risen from the dead, as her entire body begins to shake violently, causing the deep, animal voice to tremble as well, as she bends over—as she doubles over against the agony of this quaking, and I watch the energy of this flow from Adina as she backs up into my sister, with Nora's beautiful face now overtaken by an angry force of this self-same awe, as she begins to pound into my mother who remains bent over, striking against Mother's backside with her front until Mother's deep, trembling groan is transformed into a loud, high pitched cry of the damned.

Awaken! Is the voice I hear in my head, as I drift into reality from this vision, as I see again the gray clouds lit up in the lightning flashes, wondering where it is that my beloved mother could have gone.

The end of our world is dreary and gray. Throughout the long stretches of day that flow seamlessly into night, where the sun is darkened from our sight, and the Moon can no longer give her light.

It is as though there has never been a sky beyond these clouds, and the deep veil of lightning that flashes across the entire land and sea. But what land there is resides now only in my memory, as I recall the icy hill tops and mountain crests that loomed, revealing that these were the high places, the points along our journey that have risen far up into what was called the sky. Even as the Ark longs to dip and sway along our watery path toward tomorrow, I have seen that lightning show the last of these mountain peaks to us, which are brought down to nothing, as lowly reminders of what once

171

was, and of what worldwide devastation was bound and meant to be. The ship has returned to its intended majesty on the face of the waters—now being the most prominent thing beneath the Heavens, as it towers above what smooth and jagged pieces of rock and mounds of island earth we see, as the tops of the highest mountains are covered, as they are lowered and buried beneath the sea.

And so we drift upon the current of this storm, upon the power that remains of this righteous judgment, of what sorrow and grief from the Lord himself hath been poured out in devastation upon the world. And even though every rock and boulder, every pebble and grain of sand, every blade of grass and flowering petal, along with every bush and every tree—even through every spot of ground is covered from the highest mountain we know and don't know, to the lowest canyon and valley down below, we bob and sway along our chosen path unaffected and unawares, having not touched so much as the branch of a tree along the way, nor the crust of even a wayward stone. And what sign is this, I wonder, that in the cataclysmic explosion of water and power, the Chaos of Roads lost forever under the wide and sounding sea—what sign is this that not so much as a scrape of earthen treachery hath disturbed our journey, as we were lifted up and through, around and above every obstacle in my visions, and of what Noah allowed me to see at the window of the Ark, where I have spent the bulk of my leisure time away from the accursed animals, and the epic and ghostly darkness throughout. Though there is room aplenty for us to roam, sometimes I feel like there is no air, and I must climb the ramp up to this window to open it, to breathe in the freedom of the misty air, and gaze upon the watery depth of this rising, falling, whirling and swirling ocean horizon.

The Ark

As the rooster crows us into the 39th morn—as we give in to what resignation of doubt and despair there must be, we accept the impossibility of the nightmare we drift and ride, all eight of us (perhaps even Noah himself) are wondering just how long it will be before the food we have stored in abundance will begin to fade. Can we truly begin to herd and harvest many of the animals we brought on board—is that the future of us sustaining what life there is that remains? The eight of us have grown weary of this storm—weary of Hope itself—tired of any beliefs that haunt our dreams, of days where there was sunshine and warm breezes on the prairie, and barefoot strolls over the green grass near the forest wood, beneath blue skies where tranquility hath coalesced in clouds of fluffy warmth and white.

In the rising of this 39th day—across the passing of this unseen sun, we are burdened by the tasks and jobs at hand, to take care of the animals and ourselves in obedience to God, who chose to deliver us from a world overrun by violence and sin, to carry us forward into a new world, a place yet uncreated, whose possibilities lie yet unseen, and deeply entombed underneath this vast ocean, under this watery wilderness plain.

39

$\mathscr{I}$ remain burdened by this end of the world revelation—which is the full scale departure of womankind from their natural gift to the rougher half—forsaking the natural use of the man, to indulge every deepest fantasy that a man's body, a man's hairy face and skin, a man's scruffy, animalistic character cannot provide, womankind at last giving in to one another's power, being the fairer sex in all that is holy and unholy, being softer and sweeter to the touch, to activate even the very taste buds on the tongue, the hunger mechanisms deep inside the physical body itself, let alone the feminine soul and spirit. I am drowned in Mother Daughter Sex, in the deepest perversions—woman to woman, as I am tormented by this revelation, that it was one of the strongest signs of our times, that the world wide spreading in secret, the pervasiveness of it preceded the end of the

world—these old barriers between women being crumbled and fallen away—mothers and their daughters being the most powerful cataclysm among them.

And what of best friends and acquaintances among the women? Of what real shock or surprise are they, having always shared secret kisses away from the light—when secure that no one else can see? Of this, maybe there is no sign more than what has always been since the beginning of time, when the daughters of Eve and the daughters of God began to look upon one another with lustful envy. But behind closed doors—behind the walls of secret—I am told, I am shown what churns beneath cultured civility, where the sisters have begun to look at one another, where even their kisses have taken on a new affection—one that travels far and wide into them, going higher than the highest mountain peaks uncovered, and as wide and deep as the calm, serene ocean green and dark'ned blue. And the Lady Lords of this new affection hath towered over and above them, in the form of woman, which is she who gave birth to them—she who gave the daughters of her womb life, and then took it so abundantly.

The desires of womankind—of those that have abandoned the use of the man—of these fires I constantly burn, of these waters I have drifted in to my last breath, until I lay consumed by the heat and cold of it, the hunger and thirst of it, the life and death of it, in my soul, and in the souls of lost humanity itself. It is the last and greatest uncovered sign of this condemned world, that mankind is beyond redemption, and faces imminent judgment and destruction from the Almighty—that there is no need for public scorn, for public hypocrisy and judgment and self righteous punishment one to the other, for it is a shame to speak of those things which are done of them in secret. But as to the friends and acquaintances alone, in this I can sense

no evil, for I believe that Love itself crosses every gender, even to render the bodies into submission one to the other.

As I walk hand in hand with my sister-in-law, somewhere deep in the outer darkness of our little world, I am touched by the love I feel for Ada, remembering the connection we shared from the first—from when Ham first brought me into the nearly finished Ark, and I was treated to the Eastern beauty in her eyes, the deep ivory of her skin, and the natural humility in her demure smile, her lips as red as nature itself can allow untouched. Ada possesses none of Seda's hardened, crystalline beauty, but had a soft, natural prettiness deeply enhanced by demurity, and a shapely, sensual appeal reminiscent of my own mother and sister. While Seda bore me little tolerance and even less courtesy and compassion, Ada took me by the hand with a smile and a pleasant, comforting manner, and guided me through every part of the empty ship—showing me every cage and stall to be filled with what she insists will be real animals—which I remember only added to the mystery of this giant construction, of what devils and trickster gods had come to this family in the night, and whispered such nonsense into their reality.

As I walk through the bowels of this dark destiny—this phantasmal hue, imbued with this cold and ghostly yellow flame, I am glad that we have decided to at last consummate this side of our epoch, to at last express ourselves in private—somewhere far and away from Seda's nosy, jealous and busy bodying eyes that stare, away from the strap she wields with the skill of a horseman. And at last, we find our favorite place to hide in the seafaring ship, somewhere deep within, while the smell of hay is the strongest, and the noise and stench of the animals is the weakest in our ears and nostrils. In this hay storage stall—we return to ourselves, Ada and me,

with no further concern for the whereabouts of our husbands, nor Seda, nor even Sara and her great man of God, as Ada and me must answer our own calling before the Almighty himself, which is to give in to our imperfection, to bring this adulterous lust and love across the days, across the many hidden lands of travel, across the chasm that separates the old world from the new—we answer the calling of the fires that burn, removing the top of our garments down from our breasts—pressing them together until the nipples are locked, until the sparks that fly are as the lightning in the clouds—and we simply hold them there—as I watch Ada close her eyes in a breathy, hearty surrender—opening them again to look beyond the ceiling of our damnation, to look for absolution and redemption in the clouds of rain.

I watch her breathe rapid, deep breaths of ecstasy in agony—of agony in ecstasy, until I reach across from where I am, from who I am, which is my mother's daughter—and I coax her lips apart with my own, until her tongue is softly, and deeply in my mouth. I can feel the trembling of desire—the quiet quaking of her entire body, which she struggles to stop, causing a single, epic twitch of her whole self from head to toe, which I know has infused her brain and nerves with a pleasure hardly any woman we left behind had ever felt—from any but another woman's lips and body. From this feeling, Ada is suddenly helpless but to lean against me in a full hug, while she breathes deeper, slower to catch her breath, as the plateau of herself has peaked and lowered quickly, while mine has only just begun.

In the depths of the Ark, my lover and me
Somewhere in the mist of the Judgment Sea
Embraced in the storm of this misty morning dawn—
Wondering where it is that our beloved Mothers could have gone

And I am again burdened by the end of the world—by the heavy weight of my own mother's bosom in the theater of my mind, as I see and feel one of her most relaxed and favorite things to do. It moves me to escort my loving Ada down into the hay on her back, her soft, middle sized breasts wobbled free, while I kneel down on all fours above her, letting my big sized melons hang free in her face, coaxing them back and forth so gently over her face, waiting so much without breath, breathlessly, without patience, impatiently while she caresses my nipples with her lovely mouth, but so reluctant to take one into her lips to give suck. And as I see my own mother's gargantuan breasts in my mind, hanging down towards me, I can no longer wait for Ada's lust to rebuild, and I place one by hand into her mouth, where her instincts take over as though she were a babe at the mother's nursing milk, or a thirsty, wayward woman at the mouth of a wineskin, drinking to her heart and soul's content.

And as she takes one into her lovely hands, to squeeze and give better suck to the breast hanging down, I see myself doing this very thing to my own mother in private, seeing Mother's beautiful brow wrinkle in that certain anticipation we all know, which flashes the lightning through her breasts to her womb, and between her trembling legs down below, each suck of my breast, each nursing pull of them into Ada's mouth brings me closer to the edge of where she herself was but a moment before—until I see in the theater of my mind, my mother lose control of her breath, and her body twitches one great and mighty twitch, leaving her energized rather than spent, while I feel the self same energy grown in both my hanging bosoms, until my body shakes one quick and mighty tremble—joining me with the spirit of Adina herself, Goddess of the Breast, goddess of me and my bygone sister. I join with the spirit of her chosen method of

completion when she does this—and I lower myself to my dear Ada, as Mother Adina lowers herself to me—and I open my legs wide to receive the power she has to give, feeling the firm length of it rubbing the outside of myself, as Mother wraps her arms tightly around me, pinning my arms to my sides. This, even after I am grown and married—to remind me of whenceforth I came, and to what spirit I now goeth.

This same spirit I ride, lowering myself down to my dearest Ada, coaxing her legs open to what it is we knew even before the first animal came into the Ark—pinning her arms as my Mother pinned mine, slowly rubbing the front of myself against the front of Ada down below, feeling myself as my mother, as though I am she, needing to press harder, to pound and dominate in rhythm with the Ark, in rhythm with the rise and fall of the dark world we're suddenly in. My hips rise to slow and mountainous heights of grandeur, hidden underneath the dress cloth, while the breasts are mashed together and fully bare—while the hips make their unswift, unhurried fall from these mountainous heights, down, slowly and far away down to the flowing sea below, until it splashes loudly, roughly against the surf. Then these hidden hips rise again underneath the cloth to their ordained height, crashing down again, again, again, and again, until I hear my Ada lose control of what silence she can contain, her voice echoing throughout the bottom part of the ship—causing the flames, the torches of this dark world to haze in my vision, my head held back, seeing, feeling Mother do the same on top of me as her eyes roll back, releasing her wailing voice into the candlelit night, as I hear my own voice gather itself from deep within, to search the ship where Ada's cry had gone but a moment before, both searching for where it is that our beloved mothers could have gone.

$\mathcal{W}$inds of Time gather together across the ocean, above the Judgment Sea, lost as to where they should go, except by the power and the will of the Almighty God, who has lifted up a part of the four winds—to send them nearby the Ark of Safety, where they whirl downward from the darkened clouds lit up by blue and white fire—whirling down to where we can see, these three. These three whirlwinds of destruction, that guard and guide us along the path of our journey, across the endless leagues of our maiden voyage to the New Age. The new beginning of mankind upon the face of the earth. And what new beginning can this possibly be, I often wonder, when the entire earth is now at the bottom of the Sea? Perhaps when the rains cease at last, the great ship will wreck upon some distant and rocky land exposed, tearing itself open to free us to stumble upon dry land, where we will struggle to survive from one day to the next—growing

what grains there are left in storage—herding what cattle, sheep and goats there are left that have not died along the way. But the animals themselves are not worried as we, having all calmed to a state of permanent sleep and half sleep, where tranquility is the meat for their bellies, and patience is the drink for the blood in their veins. Only a few of the animals aboard seem still overtaken with restlessness—most completely being the little dragon lizards, which Shem calls "raptors"—which are taller than a man when they stand upright, with mouths full of razor sharp teeth like the great dragons, with two small, spindly arms with claws as pointed as cloth needles, as well as feet with big, birdlike claws upon each foot fit for grabbing and holding down their prey, tearing open the flesh with the biggest claw on each foot, their sharpest razor talon, which they wield with skill, herds of them being certain death for the farmer's oxen, his cattle, his goats, his sheep, his alpacas, his camels and the like. These monsters are on board our ship by divine decree, as is the largest, long tailed behemoth, down to the smallest creeping thing hidden in the corners and crevices in the wood—as Noah could have made no sane decision to bring these raptors aboard. We all only stood by during the weeks of their arrival, watching the dragons walk nearby the prairie deer and pigs without so much as a sniff in their direction, with no hunger in their eyes, nor the smell of meat and blood in their nostrils.

But the vision of them haunts this unblessed sleep of mine, where I am laid beside my lover Ada, having drifted into dreaming from her loving embrace. But these dreams are as unpleasant as our world itself, where I am suddenly awake inside the dream, sensing the rapid and cunning craftiness of two raptors free from their cages, roaming the ship in renewed bloodlust and knowledge of the kill. But what killing is this—for what living thing is free in the bowels of the ship for them to find? Why haven't

they leapt over the low walls of the sheep pen—or why not the exposed herd of cattle they surely smell? In the core of my spirit, I know why they have bypassed the delectable, the fatted calf of their most treasured meal. It is because they smell a new scent of blood for their lustful instinct. They crave the taste in their mouths the scent in their nostrils—the smell of what they hate, the aroma of what they fear, of what they have lived in dread of in the forests and open cropfields. But now, the scent of their enemy is confined to the darkness—to this outer darkness where they roam as caretakers of the fire, as keepers of the evil flame. And now they must lurk, they must locate the source of this need, the new meat upon which they must feed, the new flesh which they must tear away from its bones. It is the smell of weakness and spindly fear, the smell of humanity—the scent of womankind. Primed for the hunt. Primed for the kill. I can feel these raptors lurking the corridors of the darkness around us, fast and slow, quick and quiet, until eventually, the clicking of their claws is clear, and the rumble of their purring, growling hunger is apparent in the torchlit dark below.

I sit upright. Ada and me sit upright in the approaching terror, both confused as to what could possibly be free to roam the ship in the dark—until the confirmation of terror suddenly looms, adrift from inside the darkness as two evil, glowing yellow eyes in the dark, the rest of its tall, spindly form hardly visible as these eyes focus on us, and the teeth are suddenly bared in their ghoulish, predatory grin. And as another set of these yellow eyes appears nearby, the first monster lunges quickly toward where I sit screaming, grabbing my arm with sharpened teeth and pulling me with demonic strength and power in the dark.

And suddenly, I am pulled from sleep. Yanked upward and screaming to my feet, feeling the pain of masculine strength in my arm, and the icy, angry gaze of it in my soul. My husband, in the wildness of his evil temper and indignation, grabs me by both shoulders with the top of my dress nearly down all the ay, my breasts only half covered and in motion while I struggle against him, still lost in the fog of fear and half sleep. And nearby, I hear the muffled voice of my love, as Seda stands up behind her, with one hand over Ada's mouth, and the other wrapped tightly around her waist.

"I *told* you I heard them," Seda says with deep, lustful delight—this being the bloodlust of revenge, and the punishment for secret crimes revealed. "I told you they were sneaking off together like a couple of filthy *pigs,*" she hisses, holding Ada too tightly for her to move—so much taller and stronger than either of us, but now supported by the iron muscles of strength itself. By one of the builders of the Ark, who holds me tight by the shoulders, glaring a quiet rage at me in the dark.

And suddenly, the darkness around me is illuminated by a lightning strike, but not one from the clouds of fury high above the Ark, but from the unbreatheable cloud of fury deep within, as I feel a monstrous slap against my face, flashing a bolt of pain through my head and knocking me off my feet to the haybed below. Ham pulls me upright, all the way to my feet, and wallops me across the face again, this time causing me to yelp a woman's scream of fear and death, the loss of control over myself, and the death of hope in my spirit.

"Careful," Seda hisses, "you don't want the others to hear us."

At once, I feel a tightness around my neck in part—swinging down and around to the pit of my stomach—a punch which racks me with a sickening, helpless grunt, held upright by the neck so that I cannot absorb the blow to satisfaction. Somewhere in the haze of fainting, I hear Ada

scream a muffled scream, hissed at to *"shut up"* by Seda, and hearing her say something about being *"dead already."* My husband releases me, letting go of my neck so that I can fall to the floor of the Ark, holding my stomach and coughing from the pain in my womb, and the agonizing strain in my throat. Oh, what fresh air is there left to breathe! What deep, replenishing breath is there left to take! I cough at the edges of eternity, as I suddenly feel the iron strength flip me over hard onto my stomach, tying my wrists together behind my back.

In the stench of his masculine rage, somewhere in the corridors of [sadism], in the chambers of evil lust unbridled, in the Hellfires of Vengeance, I hear a brutal slapping upon my dear Ada—in the hazing of my vision in the dark, I see the cloth being gagged around her mouth. I see the tall, beautiful Seda's hands at her throat from behind—I see her wrists being bound as well, bound by the merciless hands of feminine strength without virtue—feeling Ada's descent into hopeless despair, as I feel my garment raised up from my hips, and my husband laid heavily down upon my back, one hand clamped tightly around my mouth.

And suddenly, I feel the sorrow of the ages, in a burning fire sliding as a snake into my bottom, to burn the truth into me from behind, causing me to scream loudly and deeply into his hand, as he pushes himself into me

without mercy, driving the iron heat of himself into my backside with thrusts, until I hear the energy building in his voice, causing him to huff and puff, while Seda pins Ada down on her back, pressed tightly down against Ada herself while Ada strains to look back at me—Seda's voice soon betraying the sun's energy hidden in her own body, as her entire body begins to shake uncontrollably, causing the deepness in her voice to tremble as well, as I hear Seda's entire being released in a shaking, quaking explosion from deep within her body, as she holds the helpless Ada bound and motionless underneath her. And after Seda's depraved, deviant devastation, I hear my husband's voice take on a higher pitch, and this selfsame tremble touches his soul, and he begins to twitch and lurch harder down upon me—as he too is touched by the sorrow of the ages, and the echo of mankind's tragic past, present and future.

$\mathcal{B}$eing naked and bound to a crossbeam is the only punishment Noah would agree to—having saved both our lives as we were tried before our Husbands for our crime, after we were formally accused by Ham and Seda. Seda had tried to get Sara to make Noah rid the world of our presence—to open the tiny window above, and squeeze the both of us one at a time, out into the cold and stormy ocean, out into the raging judgment sea. We had stood motionless in the nude, our mouths gagged, our legs bound together, hands tied behind our backs, while Ham and Seda acted as though they had never done anything wrong before, as if they had never been less than perfect—as if they had no sin, and were both primed to cast the very first stone at us, which Seda had also tried to get Noah to let them do.

The Ark

Noah you should have seen what I saw—heard what I heard. The animal lust, the depraved biting and clawing and screaming at one another. The blood running down the back of Nela's leg is evidence of what I mean—Ada was pushing her fingers into the back of her like she had gone mad when we caught them, and Nela was lying there on her stomach with both hands underneath her, grinding herself while it was happening, and they were both as naked as this when we found them. Poor Ham didn't want to disturb them, he stood there while we hid crying in my arms—who knows how long they would have kept going if I hadn't insisted we stop them. They were hitting each other in the face, Noah, clawing at each other like they had lost their minds. How can we let them stay here with us after what they've done to poor Ham and Japeth—if we were back at the village they would have already been brought to the center of the main street and stoned to death for what they've done...

Think of your own God, Noah, and think about the power and wrath of this storm around us. How does God himself feel about what they've done? How long before these whirlwinds are brought to this ship to lift us up and tear us to pieces? How can we feel safe with these two harlots—these two nasty whores—these two adulterous, slutting witches aboard this ship...

I can remember standing there bound, hardly able to breathe through my nostrils, through the unbreatheable cloud of rumour—glancing once over at my Ada, who stands obedient and humble. Her pale and beautiful, shapely body fully exposed and tied with rope, while Japeth stands nearby Noah and Sara, but off to the side just a brief distance—to separate himself into just enough space—so he'll have room for the wide and fullest blast of judgment from his eyes and his soul. And before I lower my own gaze to oblivion, to see the darkness in half sleep as I stand, I glance at the sorrow

in Noah's eyes as he stares at the floor of the Ark, as if not to engage what tragic goings on have invaded his ship through the human heart.

...whipping the skin off them won't be enough, Seda says, her pale brown eyes—eyes touched the color of amber crème—those eyes on fire with wicked delight... *it's not enough to punish them for what they've done—we have to do the Lord's work and rid the Earth of the stain of their sin and wickedness—I say we gather as many stones from the sheep's enclosure that we can and we throw them at these two witches, these two perverted adulteresses until their bodies lie on the floor dead! Or better yet, lets put ropes around their whoring necks, and drag them like the she-dogs in heat they are up to the window of the Ark, and then throw them out the window into the ocean as a sacrifice to God, so he'll have mercy on the rest of us, so we can survive this test of faith, and make it ourselves into the New World that he has planned for us—a world of life and hope that these two sinners are not worthy to see...*

And with that, I lower my head away from hope into despair, and I relish the last tickle of life there is for me, which is the feel of the tear trickling through dirty skin, from my eyes down my cheek—even past my chin, to drip upon the exposed breast down below.

*T*hunders roar. Above where lightnings flash, across the Judgment Sea. Creation, Redemption, Salvation, these three…as they ride the winds of this age ending. Watching the souls rise and fall upon the waves, lying hidden in the Ark, safe from their judgment over sin. Thunders roar, lightnings flash, above the turning of the wind, beneath the churning of the wind and sea. These souls are carried by the whims of what is meant to be—over these 39 passings of the days into night, across the living ocean deep, kept from the jaws of death. Despair leaps from every flash of lightning—hope dies deeper in every blast of thunder—as the 39 days ring true to the passengers in the Ark, of the six who stand by unmerciful, unsparing of pain and punishment, as two are lifted to the high places— their arms spread outward and tied, their bodies bound to the posts stained with their blood.

Thunder roars. Lightnings flash, around the Winds of Creation—these three. All powerful eyes that look across the years from Eden, to the souls lost in the great ship far below—tossed upward upon the highest crest of wave, down into the deepest canyon of ocean water below, upon the surface of contempt, the mapping of his grief across the pages of time— these 39 days that traverse into the night—where two souls are bound to their crosses of wood, so that the shame may drip from their bodies in bruises and blood through the darkness—the darkness of the human heart. The darkness of the ship. The darkness of pitch without and within—into the unseen expanse of outer darkness, above where the whirlwinds rule, where there hath been weepings and gnashings of teeth, below where the whirlwinds rule, these three. These sparks of Redemption turn far into the night—into this passing of the 39th day, whereby his stripes we are healed, in the passing of night into day. These thunders roar, these lightnings flash, high above the Judgment Sea, where the eight souls are carried away inside the tiny ship below.

The spirits of Salvation, these three, observe the passing of the 39th day into history. To observe their coming into the 40th day of wind and rain. Thunders roar. Lightnings flash in the clouds of grieving—to light the truth of his agony to the passersby below, that it hath grieved him in his heart that he made mankind. And that merely one soul from the face of the earth was found worthy in the eyes of God—this prophet, this priest of God's final judgment, this anointed man of God, cursed with an end of the world calling from God—this anointed man chosen, this one man who walked with the Lord, chosen to deliver what is left of them from devastation. To move them through cataclysm, to steer them blindly through the Wrath of the Almighty, to the place that lies beyond Hell on Earth, which is the

Paradise of his mercy born. The spirits of Salvation, these three, gathered from the four winds of what is meant to be, coming together to whirl down from the clouds, these three. Turning and spinning. Whirling throughout the thunders that roar. The lightnings that flash—high above the Judgment Sea. Watching in grief the echo of mankind's condemnation reborn, the rebirthing of sin and bloodlust in the Ark—carried over. Across the Judgment Sea.

The earth flows the unseen Rivers of Time. Which are buried beneath the ocean waves—moving invisibly still, as currents of grief and knowing apart from our view. And these currents of bereaving flow as ghosts far beneath the ocean wind and waves, which have risen to his divine madness again, as his anger is rekindled briefly, in the morning of the 40th day of rain. This storm is the mind of God, the angry heart unleashed, to where his righteousness is as the thunder that roars from the clouds, and the lightning that soars and flashes from high above to the sea below—cracking the sky in two nearby the Ark, as a flash of white fire splashes to the violent and rolling ocean sea below.

This blast of God's voice rumbles through every speck of wood tar, every splinter of wood, and every animal and human down to the bone. And in this

morning, this stormy awakening to the 40th day of our damnation, Noah gives the order for the two harlots to be cut down from the railings on the second floor walkway, where we languished, tied to posts all through the 39th night, our arms dead with numbness from the agony of being stretched out like a cross—our breaths short from the night of straining for air in the torchlit dark.

Seda had spent much of the night back and forth below in rapture, in a satisfaction as epic as the storm itself, but in apprehension that her secret, and Ham's secret raping of us might someday become known. And I notice a renewed closeness, a new submission and affection she has for her husband Shem, as canopy of protection from whatever future rains of our private judgment must fall. It is Shem and Japeth who release my arms from the railings, untying my legs from the upright post of wood, and lowering me down to the floor below, where my husband waits to untie me from my rope prison, and return me to some form of sanity in the torchlit darkness we know.

I am barely aware as Shem and Ham cut and free my Ada from this high place, lowering her to her husband Japeth, who is more than happy to receive her from the jaws of Death, and return her to his loving arms of mercy. I lie still on the bed of feathers and down, lying painfully on my stomach, which also contains many stripes of discipline, though not as many as what was caned into my back and buttocks by Seda herself, as the rest of them stood idly by, bound as helplessly as I by the spirits of hypocrisy and fear. This fear had permeated Noah to the core of his being with knowledge, that the last bolt of lightning near the ship, that great and terrible sound had been a warning that what this was had gone too far— and it was time for him to put a stop to it, and bring our unjust suffering to a merciful end.

Here, in the rising of the 40th day of rain—Ada and me are released from our high beam crosses to bear, to carry our wounds into the next world beyond. As I lay dying, kept alive by God to suffer, I can hear Ada's voice give way to the sorrow we feel, and the quiet weeping for the undeserved pain revealed. And as I am drifted off to a profound and merciful sleep, I am engulfed by a vision so clear as if I am awake—where I can see the leather strap in my mother's hand, as she swings me around, bringing the leather in great stings upon my arms, my legs, my buttock and my back. And are these the breasts of a goddess? These are the breasts of Adina, Goddess of the Breasts, and of my sister Nora and me.

And beyond the swinging of the lash, I see the darkness, the dim, dreariness of a wealthy woman's dungeon, where my mother's former best friend is in leather shackles, being whipped by the wealthy woman who took her and her husband and her daughter in—this whipping being the giving and receiving of pleasures unknown—pleasures unheard of, outside the walls and chambers of secret, of this pleasure and pain I now see and feel, collecting every scream into my sleeping mind and body. And I am chosen to stare at this miracle, as the two women have found themselves in each other, as the leather is brought down across the breasts and stomach and thighs of Mother's best friend, until the rich woman takes her hand to the poor woman's privacy, moving it there until she writhes and screams against the post pleasure-pain which follows. I watch the woman lying on her back, upon the wooden dungeon table, writhing and screaming from what she feels, which is the unendurable, which is the ecstasy of the forbidden.

And all of this I know happened in reality, in the days and years when the new star blazed in the sky, in the year of the comet, in the year that eight souls were taken into the Ark.

Their screams echo through the night, and into the passing days, as the rains of their discontent begin to fall. My mother's best friend. Lifted from the land of my youth and years—her daughter and she the next door neighbors we once knew. Carried on the cold winds of what is meant to be, across the years to when I am old enough to be married. A willing prisoner, a slave to the wealthy woman's libido, she is, a creation of the wealthy woman's lust, in the dungeon of their hot and cold misdeed. Shaken now by another rumbling forth, this, not from their bodies crossed over, tensed and relaxed over and over again—but this rumbling from above and beneath the earth—a booming from above they are familiar with, as is the whole world in the days before the mist of rain—and a looming, lumbering lifted from below, that shakes them to their foundation, that seems to flow

through their bodies like living waves of unseen energy, to make them forget the aftermath of pleasure trauma, and make them fearful of what trauma may be yet to come. From this rumbling, they awaken from the stupor of their sin, both women having put their marriage vows away to follow their own dungeon lusts, which have more than spilled over into their daughter's young minds and beyond—from the rumbling in and around them, they emerge, climbing the stairs from a lower chamber in the great store farm house, a small but worthy castle manor, overlooking a great field of harvest soil. These two women emerge from their doings unashamed, unabated, unaware as to the source—the reason for this great rain, this greatest of rains ever seen by man, joining their daughters at the open balcony door of the upper room, the four of them amazed at the sheets of rain that pour, the spreading of these into a mist that stretches to infinity, lit up by the sparks of brilliant lightning in the dark grey clouds, and the crackle of thunder that waits, holding its full voice in all restraint, for the power and fury that is yet to come.

Across the landscape of the rich woman's farming estate, they gaze at the driving force of Devastation's echo, the briefest flash of the world's demise—in a storm that is not yet a storm, a deluge that is not yet a deluge, the beginning of a great flood pouring from the sky, that is not yet the complete and total destruction of all mankind.

A blast of thunder above the Ark awakens me from farmlands East of Eden, where the rains had just begun to fall upon the waiting soil. Sara has been an angel of mercy for the two of us—dressing our wounds with compassion and cold water, to where the burning has dwindled downward—kindled into coals rather than flames of fire. But I am unable to give place to hatred, none for Seda, or even for poor Ham, my dearest husband, who came to me at least once in the night that I remember, and kissed me lovingly on the cheek. I have not the metal inside for hatred, nor the raging fire of Vengeance—for *vengeance is mine, saith the Lord*, is the

word whispered by Noah himself when he came to comfort me. And I could see in his aging eyes the guilt and regret, even though we both realize that he may have saved our very lives, when Seda had suggested that they build a fire upon a bed of stones, and burn us alive and screaming until we were dead, as the truest sacrifices made to God, as the atonement for all of our wickedness and sin. This, I remember, was when Noah had finally stepped forward at the trial of the century, and spoke as the leader on our behalf, allowing Ham and Japeth (and Seda) to choose our bondage to the cross railing on the second floor, after we were caned to within an inch of our lives. It was the striping of flesh to bleeding, cutting our white skin to blood, until there was no pride left in our human spirit—nor was there dignity of the soul. We were broken down to nothing, to the merest shells of women, writhing against the posts and ropes where we were tied, striped first upon our backs and backsides, and then turning us around, our arms bound high above our heads—our bloody backs to the beams, where Seda's cane took on renewed energy, when she striped our bare breasts to blood. The front of our thighs, our waists, and our bare breasts to blood.

Without judgment, without resentment I lay here, drifting to where I am lost in another vision, in the days of Sharon—my mother's friend, and Sharon's daughter, Nadia, and their last days upon the wealthy woman's farming estate. Across the rainy and wicked farmland I see, over the stormy and twisted farmlands East of Eden, I see the beginnings of the end of history, when the tiny sliver of cloud rope turns white and gray from the dark'ned clouds above it, sliding gentle and serpentine—somewhere over the dusty plain, burdened down to a muddy prairie by the pouring rain. This great whirlwind in waiting, the birth of this fury starts at the horizon of their vision—far across the open field from their palace house, so that Nadia and Lizbeth, the daughters of Sharon and Diana, Nadia is the first to

point to the Horizon in the rain, to the serpentine whirled down so smoothly from the sky, then dances gracefully along the trail of its unchosen path, but seeming to remain at one point in the distance—until its presence in the world is established, and thoughts of tranquility are abolished and thrown. Grown from a single point of origin, it is watched by the eyes that stare, as the four of them gaze upon its lucid clarity, its uncharitable wickedness, having the heart of the most evil of all gods, whose name is Lucifer, the God of the Underworld, and of the Lake of Fire and brimstone.

Far beneath the raging Winds of Discomfort, I can see the vast stretch of farmland that once was, and the early formation of God's wrath and fury "Turn the Devil loose" is the call of this divine decree, as the pair of mothers and daughters stand at the open balcony doors, gazing upon what grows at the edge of a distant horizon, as the twister begins to take on the fullness of its name, whirling the rain and soil up and into itself, so quickly growing into a whirling black mass of vengeance and destruction from above, whose only purpose is to steal, kill, and destroy.

And the Mother, the Mother, and their two daughters, these four—they look out past the former dusty plains, where the dust is weighted down by the approaching rain. They look across the unknown prairie to the twister that has formed—and they can only look to the emptiness inside, the place where confidence and complacency hath departed—replaced now by the sorrow of the ages—which is accompanied by fear and despair. In a terror unknown, having never seen the wind come to life, and do a dance in the dead room of their lives—in this terror unknown, they watch this wind whirl from the white rope into a black one, growing wider and more violent with each passing moment, until it begins to grow bigger in their

sight, and less difficult to see in the windy mist, and more difficult to fathom.

Diana and Sharon, Nadia and Lizbeth, like mothers, like daughters, stare after the approaching horror on the plains—seeing it grow louder and larger from the horizon, not knowing whether it will grow to pass in fury over them, or pass them mercifully by and bye. And they watch in awe unbridled, in amazement unfettered from their souls, this selfsame awe I felt when the winds came together nearby the Ark—these four look after the growing black cloud of turning death, feeling the ground rumble the balcony beneath their feet. And they stand now, un-idly by, watching the twister grow in size and importance, wishing to be rid of the sight—wishing to go inside and escape the wind and the rain, but being unable, not caring for the whereabouts of their husbands and fathers, or where upon the condemned earth they may be.

auge the rumbling beneath thy feet, Dear Mothers, as you see the heart of your ways, the soul of your years gathered and come to life! Crossing the prairie from far to near—passing in devastation so clear. And as the rich woman Diana and her daughter Lizbeth succomb to fear, pulling away and running into the house, the woman from Poverty is propped up by bravery—a greater ability to look danger in its black and gray eyes, in its greely eyes of doom, unable to tear away from the whirling mountain of death that comes nearer, closer by then ever, seeing that it has no designs upon the house, except to pass it by in epic warning, delivered by the hand of God.

Oh, but these souls in warning—are they beyond Redemption? Is every soul left, is every human soul with the breath of life—is every soul bereft of Salvation! For what chance have they that remain—they that cannot cease from sin! In the life that lives beyond the earthly plane, what chance do they have for paradise! Oh, but what few souls there are left in this world, on this day of destruction—what few souls are there left who can have the mind of God! What few souls are left who are granted mercy of reprieve, to be saved from the fires of Hell, when their souls are taken from their bodies by the rain!

As this tall and great whirling cloud rumbles by, the woman from Poverty—the woman Sharon feels one final epic pull upon her spirit, to warn and admonish her greatly, that no pain is too profound, and no mountain too high, no valley crevice too low, no prairie vineyard too impossible to grow—no deed upon earth too wide and deep to know, that can cause disobedience to this calling, that if thine eye offend thee—pluck it out! For it is better to go into Heaven maimed, than to go with both eyes into the fires of Hell!

And so Sharon, in the Revelation of the End—in the Realization of Truth—is burdened by the wet and stench of the cloak of sin itself, wishing to gather up herself and her grown daughter from the years, from the seven years in debauchery they have lived, to flee into the rainy weather, across the windy plains, to see hope and redemption from the heart of an angry God. For their remaineth no more sacrifice for these sins—but only a fearful looking over the shoulder for judgment—and whosoever that shall be saved in the last days away from the Ark of Safety, after the Ark of Redemption has sailed—this salvation may happen by the blood of their own death, whereby the mercy of God may love and redeem them.

Oh, what souls are they that remain, that will see the Lord in paradise, beyond the earthly plane! Two souls are they, this mother from poverty and her grown daughter—a daughter raised and nurtured in private deviance and depravity, in the home of the rich woman on the plain. This woman Sharon, holding on to her daughter Nadia, grown to statuesque and lovely goddess beauty in black hair of curls—she holds on to the beautiful, cherub faced Nadia of 21 years, refusing to let her pull away from the Truth. Standing there with her, holding her still from behind in the wind and rain, watching with her the power of judgment spin, whirl and rumble so casually by. High up into the air they look and gaze, their curly, black hair blowing in the wind, blue eyes squinted in the wake of their calling. While the rich woman Diana and her lovely princess Lizbeth lie hidden somewhere inside, Sharon holds Nadia tightly in the wind, watching the tall end of the world twister turn idly by, unconcerned to feed upon the gray bricks of the farmhouse mansion. They stare intently, perceiving every deadly part of the cloud whirling within, and the great mass of prairie dirt and mud that colors it black tinted green. They watch, listen and feel as it moves past the mansion, until it spins at last out of sight, leaving the rains to fall with greater and more steady assurance, from the balcony where they stand, across their farming property, and the barren wilderness plain.

The city on the plains lies in wait. From the rain and wind that blows in from the prairie—the city on the plains lies in wait. This end of the world colossus, this great center of life and humanity, this den of sin and castle of iniquity. The city on the plains lies in wait.

The greatest of all time. The greatest there ever was, and ever will be. From Eden to a place that haunts me called Gethsemane. This twister will be the most terrible in history. Terrifying spirits, black tinted gray and green. Spirits of the dead and pure evil unleashed. Upheaval pushed down from the skies they have corrupted, churning black as the unstarry night upon the ground. To accompany the rumbling and trembling of the ground—to cause a new rumbling and quaking of the ground. This end of the world twisting thing, sent far and away from the Ark where we see. Born to exact judgment upon the barren wilderness sea. A wilderness barren of the love of God, where righteousness hath lived and died.

This greatest wind—this breath of wrath is blown from the mouth of Creation, to the prairie burdened by the rain below. Grown from the white rope of beauty that danced slowly across the horizon. Grown as the echo of desire. As a seed planted and stored. Nurtured by the elements, until what is within shall break free—to emerge from the soil of man's darkest dream. Grown from the white rope that danced from the clouds, to the black mountain that churns as an angry beast upon the ground. Eating the soil of man's misdeed along the way—the soil wet with an accursed rain—the soil drenched with pain. This, the pain of God's wrath unleashed, the agony of Creation gone bad and correcting itself. The integrity of the Almighty unfurled, as the skies uncurl in grief and mourning.

The city on the pains lies in wait. For the greatest terror of all time. A legion of life already whirled into the boiling ocean of black clouds, whirled and churned into a single black mass of death, lit up from one side to the other in lightning heat and light—this turning mass of earthen death, burning blue and black fire.

The city on the plains lies in wait. At long last, after three hours on the ground—having gone past many towns, many villages, many farms, many homes. Houses isolated on the prairie, where the sins are hidden behind the walls—hidden behind the doors of secret. This churning black mass of destruction, having gathered without effort the rocks and sticks and grass and dirt that inhabited space as houses, lifting whole towns into itself, even every brick and cobblestone placed in the ground—passing over these villages in slow, powerful assurance. Turning what is left of their day into night. Bathing the land in a cacophony of sound, the doomful, gloomy voice of the divine spark that looms, the spark of lightning in these clouds of fury—the booming rumble from the skies above, upon the ground itself,

and with the quaking that rises from beneath the earth. From the sky, the ground, and the caverns beneath the earth, these three—from the clouds, the soil above ground, and the soil beneath the earth, these three.

The city on the plains lies in wait. From the cloude as wide as an hour's ride across, from one side churning to the other. When the skies are lit up in blue and black fire, this end of the world tower of death can be seen turning the depth of its motion, from one side of the horizon to the other, from one side of the world to the other, from one side of Creation to the other. New Gotham, this city on the plains—the greatest city on the face of the Earth, nearly as wide as the approaching death itself. The great monuments of marble and gold. The mighty temples and buildings that house the rich and well to do. Those not poor and those not rich, but who are complacent in new found streams of silver and gold security to their pockets. The new class of wage earners—the new middle class—the complacent horde of New Gotham. These are they that look outward from within. From the windows of their uneasy acceptance, from inside the spaces of unsecure security and knowledge of forethought. This acceptance and foreknowledge of what is upon their horizon—to cause or accompany the earthquakes rising beneath their feet, some having shaken their lives to their foundations already, crashing, breaking and cracking their world in pieces around them. And by now, some of these rumblings have been so powerful and so severe, that more than one of their monuments to their earthen deities have fallen; tall spires of marble and stone having cracked and felled like a tree chopped down, leaned over in the wind and rain in cataclysmic slow motion, to the unbelief and disbelief of onlookers near and far, of onlookers passing by.

Oh, what crashing sound there is, along the streets of New Gotham, as the monuments to themselves go tumbling down! How the women

scream—how the men yell to the skies, how the children flinch and cover and cry! As the leaning towers of peace become unpeaceful—crashing in pieces to the city floor! See the horses and dogs and cats great and small, see them all retreat in terror from what nightmare there is that must come! What dark dream of mankind foreseen, foreshadowed by human behavior in the city and beyond—to the outskirts and surrounding countryside! Knife thy pride and prejudice, Dear lovers, suffice thine loss of life and liberty! Of what brand of new pain and suffering is this—New Gotham— what light of wrath and fire must be! When the icy stones begin to fall from blackened skies, to fill the streets with hopelessness and cold! When these icy stones begin to take their toll among the screaming, teaming masses, when many dozens of mothers and fathers have the bones in their heads cracked, falling as dead men and women at their children's feet, from the icy hail stones that hail from the cold skies of warning!

What life is there left for thee now, New Gotham, as the black mountain of death approaches thee! What fears do you bother to show, as the waters in the city fountains and gigantic pools have begun to splash and wave as the sea tossed, in keeping with the storm of the century that approacheth— what fears are there left to show! Rest easy, stay calm, let your useless fears and apprehensions die, accept thy fate that approaches in the storm! Think not upon the witch's and warlock's call—think not upon what transgressions hath called forth thine own death and destruction. Think not upon the adulteries, the family violence in tears and blood. The fornications, the lack of charity and lost compassions for the poor—think not upon the lasciviousness, the foolish debaucheries and revelry, the gaming and gambling and money changing hands of sin!

Think nothing of the gang rapings of men, the raping of women, the raping upon innocent children done in secret. Hear not the blood of the children that cries out for vengeance, for the hope and joy that was taken by thee! Think not of the fathers who have provoked their sons to wrath, disguised in the name of life and discipline—think not of the slavish work crashed down upon the sons in child labor by the fathers who lack compassion, who can feel nothing of the joy of youth, who feels no pain for the boyhood lost, of childhoods taken away by adult labour and worry! Think not of the fathers who draw the blood in leather from the backs of their sons—sons not wayward by choice and evil, but by the foolishness of youth alone! What blood needed to be drawn from the son's back, Dear Father, when the son only needed to be a child, when he only needed to be allowed to live and play!

Think not, Dear Gotham, of the Mother Daughter Dynamic—of what ills and woes are brought here by them! As the widened black cloud nears the edge of the farms and villages around the city, think not, New Gotham, of the mothers who have taken the cloak of motherhood from their bodies and tossed it to the wind. Who have gathered the young girls in secret, who have gathered the daughters in private, to teach them how to steal! Who teach them how to steal goods, and to steal grown men's hearts for pay! Think not, New Gotham, of your Mother Daughter Dynamic, that is reached from a thousand years in the past—that will reach thousands of years beyond. Think not of the mothers who have corrupted themselves by the generation, who have taken to the false creation of discipline—who grab their daughters by the ear in public, to pull them to a private place in the shade from the bygone sunlight of public view, to grab the poor girl by both sides of her head for a mighty shaking to rattle her thoughts in confusion as to what the mother means—when the mother speaks of some

disrespect unremembered by the girl, to burn the scalp of her head from the hair pulled, to burn her eyes from the heated stare.

Think not of the Mother Daughter Dynamic! Of the mothers who disrobe themselves with their daughters to begin this punishment, when they lay upon their naked girl children of any age, to hold their daughters arms behind their backs underneath them, until their fingers are shattered bone. Think not, my dear Gotham, of the screams you hear in layers underneath, below the yelling and shrieking in fear. An entire city. Screaming in fear. But think nothing of it, Dear Gotham, as the end of the world approaches now, wider than the Great City on the Plains, farther and wider than the depth of terror. Like a mountain veil colored black, it roars, it thunders its war forward. Filled with dying and dead humanity—hungry for the life in every part of the city.

The greatest of all time. The greatest there ever was, and ever will be. The rolling twister that moves across the prairie. To the city on the plain that lies in wait. The city that refuses to remember. That cannot dwell upon the voices from the recent days that have come and gone. Think not upon these, Dear Gotham—of the man who was locked in debtor's prison, because he could not find a job to earn wages, and was set about begging for food to feed his family, begging for loans that would not be given— neither a borrower nor lender be! Outstanding debts to the money lenders he had, until he could borrow no more, until his goods no longer sold,

having no skills as a carpenter or metal smith or farmer—what is a seller of goods to do, when no one will buy what things he has to sell? Not one seller of goods, not one merchant in the great city would hire this poor man. New Gotham, turn your back on this poor seller of goods, throw him weeping into debtor's prison! And then, cast him homeless into the streets, when the gates of his time are opened, when his wife and children have left him behind, when they are married to another! Throw him to the dogs as a bearded beggar, New Gotham—furnish him now without compassion! Where is he, Dear Gotham, on this dark and dreary day of destruction? Where is the woman who was his wife? Where are his two children, who saw their father charged by the moneylenders, who saw their father thrown in the chambers of Hell on Earth!

Hell on Earth is without the one you love—this poor man. Two years he spent locked in a dungeon beneath the city! Oh, but how many days did the city governor's son spend locked away, when he was known to have raped a girl in but her fifteenth year? How many days locked away did this city father's son spend—how many days in the dungeon did he go? None! How many days did the son of a judge who was caught stealing gold and silver jewelry, how many days did the judge's son spend in the dungeon? None! And what of the so-called righteous killing you know of, Dear Gotham— when the farmer's daughter was murdered by her own father and brothers because she was caught in the hay with another? How long did this father and his two sons spend in the dungeon for this killing? None! Oh, Dear Gotham, how many days have the citizens walked past the beggars, with no offer to carry them to shelter! Oh, rich citizens of Gotham, how many days did you refuse to allow the poor beggars to have the crumbs that fell from your rich tables of plenty!

Oh, city fathers, did you gather the poor unto yourselves, to lift them up to a place of dignity and comfort? Or did you turn your backs on them? Have you spat on them, have you laughed at their calamity! How many days did the poor beggar spend in the dungeon, when he was accused of stealing the fruit he ate! Fruit that would have dried and rotted away unused besides! How long did the poor beggar spend in the dungeon for this crime? And is this dungeon where the poor beggar got sick, is this where the poor beggar became ill, six weeks into this tragedy, until he was found dead in his dungeon room? But when this man was beaten on the streets the summer before—how long were his tormentors imprisoned? Were they sought after, were they captured? How long were his attackers held in the dungeon for the blood they drew? None!

And was this the same poor beggar, who was just released from his time in the debtor's prison? Who's to say! Of what consequence is it now! Just engage the presence of the Almighty, enraged, that seeks to cross over into the city—here at the end of this age of mankind! Gauge the mouth of the cloud beast that roars, whose face is lit up with blue and black fire!

As I gaze across the prairie—into the heart of the city on the plains, I see the cloud monster, the Twister of Doom, held fast at the gates of the great city, its forward motion stopped but for this brief moment in time, as the rains above the city are suddenly diminished, tossed about by the wind into a blowing mist, as the people scramble to and fro, still too stubborn to accept their fate—too unbelieving to seek shelter in the storm. Of those foolish enough to be out, they are the first hand witnesses to the second part of the truth, which is a great and violent rumbling up from the ground, where parts of the city are cracked and split asunder, with red-

orange liquid fire pouring through. And this fire is spat out from the rocks of the city in showers of bright orange sparks that are blown in the wind, and that do not die in the softer mist of rain. And there are those throughout the rest of the city in their homes great and small, in the great buildings where many houses are built together as a legion of rooms—these gaze the windows of disbelief, at the third part of the truth, which pours fourth as great white vapors of smoke from the ground, when the liquid orange fires are suddenly put out, and the clouds of white water vapor pour through into the misty air, to bathe the lower parts of the city in a mist of fog, where the people who are remiss, disobedient to the spirit of fear, scream and wade through, as if there is something that they can control, something they can possibly do.

And the rumbling around them increases to crackling and breaking, until there is movement therein abouts, and from this movement comes two of the loudest screams in God's condemned Creation, as two creatures emerge from the heated mist in rage—their eyes aglow with the color of the bygone sky, in contrast to the dark'ned gray of their skin. These emerge from the fountains of the deep that are about to transcend the earth—these two water dragons, which stand the height of the tallest city housing places, from whose nostrils pour the heated vapor of smoke, and when they open their great jaws to breathe, whose spittle glows the selfsame blue fire of their evil eyes.

In the rage of awakening, I see one great water dragon open his mouth to exhale a fiery breath, pouring a bright and dark blue flame onto the side of the city housing place, and onto the terrified inhabitants left on the streets below. And I see the other water dragon, as large and deadly as the other, exhale a breath from the wrath of God, to turn a part of the stone carved places into glowing rocks of orange, soon melting away in a fervent

heat, as the breath of blue fire burns everything it touches up and completely away in the flowing mist of rain. Even in the falling rain, the fire of these dragons is not quenched, and the worm of their rage and agony dieth not. These water dragons step about in the cracked and burning city with purpose of intention, upright upon great legs, their forearms smaller but able to grab and tear these stone built houses apart. And there are many stones and bodies fallen into the waters of the city ponds, suddenly lit up by the dragon's breath on top of the water, to make the pond appear as a lake of burning blue fire and brimstone.

And these two monsters, both Death and Hell among them—these two, these two monsters are overtaken with the lust for human flesh, as they begin to tear and bite into the stores and housing places for the ones that hide, for the ones that wait inside—the ones who believe that this rumbling apocalypse will pass. These are fast grabbed into the great dragon's teeth, these animals never before seen in the history of mankind, brought up from the caverns and shores that lie beneath the earth, brought up by the rising waters of the deep. And in the city's final hour, these two dragons take their part, until much of the city is awash in flame, burning blue and black fire in the rain.

And after this last and violent hour, when the mothers and daughters are devoured in pain, the Great Twister of the Plains begins to move again, upon what total devastation that still remains. This cloud monster moves in authority above the remains of the city, to begin breaking it up in no effort, and lifting every part and piece of man's work into loss and oblivion. Every work of man is destroyed by fire, and the elements are melted in fervent heart, and then every monster and monstrous work is taken up into the cloud, as it passes so un-silently, and violently overhead. And after

many long moments over and above the city, the great twister of the plains moves away from the walls of New Gotham, leaving only the soil and scattered bricks where walls and houses and life used to be, where the land was aflame with fires both black and blue, burning from without and within.

And there are none left, not one stone's worth of breath left to breathe, to witness the great path of churned, blackened soil that reaches from the bottom of the great twister dying, to the middle of the far off prairie, in a line that stretches to the distant horizon and beyond.

Jonathan Lovejoy

And God saw that the wickedness of man was great in the earth, and that every imagination of the thoughts of his heart was only evil continually.

Genesis 8:21

Jonathan Lovejoy

Part Four

Jonathan Lovejoy

In the heart of the Earth's memory, by the light of a silvery twilight moon, from in the confines of the Ark still tossed at sea, I see the mother with gold and flaxen hair, small waisted and heavy bosomed, so heavy with hatred for her daughter on the farm. This mother of profound and beautiful hatred, having trained and nurtured up her raven haired daughter in like hatred, until long after their father and husband has died, the two of them revel in open air hatred for one another—days and nights filled with good natured and evil resentment—days and nights filled with bitterness and back biting, one scratching the spirit and soul of the other, tearing each other up bit by bit, piece by fiery and bloody piece, until there is no good nature left under the resentment, and all that is left is whatever there is

when all love is lost—and there is only violence and discord to be. Here, under the light of this last twilight moon, before the clouds come to the hide every star in the heavens, two weeks before the first drop of the last rain they will see, this mother is called from their bitter argument—out into the twilight [lunar] light, gazing far above where the crops grow tall in the fields nearby a forest of cedar, leaf and pine.

Far out and beyond the land where I live, even somewhere above and beyond the wind and wandering sea. Two weeks before the first drop of rain, two weeks under this twilight moon, the mother remembers how the daughter had lost her fear, how the daughter so bravely walks over to her at anytime without fear and without respect, grabbing her gold and flaxen hair calmly, but with power, pulling until the mother must drop her cooking or cleaning duties and engage her daughter silently, as they struggle in heavy breathing that turns to clawing and hitting, until the hits are ended by powerful grappling that does not end, with both of their arms wrapped around one another's neck, bending each other over, until they are desperate for the tripping and the fall. *Let's take our clothes off then, bitch*, is the muffled sound from the grown daughter's mouth, so readily agreed upon by the farming mother—so heavy breasted, small waisted, so heavy with hatred for her daughter.

And in the noon hour, before the arrival of this last twilight moon, the mother and the daughter quickly disrobe in their house of pining wood. And they return to their heavy grappling of one another, their hatred rekindled in a new flame. These are the fires of lust and violence, those that burn so black and so blue. They wrestle so violently, aggressively around the room of the house, until soon, the mother's heavy breasted strength gives way, under the weight of her daughter's youth and power,

until she is flipped mightily to the floor beneath their feet, where the daughter's aggression is kindled in lust—and she holds the mother's gold and flaxen hair down upon the floor, and proceeds to hit the mother's face with her fists without stopping, until the mother can only cry out in angry, tearful rage mixed with fear. But her daughter has no mercy in this striking of blows until the mother's face is bruised and bloody, and her senses are dulled to spinning all about. And in the haze of fainting—she feels the naked daughter upon her, lying on top of her heavily, feeling her breast pulled roughly up into her daughter's mouth, whereby the pain she feels is as lightning in her body, as her breast is bitten to agony and blood.

And the mother lies there underneath her daughter. Both of them naked in their home near the pine forest, the mother's head thrown back in an enraged and pitiful scream, until she begins to hit her daughter upon the head and gouge at her eyes, until the daughter is forced to have to at last release her mother's bloody breast and let go. Then she rolls off the top of her mother, who holds her bitten breast, curled up as a babe in the womb, still weeping in pitiful anger, from the years of pain gathered at the front of her breast, and the finality of her daughter's wicked betrayal. And the daughter stands up to retrieve her clothing, stomping the mother hard on the hip, making the mother flinch and cry out in more shock than pain, holding her naked self where the daughter had just bitten and kicked her.

Oh, what seeds of motivation lie dormant in the womb! What waters must they feed upon, to grow and flourish in the moonlight? By the light of

this silvery twilight moon—the mother touches her swollen cheek beside the cut lip, feeling the ache upon her blackened eye at her cheek, and she sees the light of the silvery Moon wax crimson in her sight, until it is the color of darkened rust and blood. And she stands under the twilight moon, with resentment for the stars of beauty, of what devils or fallen angels they may be, marveling the sight that chimes her spirit with purpose, of the twilight moon that has turned to rust and blood. From this, she knows what it is that she must do. From this, in her spirit, it is done.

*I*n the pain of loss, loneliness and hopelessness, I ride. In the pain of lost love, we sail on through the darkness of this 39th night, at the dawn of the 40th day. And through the veil of this 40th rain's arrival, I am still burdened by the Heart of the Earth's Memory—where I see the mother in her bed, long after the twilight Moon has lived and died in rust and blood, and come back to silvery life again.

This is one of the out of the way places. A place hidden by the trees of sentimental youth. Hidden by the cropfields of despair planted and grown. Under the last earth moon. Under the last stars of Heaven. This is a house of desolation. A house replete with loneliness and sin. This, the sin of violence. The sin of discord. The sin of chaos. The sin of hatred.

And this is the mother who lives in the house. A woman who rests in beauty of gold and flaxen hair. Her mind has crossed over to what is meant to be. Into what was written into the stars above—when Eve was cast out of the garden. I see the woman of golden haired beauty, breasts bitten sore of blood, face scratched and bruised from what peace was battered and torn. From what peace that had tried to live, but was choked and cut and beaten until it hath departed. This is the Woman of Chaos. The Mother of Violence. The Woman of Hatred, under the shining of the approaching midnight grass and trees, and the warm nighttime breezes blown.

This woman rises gingerly from her bed, in reticence, in surrender to the curse of Fate—to go out to the midnight Moon, and look up to its silvery face, which to her is the face of feminine beauty, and the silent voice of reason. The woman is by the blood of the Lune, whose name is Mare Luna, who speaks the voice of the farming woman's future. *Take thy daughter gently by the hand, and bring her forth from her bed—bring her before me, where thou must make her as a sacrifice to me. Gather up thine cutting knife, used to kill the swine and birds for feasting. Then bring thy daughter before me, and spill her blood to me.*

This voice of the mother's last reasoning. This voice of her last unreasoning hatred, speaks to her mind in gentle power and beauty, to bathe her mind in revelation, down through her grieving spirit, and into her body and soul. The mother lowers her eyes, in the gentle smile of easy contrition, in the smile of easy acceptance, turning in the light of the midnight Moon, and walking toward their house of isolation.

In the misty light of the silvery Moon—the mother walks so gingerly, so gently, stopping so sweetly to the cooking place of their home, where she gathers up the carving blade, which is longer than the length of her hand. She goes to her daughter's room, in the tranquility of hatred, where there is no emotion of chaos, but only the tragic calm of every evil decision born and bred. She lifts the daughter in gentleness, in loving kindness from their midnight slumber, ushering her to what will be their new path of oneness together. The door of reconciliation, the portal to peace of mind. To slaughter a sleeping swine pig, by the light of the midnight moon.

The daughter arises from her deep, peaceful slumber, rubbing the hatred and confusion from her eyes, as the mother places upon her daughter a kiss, where the two of them hold the handle of the blade, under the light of the midnight Moon. And in the spirit of wicked togetherness, in secret, severe reconciliation, they are reconciled to perform this act—walking together out of the house, both in their white gowns of beauty, glowing in the light of the silver summer Moon.

And across the grassy field of their yard they glide, until the mother stops the daughter in their tracks—stepping up behind her lovingly, wrapping her arms around her, both of them gazing up at the misty light of the Moon, as the wisp of night cloud passes just beneath it, about to caress its face in a touch of deeper mist and gray. As they both touch the knife, both mother and the beautiful, dark haired daughter besides—the daughter

speaks words of such shuddering desire to the mother, of such utter possibility as to make her womb ache with the power of a desire unknown. *You know what I want to do,* the daughter says, *I want to kill a little girl. I want us to find one and take her from her mother and bring her here. Then I want us to stab her to death and bury the little bitch in the field.* And upon these words, is tipped the mother's lifetime desire, an epic glimpse in her body of what might have been, as she grabs her daughter's ear with her teeth, and her body lurches gently, against the back of her daughter. In full knowing, the daughter turns a wicked eye to her mother, and their stares meet in the moonlight, and the daughter leans back and presses a deep, sucking kiss to her mother's mouth, where their tongues meet in hidden pleasure, under their soft and fervent lips in pain. This, the pain of desire so deep as to have substance—to cause their ears to ring from the kiss, which gathers in their minds like the clouds that have begun to come together beneath the stars, and the moonlight of the Second Heaven above them.

But now, the daughter says, *I need to kill one of these fucking pigs.* And she pulls away from the mother again, and she walks away toward the fenced in mud yard, where the pigs are at rest in their nighttime slumber. And as the daughter approaches the fence, gazing over into the group of seven swine sleeping soundly, the mother unties the top of her white cloth raiment, and slips it from her shoulders to the ground. And the daughter turns to notice—agreeing to the logic of it, to avoid the mud and filth on their sleeping cloth. And the daughter too, removes her white garment and lays it upon the fence in keeping, leaning over the top of the fence unclothed, breasts high and perfectly rounded, ivory beauty in the moonlight—*Alright now, which one of you bitches is gonna die…*

And upon that question, she feels the cold stab in icy pain deep into her back to some unknown place inside—to flash a pain never before imagined, as she draws a loud and deep breath, turning to meet her mother's gaze again, this time in the agony of bewilderment, and a confusion as epic as their moonlit night. And she feels the return of this icy blade again—but in the front of her body through her womb. In breathless wonder, in the night of isolation unseen, the daughter stumbles away from the mother in fear, and terror gripped by the icy hands of death.

In the Heart of the Earth's Memory—the depth of depravity is grown. In the Heart of the Earth's Memory, the silvery moonlight is shown. And by the light of this summer mist of night, the mother glides easily across their farming nighttime lawn, to grab her daughter by the ivory wrist, to stab her once again, in the waning light from above. Then she grabs the lovely daughter's dark'ned hair, and she stabs her daughter in shrieks and screaming, by the light of the summer moon. She stabs her many times in bleeding, in the arms and legs, in her stomach and back, until the screaming daughter's resolve is broken with her body's strength, causing her to fall to the ground in weeping.

And now, the mother rides astraddle her screaming daughter, brandishing her sharpened blade with both hands—plunging it deep into her daughter's chest through her breast, and her stomach, and her face and neck, until the blood splashes out one mighty time from the neck as a fountain, to then calm down as a trickling crimson stream. The mother stabs until she cannot bring herself to lift the blade again, to cause a forty first cut in her daughter's ivory skin.

Forty lashes, forty slashes with the sharpened blade, until the daughter lies sleeping again in the night, naked underneath her mother, both women covered in blood, under the light of the silvery midnight Moon.

ere, in the Ark of Safety, in the dawn of the fortieth rain, I am burdened by a vision of pain, under the light of a silvery Moon. In my vision of desolation, there is the mother who drags her daughter's naked body in the third hour after midnight, to the place where the deep grave is dug. A grave easily dug down deep into the plowed and tilled soil of the field, deep enough to be at her waist when she realizes she must climb out, her nighting gown now corrupted with the filth of her misdeed. Her daughter's gown is now a bloody burial shroud, placed with such respect on her body tended, as she is dragged with slow, determined pace, across their grassy lawn to the fertile fields where the grain stalks grow tall and

green in the summer. These leafy green stalks of corn blow mildly in the breeze, then wildly in the cool, late night summer wind, as the mother drags her daughter to the grave and climbs down inside, then to the best of her feminine farmer woman's strength, lifts and lays her daughter down to the grave where she stands, laying her on her back with her face uncovered, so that every mark and cut on her face is visible in the moonlight.

And the mother hears the voice of Mare Luna, the voice of the night itself—speak to her of a job well done, and to... *hearken to the sacrifice that was made, and to listen to thine daughter's voice, and two weeks hence, find a girl child not yet matured, and bring her to me, to take the life from her through choking and smothering, until this child lies dead underneath thee. And then you must bring her to the field by night, when my light is diminished to half of itself, and bury this child naked in the soil, by the glow of the waning lunar light...*

Oh, what wonder are these dreams and visions I seek, in the dawn of the fortieth rain! Could these things have possibly occurred in the days before the flood, when the flaming light graced the twilight sky, with its tail of blue fire and white! I see the mother stumble in her filthy gown from their small field of plenty, from the rich and fertile soil of her misdeed—stumbling exhausted through the darkness to the empty house, where she must go to the bed of her lonely room, letting the filthy, bloody gown drop quickly to the floor. From here, burdened by the deed of what is done, and by the newness of the child that must be one with the soil, she lies upon her stomach unclothed, placing her hands together underneath herself, pressing her hands to the center of herself with hardly a motion, in slow and deliberate rhythm, guided by the voice of Mare Luna, who tells her not to move her body to a single twitch, but to rest upon her hands which press

against her private self, moving her fingers in their proper place underneath her as she lays on her stomach, charged to think of what was done to her daughter, charged to not twitch a single itch of muscle but her fingers so slowly, charged to think of the girl child she must find and kill. And upon this last and greatest thought of hers, on the night of her daughter's sacrificial death and burial, the mother who hath killed her daughter is gripped inside by the voice of Mare Luna, which caresses her to vulgarity, causing her buttocks to shake mightily, and her entire body tenses as her eyes roll up in her head, as she tries to look up while face down, to find the face of her new goddess, whose voice flows through her mouth and out into the room around her in wailing and weeping.

This, in the heart of the Earth's memory, in the dying light of a silvery Moon. And I see the face of Mare Luna, as she dies her death in grieving, in weeping for the tragic lies that must be told to the mother, for the tragedy of human existence, which is Fate—for the strong delusions that must come upon the Earth, so that mankind must believe a lie, in the hour that he is condemned, in the hour of his death and destruction.

In the dying light of this tragic Summer Moon, I see the mother return to the soil of her misdeed unclothed, having released the lightning in her body. And as the clouds pass over the face of Mare Luna, she covers the cut and bloody face of her daughter in the dirt, and then the rest of her body in the farming soil, until the deed has come and gone. And then the mother goes back to her house alone, seeing the clouds passed over her goddess, walking unclothed, in the gliding power of herself, in the wake of Mare Luna's dying light.

$\mathcal{I}$n the storm of this raging dream, I am held prisoner while inside the Ark, as the skies above us lighten to gray darkness, in the morning of our fortieth rain. And while I lay burning, my back itching from the welts and open scars from the horse whip and caning rod, the rain I hear on the roof of the Ark is the calling of the elements to me again, to give rise to the terrifying truth inside—the tragic and demonic revelation of a mother and daughter on a farm, in the wake of the Earth's fervent memory. And what memory is this, what grieving sigh is this, before my mind's eye, of the

mother in lonely complacency, in isolation upon her farm of ill and woe, her private place of wickedness and death?

These are the Winds of Tragedy. The rainy, twilight winds that blow. This twilight of the first day of rain—that was poured from the skies without ceasing, upon the mother and daughter's farm. The mother rests in uneasy tranquility, two weeks past her daughter's sacrifice, two weeks past her daughter's death and burial. Wondering when the hard rains will cease, and she will be able to ride her horse and wagon to the nearest village to buy goods, and seek the loneliest of the pretty little girls, to ride her down the dirt road of this wildest dream for a day visit—sneaked away from her guardian with promises of gold and silver trinkets or pretty dresses with bright colors. *"I live on a small farm just down the road,"* she would say— *"we'll be back before anybody even misses us…"*

In the wet, weeping world. In the drowning, pouring twilight rain—the mother sips a cup of the unfermented grape, so sweet and tart upon her lips, as she closes her eyes, to imagine the little girl that rides here with her from the nearest village…

And at the moment she imagines herself upon the little girl in full, to listen to her squirm and cry for her mother in panic, the mother's world cracks and splits in two—but not from the lightning and crackling thunder. She jumps from the crack, crack, cracking sound of a hammer force upon the walls of her cabin near her head, as though an angry, horned beast had been lost in the storm, and was driven to madness against the walls of her house. The mother opens the rainy shutters in the nick of time, to see a dark and rain soaked figure leave the side of the house, and glide out of sight around the front corner toward the front door.

And the mother stands in the middle of the room without breath, wondering what danger she is in from what stranger sent by evil, to force his way into the house and pillage her little life, such as it is, or to even attack her, or to rape her in this rain that falls so hard and without ceasing—to hide her fate from every other part of the uncivilized world...

Then suddenly, the storm declares itself in the first signs of its growing rage, in a flash of lightning brighter than day, crashing an end of the world noise in the air around her, seeming to rattle the wooden door itself to shaking, but a shaking that pounds now in rhythm, until the wood upon the door begins to splinter, and a bluish gray hand smashes noisily through. The mother screams and drops her cup of grape squeezed elixir drink, not seeing it splash wildly to the floor—not caring of its succulent taste on her palette—as the hand begins to tear in supernatural strength at the strong wood, breaking it apart piece by piece, bit by bit, until the entire arm reaches through!

The mother's screams are of the unknown. Her fear is the terror of Death. When the crashing and breaking of the door goes on, until the hole is big enough to show eyes white with merciless evil, and a face bearing the rotted, dirty corruption of the grave. The mother screams as this figure leans and reaches inside, but not to unlatch the sliding bar of wood, but to pull and climb its way inside! The mother's screams now take a deep tone—a deeper meaning, one of revelation, as to the third part of the truth, which is the end of the world—which is cataclysm.

And the mother's screams now have a name. They scream the name of the daughter she buried two weeks ago. In the field by the cedar woods and pine, in the dying light of a twilight moon. In the twilight rain—in this rainstorm like no other, she watches the creature in the form and likeness

of a woman come forth, crashing full into the house, leaving the door in splinters hanging, in the pouring twilight rain.

This woman with bluish skin—bluish skin of ashe white and mud, stumbles into the house with white eyes of evil intent, eyes devoid of a soul, eyes knowing only the purity of evil uncluttered by morality, nor delusions of mercy or compassion. In long, black hair wet with mud and grieving, the white eyed figure lunges toward the screaming woman with a powerful frown upon its face, the mark of sinister intelligence in its eyes, its burial shroud brown from the mud of its calling. This creature in the likeness of a woman grabs the mother from her screaming fit, dragging her across the floor by the hair in a violent and chaotic pulling against her, the mother screaming the name of her daughter in pleading for forgiveness, and to please have mercy on her soul.

But where is the heart of mercy, in the midst of the Judgment of God! This creature drags the mother across the rainsoaked grassy lawn, toward where the wind blows the stalks of corn with a message from the far and distant future—toward the field where the daughter was dead and buried. This creature in the likeness of a daughter corrupted by death, this creature drags the screaming mother through the rain soaked twilight. From the house, over the grassy lawn, and into the rainsoaked cornfield of mud, dragging the mother still by the hair of flaxen gold, now wet with the stench of mud and the grave.

This creature drags the mother screaming, splashing through the mud—throwing her helplessly down into the wet, muddy space that was the burial mound where her hand broke through but just a short time before. And now, the mother lies upon her back, held there by the creature who lays beside her holding her by the throat, with its other arm wrapped about the

mother's waist, and the scarred and muddy legs wrapped around the rest of her body. The mother's back is twisted in pain, lying on a lump of mud, where her head is down just enough to be below ground, where the water has already gathered, and begun to creep up the side of her head.

The mother breathes these last, choking screams. Unable to move, hardly able to turn her head to escape the water in her ears—hardly able to turn her head to gaze into the white eyes of this thing. This *it,* that has such a familiar smell of the daughter she knew, mixed with the sweet stench and corruption of the grave.

The mother lies in screaming, choking wait, as the waters of her misdeed run from the muddy ground to where she lies quickly, slowly rising up to her cheeks nearby her lips, where screams are now replaced with desperate gasps for air, and for a reprieve from choking and drowning. But this creature frowns and stares in silence, holding the mother immobile, as the mother now, still lying on her back, must close her mouth to keep out the water rising, holding her head still to try and breathe through her nose still above the water—until the first drop of mud soaked rainwater burns her nostrils inside, causing her to writhe against the creature holding her tight, and try one last and desperate scream from underneath the water.

The mother lies in wait. Upon the muddy ground her daughter was buried in. Two weeks before the end of the world rains began to fall, when she heard the voice of Mare Luna, by the light of a silvery Moon.

In the heart of Earth's fervent memory. In the aftermath of greatness. In the wake of the Great Twister of New Gotham, the bloom falls open upon the Rose of Sharon, the companion and lover for the rich woman's desire, her refuge in the storm of wind and rain. The skies delight and rumble their steady assurance of what prevails across the entire Earth, of what is, and of what is meant to be. The lightning spreads in rivers at the bottom of the thickening gray clouds, moving across the sky in slow and steady streams of light upon them—and at times sparking from the sky to the ground, somewhere near the distant horizon.

And despite the constant shaking and quaking from the ground, and the low, deep grumbling voice of doom from the sky as well, Sharon (my mother's best friend of old) lies underneath it all in defiance to what she feels, in the farm castle on the prairie plain, where the part of the great twister had gone so nearby. Underneath the skies of gray and grieving, underneath her wealthy lady lover, Sharon can hardly think of the sucking pleasure she feels, as Diana lies on top of her in heavy repose, holding her down and pulling her ample, ivory breast up into her mouth in hunger, and deep grieving to be free of the rainstorm, which is but a day come to life and living. But the two women press onward with their calling, somewhere apart from their two grown daughters, who are at the window of their upper room on the other side of the house, still marveling at the storm.

And even though fear and trepidation have taken over Sharon's mind, her body still responds to what needs are met in this twilight rendezvous, even while she remembers the sight of the widened swath of lowered ground cut into the prairie by the churning cloud—a line of rich, darkened soil to mark the path of greatness born from here to doomsday, and to parts at the end of the flat earth unknown, having no concept of the Earth's roundness and infinity of land and water, nor the fullness of where it is in relation to the Sun, the Moon and the stars, nor the vast and blackness of infinity, as it pertains to the Second Heaven. Sharon only knows the new calling in her mind and body, lit up by the lightning shears, and the rivers of it that spread so gingerly across the sky.

While her lover moves up from her breasts to her neck, her body's heat grows, along with the unknown expectation she suddenly feels, as her heart is carried above the plain where the twister line is visible. Following the road of nature west of the farm, back to the woman she was born and raised to know, the woman she was destined to meet and foolishly left

seven years ago, to be this rich woman's pretty plaything and puppet on a string. And Sharon begins to wonder allowing this thought to cross her heated mind—*what kind of a mother am I,* when she thinks of what she has nurtured and grown into her own daughter's spirit these seven years, and of what example she herself has set for her.

But as she feels the rich Lady's wiry, muscular thinness in domination, in contrast to the large and rounded breasts that hang free from the tight, white body of wealth and privilege—these big and firm, rounded breasts of a farming queen that have grown bigger and more powerful over the years, as her woman's strength has waxed as that of an earth goddess over time, as a queen of some far and distant jungle tribe of warrior women—as this goddess moves to Sharon's lips to give suck, Sharon's mind is open again to the desire of her heart met, and why she has so willingly given herself over to this farming queen's commanding and starlight beauty. She hugs Diana fully, lying underneath her as only a submissive and willing lover should, allowing the Great Twister to spin its devastation onward still in her mind, while Diana's lips and tongue spin devastation to her helpless soul and body.

And with fervence, with profound apology for her body's disobedience, Sharon separates her legs open wide—receiving the fullness of what is strapped to her lady lover's lower self, breathing in as the length of it is pushed all the way, deep inside, causing her soft and jiggly flesh to tremble all over, as her lover holds her down in loving domination, squeezing her voluptuousness tight, and taking every part and portion of what pleasure there is left to give.

Sharon lies there. Trapped underneath her lady lover. Burdened by the moaning of a queen's depravity unleashed, and the memory of nature's

fury unleashed in her mind's eye, as she remembers the twister that flowed by their farming castle, on its way to the shores of New Gotham. And despite every reluctance, resistance and revolving fear, despite every apprehension and anticipation, the pain of pleasure grows in Diana's body in proportion, as her lover's movements become more determined on top of her, settling into a steady rhythm of effort, a decision to accomplish and achieve. Sharon bereaves this decision made, holding on to her lover above her head, grabbing onto her shoulders from underneath, waiting for the spark of lightning to kick in. Waiting for the roll of thunder to sound.

And soon, in the midst of her lover's heavy motion and moaning, heavy grinding and groaning to be relieved, the rich woman's body jerks and twitches a warning, which causes the woman to begin pushing harder and faster downward, which sends the heat in Sharon's body to a higher plane—to awaken every nerve to a different place, which causes her to begin to whimper as the moaning of her lover turns into the yell of a warrior queen on the kill, an angry declaration of a victory hard fought and won. And while the rich woman slams and slides every earned ecstasy of motion, Sharon holds on in the wake of end of the world lightning strikes and blasts of thunder outside, her head thrown back, eyes closed tightly with her teeth gritted in a strain to endure, as her lovers new and violent motion sparks a flash of energy in Sharon's body to cause a scream, but where there is no mercy given, and her queen's motion moves forward through Lover's Agony—which is a second flash of energy doubled on top of the first one, which causes Sharon to cling her arms and legs to her lover for dear life and strain, her teeth grimaced to a bitter grin of pain, while the second wave of pleasure passes so powerfully and painfully through.

$\mathcal{T}$he evening and the morning see the passing of the first day of rain, above where the Rose of Sharon lies in bloom. In the wake of the Great Twister's towering arrival and departure, Sharon understands that there is no resistance to the power of what is meant to be—the power of a trip seven years in the making. As the undertaking of this journey overtakes her inside, she comes to terms with the creation of this new barrier, this new wall that has suddenly formed between her and her woman lover. Having already been a long time coming, but finished and polished in the heat of this stormy and windy rainfall, and the gigantic whirlwind's unequivocal passing by. And Diana's own instincts have not been spared, having sensed

for many days the arrival of something big, of some eventful happening in their seven year history, but resisting it by the sheer will of her privileged force and power, which the wealthy and well off are apt to do, as they cruise so comfortably down the banks of the Wealthen Stream. *What you think*, Diana believes, *is what you become.* What you believe, she thinks, is what will come to pass. And her lover's sudden thoughts of gathering Nadia up for a hasty departure in this wild rain is foolishness that she cannot take, and most certainly will not abide.

You're making a mistake, Diana says. *Nobody in their right mind is going anywhere in a rain like this. Is this just your way of leaving us?*

I'll be back in a few days, I promise, Sharon says. *There's an old friend of mine that lives in the village where I'm from. I just have a strong feeling that she's in danger in this storm. I feel like I have to go.*

Why won't you let me come with you?

I have to do this alone, Sharon says. *Nadia and me.*

Upon the long morning of arguing and discussion, is lifted the spirit of surrender to the soul of the rich woman—whose place in life is just too secure for her to care. Too comfortable to be desperate for Sharon to stay. Too cushioned in complacent coziness and coddling to be afraid of being left alone. Though their husbands have not yet returned from their business trip many day's ride from here, the two women are concerned only for themselves and their daughters' well being, having no knowledge of their husband's impending deaths in the city on the plains. Where the end of the world twister is soon to arrive. And besides this, the trip to Sharon's old village is but four hours by horse and cart, which is not a world away for Diana to suffer through. Maybe, she will be back in a few days, just like she promised. Maybe, when the clouds of these hard and driving rains have parted, when the rays of sunlight are again shining through, she will see

her lover and her daughter again on the horizon, to come in calling to her heart's desire, and to help keep their loneliness at bay.

On the crest of this noontime departure, away from the two daughters who have languished in sorrow alone—the rich woman at last corners her sensual soulmate in the halls of their farming castle, pressing her hard against the wall in full authority, not caring what servant or what daughter should wander by, and see these actions betray the feelings she's kept bottled up inside for too long.

I don't want you to go, Diana says.

I don't want to go either. But I have to. This woman—she's like a sister to me. She's like family. I'll never rest until I know she's safe.

Why can't you just wait until this evil storm is over?

Diana, you ran inside before that thing got close enough. But I stayed, and I forced Nadia to stay, and I saw it up close. It was…it was the end of the world. And all I could think about after that was… is Adina okay? Did her two daughters survive. Nela and Nora. I haven't seen them in seven years…

Her thought is suddenly trapped in her mouth by a kiss. Where the echoes of desperation taste sweet upon the lips and the tongue. When complacency suddenly gives way to chaos in brief, and cozy, cushioned comfort unraveled.

What's wrong Diana?

I should be asking you that—you're the one whose leaving. You're tired of me now. I've become old and ugly to you. And you're leaving me because of it…

That's not true—

I can see it in your eyes, Sharon. I sensed it on you as far back as a week ago. The last time we were in the dungeon.

I told you that I wasn't feeling well that day. That had nothing to do with this—I didn't even know I was leaving then.

Then what is it? What is the problem?

I told you, I have to go back and check on my friend and her daughters. I don't know why but I <u>have</u> to.

I can't stop you. I can't do what I wish I could do and have you locked up so you'll stay.

Sharon stares intently. A wave of fear flashes through.

Just… promise me you'll come back.

I told you I'll be back in a few days—

Swear it to me.

Sharon presses a kiss to her mistress. Eyes wide open.

I swear it.

56

$\mathscr{T}$he hours of the morning pass into their rainy oblivion, as the wealthy woman stands at the balcony of her bereavement, refusing to attend their departure in the storm. Watching from the safety of the open door to the upper room, just inside from where the rains have begun to fall with even more pounding and purpose—with more steady assurance than before. It seems that in league with her lover's departure, is the rising and blowing of a new and unseen wind, made visible only by the whirling masses and sheets of rain that give away its whereabouts, as the horses and sheltered wagons let out across the prairie from their stony, gray brick mansion home.

Diana watches in the unfamiliar air, the air of apprehension that rises to fear inside, and threatens to spread to make her body cold in the storm. From the safety of privilege, she watches Sharon and Nadia take their foolish and fateful ride west in the storm. She stands at the door of privilege, having felt her own daughter Danielle's hand slip away as she left to return to her own affairs, somewhere else in the farming castle. To some other affair of the heart—with a servant girl nearby her own age, and like-minded in twisted sensibilities taught and learned.

But even while she looks after the horse drawn carriage, watching it grow smaller in the rainy distance, she is made to consider the origins and whereabouts of this powerful storm, when a single bolt of lightning forms bravely from the top of the sky to the bottom in blinding rage, and a booming revelation of noise and cataclysm.

The horrors of human negativity flash brightly in the storm, crashing loudly from the clouds of doom. Sharon and Nadia both jump and flinch from the river of light that just penetrated the floor of Heaven, making its way from the top of the sky to the bottom, to blast heat onto some unlucky spot on the ground, leaving it charred and devastated to a smoking ruin in the rain. Whether it was a clump of trees or grass, or the collection of stone and wood inhabiting space as manmade shelter, she doesn't know. But Sharon is suddenly imbued with the same helplessness, the same

hopelessness and loss of control penetrating humanity from one side of the world to the other, having no concept of this storm being more than hours or a few days temporal, or a few miles in space and dimension. As Sharon and the daughter stay the course forward, as they drive the rainy road alone, they can hardly conceive of the wide and blackened path of churned up ground that stays near the road on their whole journey—nor can they imagine that this storm is but a mere sampling of what has begun in every part of the sky, across every stretch of land across the entire earth.

Whether or not the whole world is raining, she does not know. But what she does know is the pulling and tearing of emotions, that draws her inexplicably across the prairie, to a woman she has not seen in seven years, through a storm of such power and duration as she has *never* seen.

Mankind is evil penetrates the core of the Sharon mind, as she whips the horses into a dead run through the driving rain. Suddenly aware of the unseen ties that bind—the connection that exists between the wind, the bygone dust of the ground, and the heavy, oppressive sheets of rain. And though she tries not to notice, woven through the fabric of this scene is the gigantic path of darkened earth dug into the shallow ground, winding straight down and alongside her road west across the prairie.

And suddenly along the way, an hour into her struggling ride, as if to remind her of the heavy weight of circumstances—as if to remind her of how irrevocable her decision and choices have been, the road ahead is

suddenly cut in two by the wide path of shallow dug up ground winding along side, crossing from the prairie from the right side of the road to the left and off into the distance. But even so, in the cold and misty summer rain—her fear is bound and powered by desperation, lit up by a spark and flash of lightning, and a crash and rumble of thunder.

As if called forward in the storm, she gently moves the horses forward and downward into the wet, depressed path of dirt cut across the road— riding the covered wagon slowly, fearfully across the twister's word written on the ground, which is the *Wrath of God,* Sharon and Nadia both amazed at the wide and powerful lower ground they travel through, which begs the impression of a muddy riverbed unfilled. They drive the horses across this future river unknown, until the wagon is in the middle, where they can look left and right, to see where the twister has come from, and toward where on Earth it is going to. Not knowing that somewhere down east, long past the farming castle where they have come from, it has grown into the greatest whirlwind of all time, and truly the greatest of all time yet to come.

They drive the horses onward upon their road west—through the path cut across it by the twister, unaware that it bears resemblance to many paths cut across many lands around the world, where great clouds have come down from the sky in rumbling and screaming wrath, to announce the beginning of the end of mankind. After many long breaths held and taken, after she glances back and forth down the mud river, the horses firmly approach the banks of the other side, easily climbing the shallow edge—to resume their trip down the road west, and the path less dark and treacherous. Now, they gaze to the left side of the long road, where the

twister's path in the ground is not as wide, and not so deeply dug into the soil.

"The soil of the human heart is stonier," it shall be written someday, as it is now written upon the hearts of this mother and her daughter as they attempt to flee corruption—through the severe and sounding sheets of rain. Sustained melancholy is the character of this storm, across the length and breadth of it. Unlike other rainstorms that have come and gone, the weight of this one is oppressive, like an ocean of rain, where the inhabitants of the entire earth are prisoners at the bottom. And though it has hardly just begun, the power of the water weighs down upon the forests and fields, upon the rocks and the dirt, upon the mountains and the valleys without mercy from above and without restraint, until even the great fishes beneath the ocean can no longer remain at the surface in comfort. Retreating to the lowest places they can to hide, to try and escape the churning, the windblown turning of the waters, and the waves tossed here and there, the great mountains of water hither and yonder born. Around the world, many have taken to the rainy streets and muddy roads, traveling to whatever place it is they call home, not yet understanding that home is a higher ground from where they live, until the waters themselves begin to grow, and chase them to the very ends of the earth.

They ride along, these two, braving the wind and the rain toward a village already dead and gone, though doing this unawares, as Sharon's heart is burdened by an old friend, as she wonders where two beautiful daughters may be, and where it is in this rainy world where their beloved mother could have gone. They drive on, these two, past the remains of the twister's path near the road, seeing it stretch onward and away towards south and west, toward the beginning of this end of the world message written with the finger of God. They travel on, these two, into the third hour past the noon day, until the rainy

landscape waxes familiar, well past where the Great Twister of New Gotham has disappeared from memory, and the road bears no scars from the disease of mankind's moral decay.

These are the rocks and hills, bushes and trees from days gone by, and the road of her flight from the far country has now become the road to safety, which is the road to days of happiness and home. Sharon and Nadia ride this road of false hope and storm, this road of broken dreams and wind, this road of shattered expectations and ruin. Driving their fine horses down the old village road, until they come to a place that makes them wonder, where is the village? Where are the houses, and the lay of the streets they once knew? For along the path chosen, nearby this road is another message of churned up ground in lesser magnificent display— passing through where the place was once familiar, but is now the strange layout of scattered rocks and pieces of brick, clay and pottery where homes and lives used to be.

They park the fine horses at the edge of this poverty memory, at the edge of this ghostly dream, knowing that it was a different twister that had leveled the streets of this town, that had laid waste to all pretense of life and the struggle to live. As Sharon and Nadia walk the road home, seeing the miracle of this creation wind having spared what it will, she notices the houses on their street to the right of them still standing, with hardly another pebble of brick anywhere else in the village still intact. What was once a community, a collection of houses and small dirt properties, is now a collection of scattered debris, the remains of lives gathered and destroyed, with bricks and bodies laid about, where there is only rain and wind besides, and an empty landscape stretching from the shattered village flattened, to the windswept prairie and low lying hills beyond.

The Ark

Sharon and Nadia stand soaked in the pouring rain, cloaked in fine linen drenched with foolishness and false hope. No longer the mother and daughter of country poverty and simplicity who were taken seven years ago, but a mother and daughter matured by wealth and privilege, grown in knowledge of the forbidden, nourished by fruit plucked from the Tree of Eve, which bears the knowledge of good and evil. Sharon and her grown daughter Nadia, women of stature and gold, step off the muddy, rainy streets of this town, this little village of poverty they once knew, into the remains of a house they once spent many hours in, in the days before the clouds came, in the days when the sky was blue.

58

The woman of gold stands with her daughter of silver, both wet in the house of dirt, Sharon trying to fathom of what manner of storm cloud laid waste to this little part of the world. Trying hard to draw the essence of Adina from memory alone, but being unable. And all that Nadia can gather is the strangeness of their rainy journey and destination, which is like something out of a dream she once had, where she was walking the streets of this very village, which were as deserted as the dusty streets of a ghost town.

And this is what the mother and daughter of gold sense and see in the rain, inside the old poverty house where the roof is partially collapsed, seeing the rain pour inside here in rapid and steady streams, far across the room and away from them, toward the cooking fireplace so distant and so familiar and near. They stand half sheltered from the mist, these two, half sheltered from the present, feeling in their hearts the full scale departure of the life from this village, and the absence of a bygone friend.

The daughter of gold steps up beside the mother, taking her by the arm gently, looking her in the eyes without reservation, with understanding so deep and true. *Let's go home,* are the words that Sharon hears from the motion her daughter's lips make, as if in slow motion, amidst the bright and dangerous flash of lightning in the clouds, and the unquiet rumble of doom all around them.

*H*aving made quick work of a hasty departure, having disposed of an ill advised sojourn across the prairie plain, Sharon and Nadia whip the horses into a dead run, in the fourth hour after the noonday, each hour bearing full resemblance to the one before, with the light of life so far hidden behind the clouds of grieving. The rains have begun to fall with fury, as if under pressure from above, so that the world around them is covered in mist as far as the eye can see. What daylight there is carries them forward in bleak hope, to return to the place they call home, whether or not it may be a refuge of sin. But still, just as it was in the many hours

before, Sharon cannot escape the powerful tugging inside, calling her to abandon the days of private and depraved diversion, and to take her daughter by the hand, so to speak, and guide her to another place of being, another place of believing, where there is a choice that can be made between carnality and chastity, and that the spirit of mankind can commune with righteousness, as it pertains to the spirit of God.

And what is God? Who is God, may she ask? This, she cannot say on her own, except when prompted by the sight she sees glowing across the windy prairie, in the rolling and flowing land of rain—in the form of an arc of water shooting from the ground to the sky, high across the road and down to the ground on the other side—this geyser of water having already filled the great twister's path dug into the ground, turning it into the first remnants of a rushing mighty river.

In the place where the tornado's path had crossed the road before as a benign and harmless swath of mud, a curious thing to marvel at and pass, is now fed by the waters of an underground stream broke free, with the waters rushing past them with enough power to cause trepidation, moving down the length of the twister's path and far into the distance. The two women are suddenly stranded with nowhere to go, marveling at the new river formed across the road and across the prairie, and the misty arc of water glowing high over the road above them.

The mother and daughter of gold look up into the storm, out into the sea of drowning rain, perceiving the world as one big ocean of falling water, where there is no merciful dry air to breathe—where there is no end in sight. And who is God? What is God, she may ask, as the answer is laid heavy upon her spirit, as she observes the arc of water beneath the clouds, and the elegant fury of the raging waters below. But it is an intangible, a vapour without substance to grasp—a watery whiff as a fog inside, as if it

is truly there to see and feel upon the skin, but unable to be grabbed and held on to? But from this feeling alone, she is able to perceive the power of his might, and the need to say "yes" to the tugging inside, as though it may pertain to the afterlife of green, when the grasses and leaves of every tree are gone, and the breath of life is taken from every living thing.

Mother, it'll be alright, her daughter says, when she looks over and sees the mother's awestruck expression burdened with tears, which flow down her face as freely as drops of rain upon a marble wall, flowing from her spirit in a slow and steady stream. The mother of gold kisses her daughter mysteriously on the cheek, but a kiss devoid of what carnal sensuality they have known, though still being a kiss of knowledge, mixed with love, strength and virtue. And the daughter of gold perceives the soul of this kiss, that it concerns something so much bigger than desire, so much grander than themselves and their longing to be in the confined safety of the castle home beyond the horizon.

Sharon takes the reins tightly in her hand, and drives the horses to their own gingerly stepping—their careful stepping down into the steeper banks of what was once a river of mud, but is now a river of water fully grown. In the river, they drive slowly onward, the water nearly covering the wheels of their covered chariot, with the horses' legs fully covered to their undersides, so that they can still walk and pull the wagon through. And suddenly, they feel the wagon slip downward and to the side, as if a wheel were stuck in a crevice, which the horses are unable to easily pull them from. And Nadia looks upward into the rivers of lightning that spread across the dark clouds above the water arch, feeling the rain driven into her face by a mighty gust of wind as they languish in the middle of the New Gotham River.

And suddenly, they both scream as the lightning sparks bright, so close to their chariot overhead, surrounding them in a blast of thunder from the end of the age itself. And as if summoned, they are both amazed by the appearance of a rising hill of water nearby, which rises higher—until it is twice the height and girth of a normal man and woman. And this hill of water in the river begins to move toward the horses, which both react with the spirit of Fear, jumping and tugging about against the stuck wagon, but being unable to budge it forward or backward, being helpless as well to break themselves free.

And this hill of water moves twice the height of the horses, moving smoothly past the front of them, growing thinner, more slender in appearance, until its likeness and form is like that of a *woman,* her countenance and curves hidden by the substance of the river where she was born. And the two women of flesh and blood, the mother and daughter of gold, are suddenly bound by the spirit of Fear, which fills their world with screams of terror, as this *water witch* forms arms of watery intent, flowing past the horses toward where they sit, reaching inside to take hold of the daughter's arm, pulling her with unearthly strength and power away from the mother.

But the mother holds on for what dear life there is left, for what faint and feeble hope for living and breathing there may be. And after but a few moments, a few breaths taken and given, the Woman of Water pulls with the strength of her calling, wrenching the daughter free from her screaming mother's grip, flying her through the air as if tossed, and splashing her hard into the waters of the raging river below. And Sharon can only watch and shriek, calling the words "save her" over and over again to the answer of *who is God, what is God*—watching her daughter be held inexplicably at the surface for a moment, then seeing the arm of the water witch wrap

around her throat, and pull her unmercifully beneath the swirling water below.

And Sharon leans forward from inside her fine chariot, out into the rain, gazing at the spot where her daughter went under, where her daughter was *pulled* under. And without mercy, in the midst of the mother's fear and despair, the hill of water rises again, from the place where the daughter was taken, but moving away from the mother, terrifying the horses again, flowing around them toward the other side of the chariot until the arms begin to form again, with no thought for the mother's sudden calm and appeal for mercy from the arc of rain above, nor to her repeated prayer, *save me, save me, save me...*

And without mercy, in the driving mist of rain, the water comes to life again. Taking hold of the woman of gold. Pulling her from the chariot and splashing her to the water. Allowing her to rest so calmly, so mysteriously at the surface of Death, where she can see the arc of water high overhead, before disappearing beneath the waters of the raging river below.

What is this loneliness that I feel?

What of this heartache is there left to say?

What is the mercy of God revealed?

What of my wife who loves me in the Evening Day?

In the heart of the Earth's memory, the wealthy woman surveys the landscape, from her farming castle of dreams, to the far and distant horizon. For every hour of the days gone by, she has drifted on the winds of reverie, in and out of grief and longing, wishing for what might have been, and with hopeless longing for what most assuredly can never be. Remembering three days ago, when she stood at the door of this self same balcony, in the daytime darkness of the upper room—to be struck down by the surreality of the heavy storm, the departure of the one she loved, and the arrival of the earth's newest great river, flowing many days journey from the horizon west, down her property towards the castle house, rushing and raging past it like a water monster come to life, and onward towards the cracked, broken and deserted streets of New Gotham, where their husbands had so recently just lived and died beyond her vision.

What of the loneliness she feels, three days after the arrival of the Armageddon River, the New Gotham River, where there had been no river flowing before? What is the loneliness she feels—that doth not pertain to her husband, but to one who she is now married to in her spirit—the woman Sharon, who has taken this arduous and treacherous journey of betrayal through the rain? What is the division, the dividing line between love and possession? Is the longing she feels deeper than what a man feels for a team of oxen, when one is broken down sick unto death? What is the division, what is the dividing line between love and affection? Is what she

feels for Sharon any more or less what one might feel for any close friend or acquaintance—is it what the rider feels when a horse pulls up lame, and must be put out of their misery? Is it mere affection, is it mere possession, are these the connections that ache the wealthy woman's heart and soul, as she stands three days beyond her lover's journey of betrayal? What is the division—what is the dividing line between love and obsession? Is what she feels merely the jealously that ensues, when a friend displays a cheating heart, to ignite the green fires of envy within the blood, or to fill the lungs with the crystalline cold of jade ice and winter?

What of affection, possession and obsession? Are these washed away in the rains that fall under pressure—are they carried away by the Armageddon River, to the shores of New Gotham's demise? This new river carried into the Earth's condemnation of man, over 10 days journey [200 miles] from top to bottom, from here to the far city, to the city on the plains, which rises no more toward the skies in gold and marble grandeur, whose temples no longer stand in magnificent tribute to gods and goddesses without power, without a spark of control over these lightning shears, or the spears of sharpened thunder in the ear. This is the river of the First Epoch, the Armageddon River, which is the name which burns my brain, which I even asked Noah himself of, and he could only shake his head 'no' in quiet lack of understanding.

This is the river of mankind's destruction. The waters of his misdeed. The choking current of his judgment and death. This river is a sign unto them—across the many villages and towns, past the summer cities and centers of trade, this river is a sign unto them, that the heart of God is filled to the banks of this path chosen, now to rage and overflow with determination and grieving over having made mankind. This river rages past the heart and minds of those who do not see—who cannot perceive it

as more than a natural phenomenon, a great and powerful miracle of nature alone—having nothing to do with the lust of the flesh, their lust of the eyes, or the pride of life—believing this river to be innocent of accusation, having naught to do with the sins and sinister acts unseen, of those things that it is a shame for them to speak of in public. This is the River of Judgment. The tears and pain of the Almighty poured from the bowels of the Earth—flowed across the fearful and grieving landscape of watery Hell and Death.

And in the glow of night, the fires of his intent were seen, as the cracks in the ground were opened again and again, to gush more water out and upward into the Armageddon flow—where the fires of melted rock from beneath the Earth were extinguished as they appeared, so that the river flashes light and dark the entire length of its journey down east, so that at night it comes to life, so that it can be seen glowing across the prairie in the dark. And this glowing river of light appears across the dreary landscape— as the earth rumbles and trembles in grieving, for the pain of what it knows, and the agony of what judgment and death it must give birth to. In the whole of human history, there is no river that hath flowed in light glowing from within, the glowing light of pain and suffering—the orange light of condemnation, and the red light of sensuality and sin. The Red River glows in the darkness, spoken upon the lips of those who cannot see the fires of judgment that this is, that this is the River of Blood that flows through endtime humanity, on the eve of his absolute Death and Destruction.

And after three days and three nights, this river has flowed past the farming cottages and castles. This woman of wealth stands on the edge of twilight, on the balcony of evening, at the end of the third day of waiting.

Burdened by a spirit of epic sorrow and surrender, unable to perceive the reason—unable to see the cause and effect of what hath transpired. The wealthy woman stands alone, having lost her daughter Lizbeth to fear, who has retreated to the arms and comfort of the servants and their families, and not wondering after her own mother, who is queen of their farming estate and empire.

This queen stands at the precipice of Eve, and this, two fold. The mother of sin, whose sins were passed down the motherline to her, to Sharon, to Nadia and Lizbeth, to mothers and daughters across the prairie, in the valleys, and into the mountain forests and hills. This firstfold precipice is the Eve of Creation. And there too is the Second Eve. This, the Eve of everlasting fire and brimstone—the eve of Revelation, the eve of torment and doom. This, the Eve of night, to where she stands on the balcony at the evening day, seeing the glow of the Armageddon River come from underneath a new ocean, while the entire landscape is now covered in water—from where it lashes against the door of her castle, past where the new river once was, and to the far edge of her early evening world, lit up by the lightning that shines as far as the eye can see.

61

The Redeemer walks the waters of our salvation—throughout the 40th night of this judgment rain. I have seen the glowing spirit of this man in my dreams, in visions so clear and powerful that I can feel the rain upon my face, and can smell the waters of the salt and briny deep. It seems to me that I stand on the observation floor, in the hall of light far above with one of the great windows slid open, to where the great hall is lit up with the continuous flashes of lightning, with echoes of resounding thunder throughout. In this night vision upon the 40th night, I stand sheltered above, touched by the icy cold wind and rain, held enraptured, captured by the ghostly sight of one who walks upon the waters unafraid—beneath the Cross of Lightning I have seen so often. And I know that the future of mankind, our bleak and hopeless future, is watched by this power upon the waves, in whose hands is given the power to free mankind from the sins

that corrupt him, and the darkness whereby he is made blind—that this spirit will be sent to another generation of us, sent to set the captives free, and to be lifted up from the Earth, I hear him say, *where I will draw all men unto me.*

Of none of this, I understand. Only that it has something to do with the power and mercy of Noah's God, and what mysterious workings of nature and man that he has left to bring into the world. And what world can this be, which is only an eternal sea, where the last people on earth are prisoners in the Ark, drifting the four winds for an eternity? I stand in the mist, in the midst of the vision upon the water, staring at the divine spirit upon the waves, barely able to wonder at the core of this truth, that how is he able to walk on water, until I suddenly remember that it is a spirit of God, which is subject to no earthly law, and is the ruler and creator of both Heaven and Earth, and every bolt of lightning, every booming voice of thunder, and every looming drop of rainfall in between.

And I am compelled to push my fear aside, and gaze upon this figure, until I am no longer a prisoner of the Ark, but I am somehow at the side of the Great Ship, suspended above the water by the unseen, to where I can sense the tar and the wood *outside,* as it splashes the forward motion of its calling. And I am held still, so that I am burdened to see this lighted being approach me in power, these being the powers of Love and Humility, which I see upon his countenance as he approaches, having hair and whiskers as if he were Noah in his youth, with eyes of such naivete and kindness as to defy rational thought, but empowered by Divinity unrestrained, so that one is inspired to epic humbleness in his presence, and the burden of reverence undisturbed. There is only the power of his command, over the bygone land, and above the judgment sea, as the bearded man walks so nearby me as to make me want to reach out for him,

to touch his flowing garment of pure white, which is blown by the wind so elegantly against his body, to reveal his vulnerability to me, and the nature of God reconciled in Love and Humility.

I stand nearby the Ark in the driving rainstorm, held up nearby the churning waves where this man doth walk, wishing to know and call upon his name, but being unable, as he walks so kindly and gracefully past me in the storm. And I watch him step so lightly, even politely upon the waves, moving away from the Ark into the stormy distance, upon the echo of the words Lamb of God, and a single flash of blinding light from the clouds, and a blast of thunder that shocks me to reality again.

The truth of my life comes rushing back to me as I sit up from my soft feather bed on the floor of the Ark, gazing around at the dim torches lit, and the wooden support beams in the fiery darkness high overhead. Every open mouthed breath is filled with the revelation of us, which is the smell of tar and wood and animal filth, which is the end of mankind's evil and corrupted past, and the beginning of a new and powerful hope for the future. As I raise up from the slumber of the 40th night, I am drawn to the ramp towards the second floor, and then the third floor of the Ark, to where the single window is built into the side, where I can see the real world again, and watch the rain and the lightning with living eyes.

And even in the dark confines of this long and 40th night, as I open the window of the Ark, I can still see the raging fury that is the storm we know, blowing with the same uncontrolled anger from six weeks ago, as if having had no beginning we can remember, and thus having no end that we can see. It is as if forty days is as 40 years of this raging wind and rain, and at times, 40 hours is as the 40 days we have come to know. There had been times when it seemed that God's anger had finally settled, when the waves didn't rise quite as high, or the wind didn't blow with quite as much fury— or even when the lightning did not flash quite as brightly, nor did the thunder roll quite as loudly, and at least twice that I remember, even the rains themselves seemed to fall with less pressure, with less determination, as if satisfied that the breath of life was gone from the Earth, and the wrath of God had been diminished to a fiery shadow in the clouds. But seeing this 40th night fall outside our window is but a sign and reminder unto me, that the judgment of God is absolute, and his pain knows no earthly bounds, when the agony of his punishment is unbridled and unleashed. For the Almighty is a God of restraint and compassion, and when his mercy is summoned away, there is nowhere in the universe to hide.

And this sustained and fevered energy must take me back again, as I still see one of the three whirlwinds that guide us. I am reminded of how oftentimes, punishments happen over time, when there is too much anger to be given at one time—when the banks of the river overflow into the Valley of Rage, drowning the surrounding landscape in pitiful premonition. I am reminded of myself in the year of the comet, in the weeks before I married my husband, when I was still a daughter to claim, but a daughter betrothed to another, having betrayed Mother Adina to the core of her soul, she believes. I see the whirlwind outside the Ark

splashing through the ocean waves—rising and falling past this tall and elegant whirlwind to see. I am reminded of my grown up self, and my flight from the tall, elegant woman Adina, who has chased me through our tiny house in rage, where I take a clumsy fall to the floor near my sister Nora, who stares down in bewildered fashion as I scramble to my feet just in time, escaping only because Mother has stopped to find and gather the punishment stick, to finish what has begun an hour ago—this, all spilled over from a growing hatred that has overflowed, whose source is the underground river of jealously and fear boiled over, when I defied her and announced that I would marry Noah's youngest son. I scramble to my heavy hipped, floppy breasted feet to escape, bursting through our flimsy, thin-wood door outside into the daytime street, where the rays of the sun still shine nearby a cloud so high and billowy white, as to be a mountain of fluffy whiteness in the sea of blue. Underneath this cloud mountain, illuminated by the rays of an afternoon sun, I burst from inside my mother's house into the street while she gives chase—until she is suddenly upon me, one hand grabbing my hair tight, while the other holds and wields the long stick, as thick as three fingers together, this stick—and she proceeds to beat me like a stubborn mule in the streets for the entire neighborhood to laugh and leer, while they stand around to watch me try and hold my woman's scream inside from pure humiliation—because I *am* humiliated, until fear and pain take over readily, and I call the hogs forth with the loudest and deepest female screams they have ever heard, bringing forth the two legged swine to stare in lust and grief—desires unknown even to them, and sorrow that they cannot see but this once in a lifetime, as the daytime comet that has appeared in the sky, which plunges toward the evening horizon at night, burning in blue and white fire. They watch the

tall, heavy breasted woman beat her adult daughter to tears and screaming, watching her cut my white skin to blood.

Under the afternoon sun, beneath the cloud mountain, nearby the daytime star that will shine far into the coming night, I endure the great whirlwind of rage and beauty, suffering the burning passed down from Eden, through the motherline of our years gone by, down the river of blood to where I scream on the village streets, on fire by a flame so familiar, touching my soul in blue and black fire.

In this flame of agony, I stand at the window of the Ark, to remember when Mother threw me down and stormed away, seeing the lightning crawl gentler across the sky, while the thunder crashes in a fury of bygone rage, and the winds move the waves to less mountainous growth and withering. And for the first time, as the unseen sky turns toward the light of the newest dawn in creation, the rains drive with less anger through the Ark window upon my face, and the cold touch of the icy air grips my breath with less determination and power.

And in this final hour of darkness, I stand firm at the window of my refuge, huddled in layers of my cloak and garment the color of the bluebird's wing, cloth over my head, to protect me from the rising of the cold and frigid air, as the winds have continued to blow without ceasing, but without the same breath of wrath I once knew. And I am struck by a feeling I haven't known for many weeks, a feeling of hope and renewal, which makes me want to run and wake Noah more than ever, grabbing him by the hand and pulling him to where I am. But my instincts tell me to stand still, to be still and know that he is God. And in the midst of this knowledge and power, I stand at the window of my freedom in the darkness, my refuge from the stench of tar and wood, watching the water

valleys be exalted, and the wave mountains be made low. And I bear witness, in the moment before dawn's arrival, the last river of lightning spread across the bottom of the sky, followed by the last and quiet rumble of his Voice of Doom passed on. The clouds are now lit in quiet from within, with no rumbling from the sky or the air around me, while I listen to the splashing upon the waters grow softer, until I can barely hear it at all. And as the clouds are lit as bright as the noonday, flashing the glory of the Almighty from within, I reach my hand out of the window in the first sign of daylight from beyond, feeling naught but the blowing of the cold North Wind, and the tickle of a single drop of water from the air upon my skin.

The stars sparkle like treasures in the night, high above the nighttime judgment sea. In the third night after the wrath of God has come and gone, The Ark rests bravely upon the cold, dark'ned waters of still life—this being the breath and hope of every being adrift inside. Outside, there are no more signs of the clouds and the whirlwinds, but only the tragic calm of uneasy acceptance, the calming of the nighttime waters, and the shining of every star like a piece of silver treasure, like precious stones alive with hope and beauty. Among these stars is the great star that appeared in the weeks before the flood, that burned brightest at sunset like a ball of blue and white fire blazing toward the horizon. Now, it rests in calm splendor as queen among the stars in a moonless night, glowing the same fire and

power of its great calling—to guide us from the world we came from, to what strange and new world it is we are going to.

In this world thus far, there is only the glory of the sky in day or night, with the flaming blue star as our only great sign that he is risen—that the power of his mercy is renewed at the noonday, and in the fall of night. When the sun hath traveled across the sky in renewal, when it turns orange in the cold, my heart longs for its disappearance beneath the calm waters of our discontent, so I can see the arrival of the stars at night—so I can see the sign of the great star that guides our path across the waters, under his glory from the Second Heaven. *The Heavens declare the glory of God,* I heard Noah say, *and the firmament showeth his handiwork*. He worketh all things in Creation great and small, from the highest mountain covered beneath the waves, to the smallest grain of sand—from the great behemoth with legs as the trunk of a treetop tall, to the lowliest ant that crawls unseen. The glory of God hath set us adrift upon the waves of his wrath—which has blown the course of his might, until there is left only the beauty of Creation—as it pertains to the stars that rule the night.

More than I ever had as a girl or a young woman in the fields near my mother's home, I sense the power and presence of God in these stars that shine, knowing in my heart what messages they must bring. And among these are a group of them that rise high above the window of the Ark, nearby the blue and white fiery star that rides. These stars burn bright in the shape of a cross, I see, where I am told is the shape of our Redemption, as it was told to me about the crosses of lightning that once burned from the clouds of grieving. Oh, how I long to walk the field of dreams again, far away from the smell of tar and wood, nor the sight of wood fashioned as a boat! How I long to see the glory of the blue and white star in the day that glows after sunset, as the world fades toward something called the

Evening Day, where the prophecies of God burn the brightest in the hearts and minds of men. At the nighttime window of the Ark, underneath where the star burns bright and blue, the eyes of my truest love doth burn brightest in my heart and soul—this being not the husband of my youth, whose pleasure is the losing of his evil temper toward me over and over again, for no good reason under the sun. My desire is to the soft hands of my dearest Ada, whose touch hath been taken from me at the moment, though the sweet milk of her still touches the taste of my tongue in memory. My long breasted Ada. Who hath suffered in life such as I, which makes us both ripe for the picking, I suppose.

The firm breasted, tall and beautiful Seda could smell the fear on us like a she wolf when we both came into the Ark—Ada 10 years before me, having had to suffer under Seda every long year of it. My Ada is at least 10 years older than me, but carries with her a softness and humility that touches my heart in grieving. Not the shyness of fear, but the humbleness of a kind heart, burdened by the need to make everyone around her feel no suffering, and to do good to those that hate her, even to love her enemies, so that she hath no bone to pick with any other, even the mighty Seda on the prowl.

And even among the stars that twinkle in purity, that sparkle the light of the glory of God, as the light of one touches my eye, it gives rise to my body's impurity within, as it reminds me of a droplet of milk—a drop of white at the tip of the dark'ned circles at the front of Ada's breasts, where I have lain many a time in secret, and nursed her until I was full. How Seda believes that she knows—but of Ada and me—she knows nothing! Ada's husband Japeth, he knows nothing! And I wonder if even the prophet himself knows, our silver haired leader and guide into this strange new

world. Even while my back still burns from the lash, even while my arms still ache from the binding to the second floor guard rails—even while my thighs bear the bruises from the ropes and the scars from Seda's cane, my desire is still toward Ada, where it has been this entire year since I first came aboard the Ark, and where it remains throughout the days, and into the fall of this bright and fervent night.

$\mathcal{I}$n the heart of the Earth's memory, in the messages written in the stars of heaven, mine eyes hath seen the glory of the coming of the Lord, to rescue mankind from the wages of sin, and the behind closed doors depravity we are in. I see the youngest child of a woman named Sylvia—this child being named Ada, who has grown to marrying age already, with a softness and sweetness about the eyes, and a kindness that colors a humble expression. Skin tanned like time in the sun—hair black as midnight, with eyes that imagine to be the color of the sky at noonday—she is the apple of her mother's eye, the sugary sweetness of forbidden fruit partaken, the youngest and most beautiful jewel stone, in her mothers crown of poverty.

Two of Ada's older brothers have married and left already, and in the house are only Ada and her brother next to her, who is but a year older— shy and sweet like his sister, under his mother's beckon call and control. Not close to his father who works the fields—who sees Sylvia's youngest son as a weakling disappointment, likely not to even get married or amount to much of anything in life beyond a dirt field and a small space to call his own.

Neither the father, nor the son are aware. Neither the father, nor the son are privy. Neither the father, nor the son are savvy, as are the eyes of the Lord that stare. Neither the father, nor the son are struck with the hint of truth, that leaks from the mother's breasts as she sits with the top of her garment down, so that her large and long breasts swing free as she pulls Ada's breast hard into her mouth, savoring the pulling of them that stretches them a great length, before she releases them to flop back to her daughter's body. The two of them are half clothed in the noonday sun, shaded from the light under the roof of their home in private, behind the walls of grieving in secret—as the mother grieves to nurse her daughter's breasts until they make milk, but being unable. In disappointment from the many days and weeks of nursing, from the hours spent suckling them to swollen redness until they are raw and sore—this disappointment grieves the Sylvia mind—until she knows what it is she must do.

After dinner this self same evening, with her son Jeb at her side in the evening day, 10 years before the Great Blue Star, 10 years before the first drop of judgment rain—

I want you to lay with your sister until she is with child.

And this travels hard and fast through the Jeb mind. Touching him somewhere far, wide and deep. To touch him in a place beyond desire, to where the tree of knowledge grows in the soil of men's darkest dreams.

Every day for two week's time, the mother says—*But you will not touch her to caress her, nor will you kiss her nor see her nakedness—you will spill your seed inside her for seven days twice, to see that she is with child.* And this, the son does to his mother's bidding, where his sister lies upon her back in tears and confusion, as her brother works himself to sweating and a high pitched moan seven times twice, until the mother sees that Ada's curse does not come in this month, that she does not bear the curse of blood. But her daughter's chastity was sacrificed upon the altar of sin, for the pleasures of sin for a season, which reach into the body somewhere past the mind, to where there is no judgment or resistance, and where instincts are driven forward as an unstoppable force without mercy.

Ada is disgraced before her father and her brother, accused of having lain with one other in the village, which the mother makes sure is true—forcing Ada to lure him to a secret place, for one single time in sin. So that Ada's sin is covered when this poor boy is accused of rape by Ada's mother, which everyone believes because of Ada's sweetness. And this poor boy and his family have to steal away in the night—to prevent him from being killed by Ada's father and two older brothers. And all the while, Ada's mother revels in secret joy and glee, at what luck was had in her master plan—completed when Jeb suddenly allows himself to be taken by a girl in the village—who had always seen him as a kind and gentle, hardworking prospect for a husband.

And in only the third month of Ada's child in her womb, her brother is married to another—and leaves the village far behind, lifted upon one of the four winds to parts unknown.

It rains upon the just and the unjust, is the ironic message in the stars, and I see that even Divine Luck has no morality. It does not matter the individual, who it is or is not, for God is no respecter of persons, I see—and all of his judgments, all of his blessings are part of his righteous plan, and part of our unrighteous planning. When the thief and the murderer are not caught it is the same white rabbit that hops when the hard working, law abiding good man finds a good job with good wages. Over what humble abode hath the dove and the bluebird flown! At what door doth the white rabbit play, when the mother's luck hath put such a powerful smile upon her face, and such a perverted place in her soul! This, as she relishes in the beauty of her life, the beauty of solitude—the beauty of a newly absentee husband, the beauty of three sons married and gone,

and the beauty of her sweet and long breasted daughter with child, who stands before her now, the mother completely clothed, with Ada's garment down from her breasts and her stomach exposed, being heavy with child, and both her breasts heavy with milk. This is the milk of human depravity that flows through the motherline, when the mother must pull her own elongated breasts out to wobble free, then lower her head to her daughter's belly, to lick upon it from the bottom to the top, tasting every sweet and salty [inch] of her daughter's belly raised with child, until desire takes over to the purest center of her need, and she stands upright beside her daughter, and begins to squeeze her daughter's breasts in milking fashion, until the milk appears in a single droplet against the darkened nipple like a star against the dark'ned sky, in the beauty and wonder of nature, and the innocence of Creation itself.

The mother's face, the mature and careworn face of sensual beauty hidden in poverty—the woman's face washes over with awe and anguish, when her daughter's nipple begins to spray the milk in multiple streams, as the darkened nipple is raised and bulbous, to where the mother cannot take her eyes from it. She stares at the nipple flowing with milk as she squeezes, holding on to her daughter tight, watching Ada stare down at her flowing breast in curiosity and partial naivete, lips tucked in, but not in total misunderstanding. The mother's breathing becomes very deep and rhythmic, to match the rhythm of the milk, that flows in the abundance of her deepest longing and fulfillment. And Sylvia notices a curious sensation growing at the corner of her own body, as she studies the beauty of her daughter's eyes and lips—as she feels her daughter's breast milk wet her hand, as she watches this milk drip so abundantly to her daughter's rounded belly below, she notices the most curious sensation that grows in

her body, until the feeling flashes through her womb and into the rest of her, causing her to twitch once against Ada, which makes Ada look at her mother, who can only stare down in the same anguished wonder as before—still squeezing the milk, her lips relaxed now in the aftermath of a secret trauma, her breath trembling in a louder fashion. Sylvia lowers her head to Ada's breast to give suck, not releasing it until her mouth is full, surrounding them both in a single, big gulping noise, then raising up to kiss Ada firmly, and deeply on the mouth. From this kiss, she continues to massage both of Ada's milky breasts, rubbing it onto her daughter's stomach. She soon takes her daughter's face into both hands, and she licks her daughter's face in the deepest lust possible, washing it with her tongue from her chin to her eyes, covering her daughter's lips and nose with a kiss, until her domination of her child bearing daughter is complete.

And when she places her hand underneath her daughter's belly, touching her deeply, Ada can only close her eyes in a reluctant surrender, her brown wrinkled as she takes a deep breath. Her mother backs off for just a moment—holding her daughter there, whose body is heavy with child, and new desires forbidden and unknown. *Take off my clothes,* Sylvia says. And the mother stands still and in waiting, as the daughter obediently tends to her removing every cloth thread of clothing from her long breasted mother, who is able to take her own breast into her hand and raise it up to her mouth, to taste the contrast of her own milk and desire. When she is naked, she takes both her daughter's breasts into her hand, and she gives long and heavy sucking to them—letting her mouth fill with milk, then letting the milk flow freely down her mouth and to her daughter's stomach below—repeating this until the milk drips from her daughter's skin to the floor.

Ada stands still, looking down at her mother, then closing her eyes to feel the sensation pull up from her [groin] to her nipples, as her mother sucks, until her mother stops abruptly—*squeeze your milk into my mouth.* This, Ada does. Spraying the milk as droplets of white rain onto her mother's face, onto her mother's closed eyes, her mother's closed lips, then into her mother's open mouth. From an endless source of grieving, an eternal stream of want and need, Ada's milk flows onto her mother's face in drowning, until the mother must stand up and latch onto a single one of her daughter's breasts. Sucking hard and deep upon it without compromise and without remorse—pushing her lower self against her daughter's leg, her eyes half open to glimpse her daughter's belly, then closed to better see the arrival of Perversion's ghost at the gate, which arrives in flowing white robes of beauty and ecstasy. She breathes, she drinks, she suckles, she breathes her life's air again, until the feeling at the center of her body returns, and her voice grows a long and deep bellowing sound, which is muffled by her mouth clamped over her daughter's nipple, and trembled mightily by the deep quaking that passes through every muscle in her body.

In the heart of the Earth's memory, from this afternoon of revelation, from this daylight of mother daughter pain revealed, I see the turning of day into a starry night, where Sylvia and her daughter walk together in the field of dreams, until the mother stands behind her daughter in a loving embrace, wrapping one arm about her daughter's rounded belly covered in modesty, underneath the treasure of white lights that burn and twinkle through the night. This, before the rising of the Great Blue Star that was placed above the Ark—this selfsame star that I see, that glides us to a place

above the sea, to a place beyond the sea. This, the glory of the Almighty God. Burning blue and white fire.

Jonathan Lovejoy

And the waters prevailed exceedingly upon the earth; and all the high hills, that were under the whole heaven, were covered.

Genesis 7:19

Jonathan Lovejoy

Part Five

Jonathan Lovejoy

he God of the Heavens and the Earth. Along with seven other souls,
I ride the wind and the night, confining so much of my prayer time— my
alone time, to a place beyond the stars, when the sun goes down behind the
Horizon Sea, and the sky becomes invisible again, so that I can see the
truth that rises above the wind and sea. I open the door at the top of the
Ark—climbing from out of the bowels of Hell, to breathe the wind of cold,
fresh air that blows through the roof room, through the Hall o fVoices that
goes from one end of the Ark to the other, where there is not a single bird
of butterfly to keep me company. But here in the cold, carrying the torch
that is lit—I have cast just enough light around me to see the long and
lonely emptiness we face—and I am able to better see the small white
rabbit I could no longer resist, that has now become a part of me as I roam

about the ship, and as I come to the Hall of Voices to hide. And what exactly is it that I am hiding from, as I close the door in the floor behind me? As I cast the orange light through the upper windows and above the open sea, what hidden sorrows from below beckon from whence I flee?

My white rabbit holds court with me, and the sparks of loneliness that keep me company. I place this furry little hopping creature at my feet, and I am inspired to take the damp cloth the handle of the torch is wrapped in, a cloth dyed as red as the blood of a lamb, and I douse the flame of my distraction, to better see past the wood of the Ark, and into eyes of the spirits of the nighttime wind and sea. These spirits have drifted with us, in these many months since the clouds have departed, and the last drops of rain fell upon the roof of the Ark. *Leave them alone,* is the blessing that Ada and I received from Noah many weeks ago, when we had begun to talk and see each other again, when Seda tried to stir up another hornet's nest of trouble. And although our backs were burned with bruises and blood from the whiplash, and our buttocks and thighs were cut by Seda's cane—and even though the muscle and bone of our arms and legs were pressed and pulled and stretched beyond reason by the ropes of discontent, the spirit of mercy hath intervened, and our husbands and Seda have lost their power over us for the moment—though she continues to lurk in the shadows of our weary days and nights—leering at the two of us in a secret anger that burns her blood to lust, to where she tosses and turns in her featherbed at night, to wonder what manner of torture she will place at our feet again. And though she is but one and Ada and I are two, we still languish and lurk about in something close to fear of her, at the thought of confronting this warrior queen in the bowels of this war ship, which it seems that above every other man and woman, she is ruler of the night, and

of whatever fight that may ensue. I think that even Ham and Ada's husband Japeth are wary of Seda, knowing in their hearts what she may be capable of when they least expect it, maybe even while they are in their sleep.

But as I look over the beauty of the stars that beckon, over the lights that mark the whereabouts of the Second Heaven, I try and turn my mind away from Seda, the Goddess of Fear—and I am again enraptured, captured by the heart of the Earth's fervent memory, where I can see the lovely Ada on her back in the middle of the night, screaming and weeping the curse of Eve, to be delivered from the torture of childbirth, to be rescued from the pain of blood that flows when the head of the infant pushes itself free, and then the rest of the body slides screeching into the world that has come and gone. And this child, this seed of her brother Jeb, son of Cephus, this child that has no name, is taken quickly from Ada and given for *thirty pieces of silver* to a wealthy couple from the far city, who received word that there was a child of a beautiful young woman to be sold for not too great a price. And I am compelled to believe in the power of this number, that there were not thirty one pieces, nor twenty nine, but that this is the harbinger of mankind's betrayal, the harbinger of his treacherous dealings with the Spirit of God, and his choosing of money over love, and pleasures of sin over salvation. I see Ada's mother watch the couple speed away in their chariot, the bloody child wrapped tightly in a blanket, where Ada's mother relishes the tingle in her long breasted bosom, as she closes her eyes when she looks up at the stars that shine, in the hour before the first light of the morning day.

In the satisfaction of victory, in the tranquility of wants and needs met, she goes back into the house of horror, where Cephus lies sleeping through the pain of exhaustion and overwork and disillusionment. Sylvia walks

past the quiet man, through the empty space of lives lived and died to her daughter's space of post trauma—to where she had lain and given birth in blood. She places the leather drawstring bag of silver upon the small wooden table nearby, hiding it under a cloth dyed as red as the blood of a lamb slain by wolves, as red as the blood that stains the white fangs of a wolf in the killing. Under this red cloth, Sylvia places the silver in mild hiding, staring at her daughter in a longing so deep as to touch her spirit, a lust so deep as to touch her soul. As Sylvia stares down at her daughter who sleeps in post trauma, who sleeps the sleep of the dead, Sylvia dreams of the days and nights of nourishment, one to the other, when she will lay securely in her daughter's lap, and nurse deeply from the milk that flows from her bosom. To have Ada on all fours—so that she can milk her as a cattle of the fields—this is one of many desires risen and nurtured, and placed as a heavy burden on the shoulders of Ada, daughter of Sylvia, burdens nurtured and laid so heartily at her feet.

Sylvia loves when the father Cephus is away, to buy and sell goods, so that she is free—free to relax in the behind closed doors rituals and bathing, where they take much time in washing one another fully unclothed, to partake of hidden pleasures within. Among these hidden treasures, therein, are when she has gathered up their clothes from themselves, and they are together naked near the bed, or even in the place where they prepare food and eat. It is one of Sylvia's best pleasures to have her daughter unclothed and on her hands and knees, both her daughter's large and long breasts hanging free. Herself unclothed, she will gladly place two small, carved wooden drinking cups to the floor, and she will pull and squeeze upon her daughter's breasts until they are dripping with milk, until they are flowing with milk, until the milk trickles into the cups

in two separate slow and steady streams. And this, she will do until the cups are nearly filled, continuing for as long as it takes in the hour—even while her daughter begins to lose control of her breath, or when she may appear to have no feeling at all, but suddenly twitches mightily, lowering her head as though ashamed that she lost control again, and that her body betrayed her as to the violent pleasures she feels coursing from within. Ada can hardly admit to herself, that what rhythms her mother plays upon her body often devastate her, creating within her a rising mountain of needs met, stretching up, up and upward to a sky of infinity's lust and regret.

In the confines of her tortured body, Ada is indeed her mother's daughter, taking intense satisfaction in every nerve, in the chiming of every muscle and bone. Ada herself will often shake and tremble from her mother's skilled touch, whether laying upon her back in tortured waiting, or as it is this bright and fevered noonday, where she is on her hands and knees in private, as the village people mill around outside unawares, past the house and field—while her breasts dangle in her mother's hands and drip milk for them to sip. And when Ada's twitching and milking is done, the mother must often come down from the heights of what mountain she has built for herself inside, and she will move their ceremonial cups to the side and away from them filled with her daughter's breast milk—and she will kneel behind her daughter unclothed, the both of them, and she will slam herself in tortured rhythm against the back of her daughter for many long moments—stopping and starting as it is necessary for her own body's pleasure—sometimes in awe of the sound of heightened torment that will come from deep inside her daughter's breath in a quick, forceful wailing, where her body gave no signs as to what storm of pleasures were raging within. Ada's way, it seems, is to try and resist what pleasures there are to be had, but she cannot, making her body's reactions all the more

irresistible to Sylvia, twisting her own expression into the tortured precry, into the look of energies building as lightning in the clouds, or as the volcanic rumblings beneath the earth.

These energies take hold of the Sylvia mind steadfastly, as she holds on to her daughter's waist from behind, looking away and up to the ceiling of the house and beyond, trying to endure her bodies' separation from itself, and the ghostly trip through the roof and up into the fluffy white gathering of clouds nearby the noonday sun. Upon this, her body stops its tortured slamming against her daughter, as her voice exclaims loudly as to what power she must endure, as to what these forbidden fruits hath done to devastate her both body and soul. She exclaims to the heavens in trembling, trying to hold still behind her daughter, until she must fall forward heavily onto her daughter's back, panting out of breath from the action of labor, from the satisfaction of torment most welcome and endured.

Sylvia reaches over to where the wooden cups sit nearby, to where the wooden chalices lay, picking one of them up and drinking it in a gulping hunger, in a thirst unknown and unseen until every drop is spilled down her throat and into her body. She takes the other cup, admonishing her daughter Ada to drink, of which Ada swallows but just a bit, so that the mother can finish her ritual, taking the second cup to her lips as well.

*I*n the heart of the Earth's fervent memory, I can see the mother Sylvia at the gate—this, the gate of another of her husband's many departures in trade. Hugging him as a loving and faithful wife should, giving him the long and reassuring kiss upon the cheek, as he whips the horses and rides the empty wagon away, which will return loaded with goods they don't really need, and what few they need to survive. I see the mother Sylvia stand longingly nearby the road—gazing after the wagon as it rides away, with the husband believing that it is a look of longing for him, a look of regret for his departure. O Cephus, what secrets thou hast not known! For he doesn't know the look of tortured anticipation, the impatient waiting, the hurried and fevered wishing that he would whip the horses into a froth and frenzy, and hurry up and get out of her line of sight.

Upon this impatience, she waits. Until at last her husband is a speck of dust on the horizon. *Ada,* she says when she gets inside the house. *We need to go to the barn. That cow needs milking.* And this, she says without apology—with neither a trace of laughter nor irony, with no thought as to what doth cows and milking may entail. She prevails upon her daughter to remain clothed, whispering in her ear as to what doings there will be in the barn, and whether or not here is any milk there to be had.

And they go to the barn in the early morning light, on the edge of the red light of a rising sun, as the Song of the Lark sings a morning lullaby. In the Tranquility of the morning day, they walk together in the public guise of motherhood and family, disguised in community, so nearby the houses that watch and see, yet so far away from those that might wish to know the depths of hidden humanity. They go inside the barn, where the cow and the chickens and the pigs live and wait for slaughter.

Take your clothes off, she says, locking the barn door, unashamed in front of the animals nearby, as to what they might possibly say in their animal minds, through unknowing eyes that stare. Soon, the mother and the daughter are both naked before them, secure in their dominion over the animals, and their rule over them in fear and blood. With the cow nearby unawares, standing a prisoner of tranquility in her stall, the mother places her hand upon the fence, with both long breasts hanging over the railing, as Ada pushes her finger deep into the mother's backside, the smallest worm of feeling inside the mother, causing the biggest exclaim of noise she can make. Loud and long is this scream of false pain—a pain created when lust of the mind is satisfied. A phantom pain felt throughout the height and depth of her body inside and out, as her daughter moves her fingers inside

her mother, up into her backside, to cause her mother to yell in a voice of phantom weeping, as though she is being tortured to tears and sorrow.

And after this pain is done—when the daughter's finger is removed, Sylvia moves Ada to the middle of their tiny barn, telling Ada to bend over while standing, to bend far over so that her breasts hang big and long. Then she says *put your hands behind your back.* And so, in the aftermath of grieving, she watches her grown daughter, hidden from the light of the rising of a crimson sun, standing upright, but bent far over, with her hands clasped up behind her back. Leaning patiently, obediently for what needs be, for what needs must be risen and met.

Undeterred by the staring of the cow, undaunted by the grunting of the swine nearby, she stands up behind her daughter and begins to pound away, as if to drive in the phantom member of her body into the back of her daughter—taking her time, to see her daughter pretend to have no feeling, watching Ada's body then jerk and fall backwards against her, then hearing her daughter grunt but once, in the wake of what light hath flashed through her body again. And this rises what feeling there is in the Sylvia mind to a quiet fury, to where the Grapes of Wrath are stored, and she takes hold of her daughter's clasped hands and holds them together, while she slams her body against her daughter in something close to rage, until her eyes are closed in an angry expression, and the barn is filled with the voice of wrath, causing her mouth to open wide in this angry scream, from where before there had been only weeping, and gnashing of teeth.

$\mathcal{W}$e drift the cold waters of our discontent, in the sunrise of a new day. Not knowing from where it is we have come from, nor where it is above Earth we are going. In the six months since the last drop of cold rain fell, we have seen not a speck of dry land, except for what lies in melancholy regret, in the heart of Earths' memory. And we've all noticed the biting winter wind at the window of the Ark, but realizing that even though the air outside is as bitter and uninviting as the raging storm had been, the air inside the Ark is as warm and stable as what can be expected or imagined, so that we are not touched within by the blowing of the cold winter wind.

My little rabbit and I spend less time up here since the arrival of these winter months, being that this window room does not carry the same protection from the cold. But there are times that I must come here, glad to breathe the freshness of the crisp, winter air. Glad to see the world in the clear light of day, to gaze upon the waters of the winter sea, to watch my breath appear before me as a vapor of smoke, then disappear as quickly as it came. Today, I notice that the blue sky is hidden from our view, but not he same as the gloomy, gray skies that preceded the storm. These are the pale, melancholy skies of winter gray, that seek only to hide away the light of warmth from the life and sea, while casting a veil of hopelessness across the scope of humanity's final hour.

As to what hidden scrap of island that may appear, what cold and frightening stretch of ocean rock that awaits us—how can we possibly know? Or perhaps we are adrift in our home forever, where we will learn to live on what animals and grain for making flatbread there is—as it seems we may have enough for 20 years of this misery. But what of when the nuts and grains are gone? We will live high on the hog then, I suppose. Becoming eaters of meat alone, with many eggs and plenty of milk to suffice. I suppose there is enough edible life to keep us alive for too many long years in waiting. But it dawns on me suddenly, like the veil of gray that descends over the natural dawn of the ocean around me—that even the animals we choose for ourselves to eat, far into this unknown future—even these animals will need food to survive. And we carried no soil from the condemned earth with us, here upon the Ark, not even enough to grow the roots of a single fruit tree, nor even to shelter what crawling and creeping things that hide among us in the shadows, in the dark and out of the way places unseen. There is simply not enough food stored to last the animals

far into the years—except if we began to take food from the mouths of those creatures of no benefit to our survival. Then, maybe we could stretch the food grains and dried hay to our necessary infinity. For how long can these animals doze and languish about in half sleep, before hunger awakens their appetites to what they once were? How long before the many thousands of creatures begin to fully awake to the same reality as we, that soon, the supply stalls and storage houses will begin to diminish, and the devil of true hunger might come to lay claim on the last hope we have? Feed only the animals that are meant to eat, perhaps. Let the bloodthirsty predators die—with their glowing yellow eyes of instinct unrequited—let all of the deer creatures and ox creatures and horse creatures die, so that the cattle and the goats and the sheep can be nurtured and fed. But even then, how long would they last? How long before the storehouses of hay and grain go empty? Which of the blood beasts will be kept alive by the slaughter of the innocent, the hay and grain eaters—the beauties that walk in humility among us, wishing us no harm and no ill will? Should we destroy the behemoths now, before they grow to their mountainous selves, with tails and legs like tree trunks, and long necks that rise as high as the rolling valley hills of Earth's distant memory?

A glimpse at the rabbit's fur speaks volumes about the cold. This is white cold. Cold that dispenses an icy pain to the touch, that delivers a pricking of needles to the skin. It is a cold unlike anything I have ever felt, to remind me that for now, the Great Ship beneath my feet is my home, and yes, the Ark is my refuge from the bitter cold. And even though I cannot sense the coming of a single drop of rain, the air still smells vaguely familiar, with a lonely, dusty scent of approaching devastation and doom. It is as if we are reminded that the world has been destroyed, and God's

sorrow and regret is as wide and deep as the icy waters of the deep blue sea.

The gray of futures is in my eyes as I stare at the hopeless clouds—which bring to mind the infinity of gray birds of every shade and size, with their dull and lifeless feathers in every shade of gray. By contrast to them is burned in my memory the bright red birds that roost and fly about in beauty without vanity, and the birds of the deepest royal blue beauty known to man. And there are birds as bright and yellow as the flowers of a summer field, and the wings of the snow white dove, whose feathers are as bright as a fluffy silver white cloud in the noon day sun. Among these are the Creation Animals, I see, the animals that burn brightest in my heart and memory.

The crown of the King of the Beasts is the lion's mane, which makes him ruler of the jungle and the prairie. And no creature can match his strength in the moonlight, as he peers across the night plains, in eyes that glow with an angel's light. And the stripes of a tiger's fur glow bright in the forests of the night, as this cat kills in blood and beauty, wrought by the hand of God. And I see the size and strength of the great bear, with their giant curved claws of grisly intent—whose ferocity in anger is unmatched, and certain death for any unwary beast or man. And I see the stripes of the horse that no man should ride, the black and white stripes of what I hear is called a *zebra,* whose fur captures the eyes in wonder and awe, until the stripes are a dazzling and dizzying display. And last, I see the elegant and long-necked thing with blinking eyes, standing tall on thin legs of clumsy gracefulness, legs of graceful clumsiness. It stretches upward, its long neck rising its head into the trees, to feed upon the leaves of treetop tall. The lion, the tiger, the bear, the zebra, the giraffe—these are the five Creation Animals that burn the brightest in my spirit and soul, that testify of God's

grace in Creation, as the lion itself somehow bears the face of Divinity, with divinely inspired authority.

As I think of the feathers of the white dove, soaring adrift in the prevailing winter cold, I must remember to take a breath—for I am held in breathless surrender here, as I watch icy *flakes* of crystalline white begin to fall freely from the clouds, to gather as flakes of newly fallen snow upon the Ark.

"*N*oah!"

I hear the natural, ghostly wail of my voice echo through the bowels of the ship, as I kneel and lean down to where the door in the roof floor is open. I call once in something close to fearfulness, a shyness that I don't fully understand, until something in me brings a realization—a sudden awareness that so what if every man, woman and beast left in the world should hear my pitiful, plaintive wailing. *"Noah!"* I call, but with much more purpose this time—not moving until I see a figure at the bottom of the stairs. I raise up again, still holding my rabbit from days gone by, which is so much bigger and heavier than he once was, being that much more a comfort for me. Soon, the dark, curly headed handsomeness I married appears through the open space in the floor, climbing up into the cold window room.

"What is it?" Ham says.

Without a word, I simply look out the window of Winter's Discontent, so that he may gather his own words, and feel his own heart's nervous fluttering in the cold, winter wind. He walks slowly to the window, leaning both hands onto the wood, staring out at a sight we had all once heard of, but had never seen a day in our lives. Down below, our prophet, our leader hears the voice of his younger son—the word "Father!" echoing loudly through the ship, until he must leave his attention at the lion's cage. He cannot imagine what foolishness, what nonsense his youngest son and his wife could be bothering him for, in regret that he has to leave his communion with the Lord, as it pertains to something about the King of Kings. *The Lion of the Tribe of Judah*, is the mysterious happening in his brain as he hurries toward the third floor of the Ark, hair glowing, in flowing silver white mane about his head and handsome old face.

Staff in hand, which he carries everywhere as he roams about the ship, he is the next one of us to reach the steps that incline up to the big door, climbing the stairs into the room where we stand gazing out the window. As Noah steps over to the other window, Sara soon appears in the room as if from nowhere, as I did not see or hear her arrival. My Ada falls close behind, followed by her husband Japeth and his older brother Shem, and then at last, Shem's beautiful wife Seda, whose eyes are as cold and bewitching as the new fallen snow.

We all stand at our perspective windows, our four windows of grieving, where each couple is provided their own private view of the world. I am suddenly thankful that these windows did not allow the hoarde at our ship to get inside, knowing that the few that had been smart enough to use the trees to get in were soon gathered up by the wind itself and swept away.

"Its beautiful," I say.

"Its him," Noah says.

"Who?" says Seda sharply, in the true and angry bewilderment she is known for .

"You *know* who," Shem says sharply. Seda takes this admonishment to heart, as the memory of our plight re-dawns upon her in revelation.

On the opposite side of the room stands Shem and Seda together, beside them are Ada and Japeth. On our side of the room, Ham stands with his mother at a window. Beside them, I stand with our father, us together at the same window, as if I am the daughter he had never had, as if we share a bond of understanding—a sense of knowing that the others simply cannot feel, concerning the mystery of God's creation and the mysterious working of his mighty hand.

Seda is the first to acknowledge the oppressive cold, saying "Its freezing up here," as she turns away from the window of winter white— pulling her obedient husband along with her, back to the dim, dank darkness and loneliness below. Japeth and Ada follow behind them, Ada glancing me a look and a smile, to remind me that there is always hope for us, and that the fire we have is not quenched, and that our secret remains burning in the shadows forever.

"Are you coming Mother?" I hear Ham say, as I watch Sara turn with him in sorrow, without a single glance toward either Noah or me, disappearing beneath the floor of our new truth, until her and her youngest son are out of sight.

"What is he saying?" I say, warm white rabbit in my arms, as the cold breeze touches my cheek from beyond the Great Ship.

"I am," Noah says. "He says, *I am.*"

The Winds of this great storm blow without ceasing day and night, until we are at the dawn of the seventh day of this world wide winter, where the skies are in grieving for what has come upon the earth. I am the God of Creation, I hear, I am the God of Heaven and Earth—I am the one true and living God. I feel this drift through what is left of our Creation, as the waters themselves cry out for renewal, to rid themselves of the stench of dead humanity, the corruption and filth of what billions of lives were taken and destroyed.

The Ark drifts these icy waters with so much less speed and power than before, as though it has given up its quest for a destination, and is content to surrender to the will of the Great I Am, the will of the Almighty himself. And as the winds blow the snows of our despair high and low, the skies are

lit up from within in glowing white and blue, as the lightning charges forth down to every horizon, and the thunder rumbles in a quieted voice of remaining doom. The voice of God speaks in rhythm and melody. This, the rhythm of the thunder, and the melody of the lightning. And these two intertwine and establish their places in song, as a chorus of music plays the rhythm of the rolling thunder, or the rhythm of the flashing mountains of hidden light. These cascade above and below the melody of the angel's thunder, and the melody of their deadly lightning shears. All of this tumbling free without stumbling, in the glowing, flowing winter storm, which rises the snow that falls around us as a whirlwind too far and wide for us to see, as we are prisoners inside of it, and the endless gathering of them across the wide and windy sea.

For seven days, this icy storm has blown, until it seems that the Ark is weighted down underneath the piles of falling snow that have gathered upon it, covering the roof and the deck with many frozen daggers of pure crystalline beauty hanging down in places all around. Across the windy calm of the quiet, unraging sea, what tiny waves and currents of effort there were have ceased despite the wind that blows, until I can hardly see the dark of the waters at all around the ship, across the wide, white expanse of ice and frozen sea. The noises bumping and scraping against the outer hull have unnerved us these last two days we have felt it, wondering how it is that such a thing is possible, none of us having even seen as much as the waters of a puddle turn icy in the cold of a winter morning. As to the power of ice and snow, we are but listeners and hearers of stories, as some travelers and great hunters have told of their journeys to the frozen north, where the snows are piled as high as a man's chest, they say, and where they are melted in an instant by the fervent heat of the fiery dragon's breath. As to these stories of dragons that breathed fire upon the earth, to

burn whole forests of the north in blazing blue flame, I had never bothered to believe the stories were true, nor to even imagine such a thing as a land covered in crystals of snowy white.

But as the scrapings against the Ark grow louder, until it becomes a ghastly scrubbing throughout our dark world, I am inclined to believe that there are wonders in heaven and earth unknown to man, and I shudder to imagine what demons in claw and fang we have brought aboard our ship unknowing. What might emerge from the eggs they lay, from the calm of their long and perverted sleep? What might become of the ashes of our false hope, as we seek to go down in a future flame of grief and sorrow? I am burdened by the terror of sound that swallows the reasoning of the mind, as the roar of a great creature risen from beneath the waters, as suddenly we are all thrown to the floor of the Ark from where we sit or stand in great yelling and screaming, until suddenly the great, beastly roar ceases to be, along with the chiming of every bird and beast aboard. Only the breathing from our own lungs can be heard in the darkness, set to the rhythm of our beating hearts within.

I do not presume to leave our little living space, the room my husband and me call our own, to hurry up to the third floor, up my favorite incline of stairs, to open the roof of our judgment and refuge, our suffering and safety, climbing up to the hall of voices above, to brave the iciest cold the Earth has ever known—a cold so bitter as to have claws, that scratch and bite the skin with unseen tooth and nail. And before any of the other seven can disturb my revelation, I gaze out upon the seventh morning of this raging storm of God's wrath in winter white, to savor the beauty of a land of white ice from where the Ark rests still, to every gray horizon as far as the eye can see.

*F*ar into the seventh night, the wind and rages blow, until the Ark is frozen into this part of our epic journey around the Earth. I languish here in the hall of voices, gazing across the eighth turning of the winter days, across the eighth field of sunset, the first one that we have been shown for many days, where the sun appears as a great portal of orange light in the hazy blue sky, as it rips far below the distant horizon. It is the strangest set of sunrises and sunsets that loom across this eighth, ninth, tenth, eleventh, and beyond the twelfth day come and gone—for the sun rises low into the sky and hangs there all day, before it falls slowly into its orange self again, and slips back beneath the snowfield towards the night.

From the eighth day—after the snowstorm had blown for seven days and nights—from the eighth day to the twelfth day I arrive, to watch the daylight begin to fade into the night, as the Earth turns toward the evening day. The faded blue sky has deepened over the days, until it has become the deepest blue mankind has ever known—which has now darkened before my eyes to a violent and purple dream, where I can see the bright and evening star that shines, to rule the nighttime heavens over the field of snow. When I awoke early this morning, on our twelfth day frozen in God's immortal plan, I saw a vision of the Ark, resting upright in wooden beauty and splendor, the roof and the deck covered in snow, with many crystals of sharp pointed ice hanging down. I am a prisoner of this ghost world, in this ghostly reality that is us, the only eight souls left anywhere on this frozen Earth, waiting to either live or die. I watch the evening day fade into the night, where the few stars I see have turned into what no man can number, in lights that twinkle and glow from the top of the sky, down to every horizon.

There is one group of stars I see that always catches my eye, that will not allow me to gaze into the heavens without looking for its whereabouts over the snow—this set of stars is as a large drinking cup with a handle, that we used to dip into the waters of the fountain on a warm summer's day. No matter how hard I try, there is no other shape these stars will form in my mind. And on the other side of the sky from them, I see a great warrior, whose shoulder leans forward in battle, with three bright stars in a strange line across the middle, where his belt and dagger must surely be. These two groups of stars dominate my fancy like no others, except for the stars I first saw on my journey many months ago, that stretched across the

top of the sky like a great swan in flight, whose body and wings formed the shape of a cross.

Have we suffered so many things in vain? Of what power doth the swan bestow to my spirit now as I think of her, and the cross of stars that bears her up in my memory? I am burdened by the vision of the Ark frozen in the snow, and I wonder if this is the fate that God hath wrought for us— to live here in the ice field until our supplies run out, to take an axe blade to the side of the Ark soon, and open the cages and the stalls, and let the animals fend for themselves in this brave new world frozen in ice and snow. Already, Noah has had to stop Ham from working his brothers into a froth of folly and foolishness—wanting to tie a rope to the wood of this upper room, looping it through these two very windows nearby, then lowering the rest of it down from this tree top tall place to the field of ice below. Then going off on some ill-advised trek across the ice, to explore this new world God has brought us to. But Noah told them to have faith, and to wait on the Lord, that the end of our journey is not yet. *How can you sat that,* I remember Japeth saying, *when we haven't moved from this spot for almost a week? We're not going anywhere,* Shem had said, which caused Noah to look at him with good natured shock in his aging, blue eyes, as if Shem should have known better than to doubt the hand of the Almighty God, especially after the miracles we have seen.

The only miracle is that we're still alive, Seda had said, which all the three sons most surely agreed with, as they all left Noah's chamber room in frustration, having considered tying the rope up here without his permission, and going out on their own. *Why do we have to stay here in this floating death trap if we don't want to,* Ham had said as they met secretly. *We should go ahead and prepare ourselves to leave and go looking for a place to settle down—there has to be land somewhere out*

315

beyond this field of ice. We've come to the North country is all, and there's probably a forest of trees nearby—a place where we can build houses and hunt, and maybe even grow our own food, and raise children—and why do we assume that everyone's dead? There's probably whole villages of people still alive. I mean, look at where we are—this is solid ground. This is dry land, and we're probably at the edge of it right now. I'll bet if we got started, we could find a place to settle within a week—we've got plenty of food and water to take with us. Why don't we forget Father's foolishness after all these years and strike out on our own? Now's our chance...

I stand here in the Hall of Voices, hearing the bygone words of my husband's lack of faith, my husband's disobedience—echo the corridor of darkness. Outside the Ark, the snow field suddenly glows with blue and green light, as a veil of color appears in the sky like a great curtain of silk blowing in the wind, flowing above and around the stars of the great warrior and the drinking tin, shimmering in such eternal power and beauty as have never been seen underneath the stars of Heaven.

High above the twelfth night, the veil of blue green light shimmers the colors of Creation, waving like an angel's cloak in the chiming winter breeze of night. There is a message that sings in the whistling wind, as the snows begin to whirl above the ground, to threaten us with a blanket of drifting flakes again, but this time from underneath as the skies above remain as clear as they can be, unphased by the haze of the blue green light veil I see. This, the twelfth night since the first snowflake fell, twelve days after the snows began for us, the twelfth day of our calamity.

I stand in awe at the window to my world, so sad that the veil of light must flicker to its ghostly end, until every bright star is again visible without the angel's cloak to try and hide them. And soon after the veil of

light vanishes away, I notice the fading of the whistling wind, bathing our nighttime winter landscape in an eerie calm of waiting, until I hear no sound from the animals below, nor even the voices of human life that drift among them.

And from this icy cold darkness below, I hear a set of single footsteps invisible, coming for me. Sounding in rhythm and echo through the ship reaching the stairs, then taking each step in slow purpose and determination, as if to announce the death of Tranquility, and the coming end of the world I'm in. Appearing suddenly without fear, are the eyes of serpent green, the eyes of uncompromising evil capacity, the eyes of compassion seared with a hot iron. These are the eyes of the oldest of seven sisters, brought aboard the Ark as one of the chosen few, who knew not the whereabouts of the six lovely women she raised with her mother alone, nor doth she know to what place underneath the ice hath flown, into what land was so unbravely shown—of where it is that her sisters and her beloved mother could have gone.

73

The eyes of Seda take hold of me. Stalking my soul with poison fear, until I am held prisoner as a ghost in the wind, in the heart of the Earth's fervent memory again. Here, I see her, I feel her and her mother's epic power, great partners in the crime of their perversion. Daughters of Eve, tasting the bitter knowledge until their bellies are full, and their souls are filled with wickedness and scorn.

I see the thin, sixteen year old Seda naked, black hair down the length of her back—sitting in raptured and pleasured obedience to the bigger, stronger warrior woman—upright on her knees in front of her daughter, with only a small cloth tied about her strong, heavy hips, one of her firm and rounded breasts in her young daughter's mouth.

The mother's hand is down the front of the tiny cloth she wears, a hand in motion, to play a melody of futures, a tortured warning from the end of this age, that the pleasures of sin are for the season of man, and that judgment from one another is no longer man's to give, for the imagination of his heart is evil from his youth, and there is no hope beyond Redemption, which is the future mystery and mercy of God. The mother stares at her skinny-pretty daughter, her breast deeply and firmly in her daughter's mouth, as she begins to breathe and tense to a mild shaking already, though the lightning has not yet struck inside her body.

And when her daughter pulls the breast out, when young Seda releases the nipple in the hard, smacking sound, the glow begins somewhere in the clouds of her mother's womb, to wait for the sucking to begin again. And when Seda begins to nurse this pleasure again, the lightning bolt flashes from the Mother's hand to her womb, to her breast and back again, and she begins to grunt loudly in the pitch of grief, which is neither high nor low, until the lightning in her body strikes full, causing her to lurch forward, leaning hard and heavy against her daughter, who must struggle to hold her up, and keep her mother's breast in her mouth. The mother's voice grunts its travail, suddenly pitched low and animalistic, to where the masculine lust pushes through the feminine, so that the power of her body's rise and fall can be heard. She grunts this agony until it passes, until she can take it nor more, removing her breast from the daughter's mouth by necessity, so that she can lean heavily on the young Seda for support, holding her tight around the neck, and breathing the aftermath of this trauma. This, the trauma of a buried and repressed desire unleashed—exploded into her world like a fountain from below.

And this is the beginning of sorrows for them, for the seven sisters left behind by a father dead and buried—the beginning of the end of their hope and time. From this recruitment, from the ashes of this fire unleashed—the question is asked and answered, that yes, Mother, I will gather myself unto thee, and I will subjugate my six young sisters with thee, down to the merest babe of them, until their life is taken from them, until the light of hope is stripped from their souls, until they understand that to be born to be cursed, and to live is to suffer.

Yes, Juna, Goddess of Mothers and daughters, I will surround myself to thee. And together, we shall surrender all six of my sisters to thee.

"They're leaving tomorrow," I hear a voice say, which reaches into the heart of the Earth's memory where I am, to pull me back to the icy present day. *"I just came to tell you that your days of hiding up here are over."* And I notice a strange and powerful sweetness in her voice that unnerves me, an attitude of niceness that betrays her words, and the look of sinister intention behind her eyes. She steps up to me serpentine, without the smallest trace of fear or reservation, until our noses are almost touching, and she looks down at me bold and strong. "What Noah doesn't know, won't hurt him," she says. "I promise you Nela, that what you went through before is nothing." She steps up against me, taking hold of my arms against my own strength, pushing them behind my back without

effort. Then, the calm of a winter's night, she places her lips firmly against mine, squeezing my wrists with a power I would not have thought possible for a woman, until I have to cry out, but with a voice muffled deeply by her lips pressed against mine. She squeezes my wrists again, until I have to scream into her mouth, and she tightens the kiss, softening her hold on my wrists just enough to release the pain, but not the fear. She writhes herself against me just once, moving her head with the kiss deeply, then releasing it when she is satisfied that I understand, that I understand that what she has planned for me has nothing to do with a mother's love, but only with a sister-in-law's bitter contempt and hatred. She stands tight against me, staring down without shame, tensing my wrists one last time, until my eyes begin to water, from where the river of tears has threatened to flow.

"It hurts," I say. *"Please."*

"I know it hurts. I know. And you're going to know it too, Nela. Because I'm going to finish what your mother started. I'm going to tap into what I know you understand. I'm going to bite you until I can taste the blood. I'm going to lick the tears off your face and spit them onto your tongue. I'm going to make you scream while I'm on top of you. Not whimper and moan like you did with your little Ada. And I've got plans for that mouse little bitch, too. But not before I'm done with you first. Because you and me, we're going to get to know each other. And I'm going to teach you what pain is. I might even show you about pain...and donkeys. Or dogs. Or how about one of the horses, as if you didn't know. As if you didn't understand about putting things in your mouth...

"You play innocent. You play sweet. But inside you're just the same, whorish little slut they all are. Just like my mother was. Just like all my sisters were. I can see it on you, Nela. I can feel it on you..."

322

And suddenly, my breath is cut off again, by the deepest quick kiss I have felt since before the flood. *"I can taste it on you,"* she says. And with that, Seda backs away, slowly, then turns to go back toward the stairs, staring curiously at me. Looking me up and down, as if to try and figure out what I am, where I came from, and where in this icy world it is that I think I'm going. She snickers involuntarily, an involuntary laugh erupted from deep within and stifled. But as she takes the first steps down, as she descends to the darkness below, she laughs out loud without restraint—a skin itching, soul twitching, full blown witch and bewitching laugh that runs ice into my mind, down my spine and into the blood in my veins.

And the second she disappears below, the twelfth night is alive with a familiar rumble as thunder, though the night skies are clear and filled with stars. And this rumbling grows louder, until the ship begins to shake violently—enough to make me have to grab onto the cold window and hold on. And as if I am shown, in the dark of night, upon the faint glow across the field of white, I see the earth begin to crack open, in a line from the horizon to the Ark, reminding me that what was once the earth is no more, as the water underneath the ice splashes darkly through, pushing the great sheet of ice we rest upon, leaning the Ark sharply over toward one side, causing me to have to hang on to keep from falling and sliding to the other side of the room.

What is left of the earth cracks around us and breaks the ship free from its standing position, rocking us back and forth, until I feel that I may be thrown free of the window and out into the icy cold ocean that has reappeared far below.

Jonathan Lovejoy

74

As I stand beneath the Seven Sisters

   Gazing into sparkling light

   I watch the Earth Stars blaze a trail

   Across a fervent winter's night

   Seven stars glisten through the ages

   Above the rise and fall of men

   As eons rule the Great Beyond—

   Turning time and time again

   I stand beneath the Seven Sisters

   Underneath a fervent winter's night

These are the words that blaze through my spirit, as the Ark hath set sail again, many evenings after the twelfth night. The ice had rumbled and begun to break up on the twelfth night of our captivity, splitting and cracking throughout the night, always in a great noise, nearby and far away from the Ark. In the dawn of the next day, as the Ark drifted free from the field of ice, we witnessed the rising of the truth in the broad light of day, as another great line appeared from the horizon, rumbling toward the Ark where we had settled again as if we weren't really going anywhere. And up through this opening burst forth the sea in broad daylight, spraying wrath and blue ocean up through and out into the field of ice, spraying down across the landscape as great drops of rain for a brief time, rocking the Ark again to its foundation as though it might turn over and sink beneath the waves. But such a seaworthy vessel hath never been built such as this, I suppose, as the Ark splashed and turned itself upright again, floating further away from the dying bed of ice that had held it captive. The first break had come to set us free, on the twelfth night of our captivity. And then, we saw the second coming of the truth, more violent and spectacular than the first, spraying a line of ocean high into the air as we departed.

Many days past the field of water, from beyond the many veils of blue green light come and gone, we sail again into the unknown nighttime, guided by what messages that were written into the stars before we were born, when the Almighty had already known that mankind was beyond redemption, and was going to have to be destroyed. Somewhere among these stars I know, to have not yet seen, a cluster of seven sisters, shown to me so many times in my dreams, but which I have not yet been lucky enough to find and see. These stars bear the mark of a question, I am told:

What is the way of woman? Woman is wayward. From the garden of antiquity, to the rising of the Judgment Sea.

In the Heart of the Earth's fervent memory, as we sail on into the frigid cold and night, the frigid cold of sensibilities frozen rise up in my soul, of Juna and her seven daughters—mothers and daughters incarnate, the spirit of sinful jubilation, souls of secret corruption in glee, the perverted happiness that comes with the rejection of any kind of moral code, that code which inhabits secret desire—this code of morality, that makes one understand that there are barriers that need exist betwixt humans. There are guides and rules governing human behavior that must be observed, as Noah says, that need to be written down by the finger of God, then burned into the core of the human soul. I see the mother and her seven daughters, the oldest Seda, 12 years beyond sixteen—raised and nurtured in that admonition of the lash, until she hath learned of its whereabouts, whether to give or receive it with fervent energy, with the thunder of effort and the lightning of effervescent tears and blood. She is the prodigy with the whip, the cane and the paddling board—which hath delighted her mother to no end, having watched Seda take it upon herself to aid in discipline—to help her mother with all six tragedies of birth, down the youngest of seventeen, whose beauty is as the stars of a fervent winter's night.

And it is nothing for the mother to engage her own anger, which grows the lust inside her to volcanic proportions—which reaches out to her oldest daughter and grabs her inside, until sometimes, Seda is able to make suggestions how to make her sisters suffer more diligently than they normally would have, even down to the most unimaginable humiliations, which tear into the souls of the seven sisters. This, in the last year of

Seda's training and captivity, before she was unchained by the freedom of a man's love, and carried away to the Ark.

These are the last days of Seda the daughter, Seda the mother in spirit, the mistress of her six younger sisters, as her mother is mistress to she. And lo, what punishment is this I see, that must be conceived for the youngest daughter, whose beauty and stature rivals their own, that of Juna and Seda—having the face of such extreme beauty as Seda, and the fully curved strength of the mother Juna, but having a soul of virtue and independence, to where she is a young tower of sweetness and good, burdened by the need to be a help to the family, escaping the pain of the cane and the lash more than her other sisters. Saphron, Goddess of Compassion, embodies the soul of youth and beauty! But not being the favorite of her mother, who despises Saphron because she is good, who spits in repressed hatred to the ground her daughter walks upon in the beauty of feminine strength and virtue. And in her heart, there deviseth a plan to begin the final breaking down, the final unraveling of the cloth that binds, to strike fire to what strength of beauty there may be—this, the beauty of a Soul of Goodness, embodied by the face and figure of a goddess born.

I see the lovely Saphron, end of the world curves and bewitching beauty, charged by her mother to work beyond endurance until one day, exhaustion gets the best of her obedience, and she must rise up in defiance to her mother that no, she cannot sheave another stalk of wheat from their field until she rests, letting the pain of overwork come through the voice in disrespect, until the other sisters are a witness to the conflict, watching their mother and Saphron at odds in the field, until Juna grabs Saphron by the hair and pulls her head downward as she slaps her in the mouth, screaming at her to go to the house and wait for her so she can get the

punishment of her life—this end of the world punishment that must be—this behind closed doors revelation of deeds, of those things that are a shame to speak of. And this was a planned decision by the seasoned and mature mind of her oldest daughter, who had dreamt that Saphron was becoming rebellious, whispering this into her mother's mind under cloak of night, when they were engaged in their deepest perversion, as the mother had shuddered with realization that this is the beginning of the end for her youngest daughter, that the ring of her daughter's control must finally be sealed, that the circle must finally be closed and forged to outright completion. Live to break her down, Seda had said, and make the bitch understand who rules this house. Make her understand who is in charge. Who tells her what to do. Who it is that she must obey. And the rising of this new day has turned, until the sun makes its journey across the sky toward the long afternoon, when the other five daughters remain in the field. I see the lovely Saphron standing tall, in tears and pleading already, as the ropes are gathered and brought into the mother's bed chamber, along with the wide and unruly paddling board, which bears the stains of phantom skin and blood.

Saphron is made to strip down to nothing, to where her fair skin is exposed in the late afternoon house light, in the daytime darkness, where her mother and oldest sister too are naked and without shame, as they tie the youngest daughter's legs together—secretly in awe of the magnificent spread of wide and firm hips in such a youth as she, the waist of curved and cunning craftiness of Creation, to draw the eye to the corner of what form is woman, as pleasing to the eye as the line of plush, green trees that line the banks of a mighty jungle river. The mother and the oldest daughter look on in contempt, Envy and Jealousy, of the beautiful Saphron, and the

blessing of beauty they see bestowed—beauty in the face and form, whose appearance is like that of men's most fervent imagination and desire, of the fertile statues carved and raised to be worshipped and looked upon.

They tie Saphron's hands tightly in front of her, that what must happen in back of her be not inhibited, as the mother takes Saphron by the neck first, while Seda begins to hammer the wide, flat paddling board into her youngest sister's backside, as the widened hips shake and jiggle this painful course of their latest calling—even while stubbornness, shame and fear caused Saphron to stand stone faced and teary eyed while it happens, unable to allow the disbelief to come out in her voice yet—just the choking grip her mother has placed around her throat. The lovely Seda pulls back and upward, bringing the paddling board down in full swing while the mother holds her daughter up by the neck, which enrages them both, making them hold her tighter and hit her harder—until the mother releases her throat and takes both her daughter's breasts in her fingers, two breasts of young and perfect beauty, and twists the front of them without mercy, until the voice of agony within must finally erupt, and flow out of her mouth as the river of glowing, melted rock must pour from the Earth in grieving, in the days before the first drop of rain will fall.

Mother, please, are what words this voice of pain must form—as Seda knows to stop her paddling just long enough, so that Saphron's body may absorb the sting and fire of having her breasts twisted, which causes Saphron to break down to a pitiful and powerful river of weeping. In the satisfaction of tears that flow, the mother embraces her daughter's body in full, but not in love and comfort, but in lust and control, holding her upright and still, telling Seda to *burn the skin off her. Don't you stop until I see blood.* And this, the mighty Seda does with power and glee, holding the paddling board by two hands, concentrating the wood onto different places

on her sister's wide and ample hips, until the skin is raised and bruised blue and black, and begins to crack and split open just enough, to betray the presence of brokenness and blood. Yes, beat the blood out of her, Juna says, holding her daughter's head down now by one arm, causing Saphron to be bent over forward with her head locked in her mother's arm grip, while Seda wails the paddling wood tirelessly, as a woman possessed, the muscles in her nakedness tensing beneath her femininity, to reveal the body of a warrior woman, whose breasts are firm from labour and strength, and whose hips are tight and formed as those of a woman built for work and battle.

In the strength of her body's calling, Seda beats the blood from her sister's body, until the landscape of her sister's backside is a meadow of bruises, with hills of melancholy intent nearby, raised portions of flesh where the skin is no longer present, which Seda is not shy to concentrate upon, noticing that they cause Saphron to writhe and cry out the loudest. This, she does until her own exhaustion is apparent—then giving the paddling board to Juna, who finds new places to raise bruises and blood on her daughter's backside—even down to the top of her thighs, while Seda holds on to her sister in the grip of a lust more powerful than what she had thought was possible, a feeling that churns beneath the surface, as an underground hot spring of hidden water, that bubbles and boils with a power never before gleaned by the hearts of men. And Seda readjusts herself upright, so that the front of herself is pressed tight against her sister's bound hands—so that she may feel the pounding of the paddling board rattle her sister's body to oblivion, and feel the rumble and roar of horse screams pour through her body in waves of grief unknown. And as fate would have her day in cruelty—the mother ceases the paddling, only

the fewest strokes away from what would have sent the spark into the forest of Seda's wildest dreams, and set the trees of her lust on a blazing fire. The frustration of this woman interrupted, the anger and irritation hath raised the oldest daughter's ire, and she forcefully, gladly forces her sister over to the mother's low bed, lying Saphron down on her stomach, then straddling her back, telling her mother to finish her thighs, which the mother does in anger and exhaustion, allowing herself now to be controlled by her oldest daughter and told what to do.

Seda watches the mother raise and lower the paddling wood as a carpenter driving a spike into a wooden beam, grunting through gritted teeth until new blood is born, and Saphron can only tremble against the pain coursing through her body. At long last, the mother can raise the hammer of this no more, and she stands upright in strength and power, holding the paddling wood by one hand, body curved to goddess infinity. *The oil,* Seda says, which causes the breathless mother to look bewilderedly. *The oil, Mother,* which causes Juna to turn in obedience and walk to where the olive oil is kept, bringing it to her daughter. Seda pours a generous portion to her hand, then rubs it into her sisters bottom, deep into the middle, then she pours a portion onto the handle of the paddling wood. She opens her sister's backside, and admonishes her mother, *push it in.* This, Juna obliges, by the decree of her oldest daughter Seda, into the bottom of her youngest daughter Saphron, to hear the wailing of her youngest daughter take on a renewed hopelessness, in a place beyond despair, to where the spirit is tattered and torn, and the heart is cracked and broken in two. *Push it,* is the order from Seda, who sits astraddle her youngest sister, watching the mother push the handle of the paddling board up to its rightful conclusion, up to its unrightful place—holding it there, until they are satisfied at the scope and width of Saphron's weeping, which

betrays a soul of hopelessness and despair unknown, where there is no longer reason to push forward in life, where the journey uphill is too high and far to bear—and the burden must be let go, so that one tumbles back down the hill in sorrow and defeat. *Take it out,* Seda says, unmoved by the presence of blood upon the handle, and the new scream of pain in her sister's voice as the handle is removed.

Seda lays down upon the bed, upon her back, lifting the broken Saphron on top of her, where the hands that are bound are again touching Seda in her proper place, her improper place, as Seda lies renewed and ready underneath her. Get on top of her, Seda says, which delights the mother to the greatest lust she hath yet achieved, knowing instinctively to press the front of herself hard against her daughter's bruised and bleeding backside, showing the daughter's skin no mercy as she begins to bump and grind, to writhe and slam herself against Saphron's sorrow, until the rhythm of her motion is steady, and apart from her ability to cease the hard slamming downward from within. Underneath Saphron, Seda lays in confidence, in the renewed splendor that is her birthright, to achieve the rising of the Witch's Crown, the trembling that explodes into the body on its own. Seda watches the mother, she feels the mother's hard concentration and fevered pushing against her sister's backside, again perceiving the waves of motion through her sister's body and into hers—the hammering of the carpenter's mallet, the swinging of the woodsman's blade, all to achieve the means to this powerful end, to where the beams are held tight to infinity, and the tree may come crashing from high above, in thunderous revelation to the forest floor. And as the mother readjusts herself, as she grips her daughter tighter, as her pounding takes a purpose of action all its own, Seda's body can bear no more, as the ground beneath her opens up, and she is a creature

tumbling fearfully into an abyss, from where is heard the wailing of a woman in travail, as the waves of pain and pleasure erupt into her body in spasms, passing through her in more power than what she has ever known.

And this power flows outward, to finish her sister's descent, as too with the mother, as Juna is suddenly unable to stop her own motion, which transforms to a rolling barrel of feeling from her lower body and into every muscle and bone, causing her to tense up, and yell angrily the pain of this end of the world trauma into her youngest daughter's ear.

*I*n the heart of the Earth's fervent memory, I hear the song of the lark in the evening day, in the world beyond the setting sun. The seventeen year old beauty steps unlively, a trembling soul of grieving, who hath looked far into herself, to find the strength of life's renewal, realizing there is none to be had, as she looks to the evening star. She gazes into the nighttime stars that rise and appear, that look down upon her fear and grief with compassion. Calling her to a place none other hath gone, to a place where her Redemption draweth nigh. And in her heart, she hears that there may be a single God of Heaven and Earth, who hath called to the souls of mankind, but hath been rejected, and looked unkindly upon. Beyond this barrier, Saphron is taken, until she agrees in her heart that there is one God, the Creator of Heaven and Earth, and that she loves him with all her heart.

Saphron goes to bed in this grief, in this renewed wandering through life, having not slept a wink through the night, but passing into a brief drifting morning light. She opens her eyes to the morning day, to the crowing of the rooster's voice, which confirms to her what must be done, to where it is she must go. Saphron gathers the sharp blade, then steps out into the early morning light, far into the open field of wheat harvested away, looking past the grove of trees to the horizon, where the orange sun rises to a new day. She walks to the storehouse, where the birdsong doth call to her again from the sunrise, as it hath done the night before, as the world had turned toward the evening day.

She steps into the storage house of wheat, going to where the rope is gathered in secret. She climbs to the left of this storage house, to the upper place within. Tying the rope to where it must be, with the loop ready for her long and lovely neck to see. She undresses herself, down to where every part of her sin is laid bare, and she is one with the spirit she hath known. This divine spirit she met in the Evening Day, who hath beckoned her in the midst of sorrow, to take away her fear of death, and give her the power to do this thing, that she may not be upon the earth 20 years hence, when the first drop of rain will fall. She stands high above, with the sharp blade in her hand, and the rope around her neck, knowing where to pierce her neck with the blade, to bring forth the fountain of sorrow and blood. Saphron raises her hand, stabbing the knife through in bravery, her eyes closed, to not see what it is the cold and sharpened blade hath done. Then she falls forward, swinging high above the ground in loveliness and blood not kicking, not trying to breathe or pull upon the rope, losing the blade from the grip of sleep as it falls to the floor of the storehouse, above where the body of the young woman hangs lifeless and still, her fair skin tickled by the trickling of blood, as she drifts to where the angel of the Lord

335

awaits, to gather her up from her body's grief, as it hangs still in the sleep of death.

The eyes of Seda loom throughout the ship, in the gloom and fiery darkness of our winter sojourn. I walk and work and sleep and breathe in perpetual fear, wondering when she will jump out of the shadows like one of the raptors, grabbing me from behind and sinking her teeth into my neck. Oh, but what more subtle and beautiful ways hath she planned for me, that will leave me both trembling and weeping in the dark? I do what I can to avoid her now, which often means avoiding Ada, who has allowed herself to come under Seda's control without defiance, as if she understands that having Seda's bitter approval is better than her honey sweet disapproval, which is what I now have in abundance. Whenever we pass or come close enough, she never misses the chance to catch my eye, then cast something like a smile in my direction, one of such deep

knowledge as to be terrifying, with such dark and bitter intentions. But I know that already, she has turned her attentions away from me, and she is working on her sweet and subtle plan to have Ada in private, somewhere far away from Noah and Ada's husband Japeth, to work that which is unseemly, and to press and stress this end of the world sign before God in secret, that women are leaving the natural use of the man behind, returning to them only as it is convenient for emotional and financial security. A man is the money, a woman is the honey.

And women have discovered and learned the power of our fair sex, that to engage one another's eros is to engage the depths of the forbidden, which unlocks the secrets of our bodies' capacity for sensual pleasure. I love my husband, to be sure, but he has never brought such eruptive feelings from my body as have my times with Ada, and even back in the days of Adina, and my private times with my sister Nora as well. Men are to be envied, to have women as their natural object of desire, for the sensual pleasures of a woman are universal, and absolute under the passing of the stars at night, and the traveling of every morning and noonday sun. And I know that Seda has tapped into this like a tree root into an underground riverbed, where her soul is fed day and night with fantasies of female sensuality, from the Earth's fervent memory, to our long and lonely present over the sea.

I have already been shown the vision of Seda's mind, where she is standing naked behind a naked Ada, having Ada bent over with her long breasts hanging and arms pinned to her sides. This, I know burns the Seda mind to no end, so that she can claim her body's gift again, to bring herself to magical pleasure by the infliction of naked pain on another woman. I know that for now, she has left her intention for me on the side of her

chosen path, which is to have Ada naked in her grip and weeping, somewhere deep in the hidden bowels of the ship.

And it seems that today might be the day it could happen, as I notice Seda's mood darkening, until when we are away from Sara and the others, I see her grab Ada by one arm and spin her around angrily, then grabbing Ada's face with both hands to the song *"I have had it with your disrespect."* I suddenly feel the heat of bravery flow into the cold fear which is my soul at large, rising a strength and power within that I have never known before. I drop my basket of grain to the floor of the Ark, and I rush over to where she stands threatening my Ada, whose eyes are filled with fear and humility, and I grab Seda's hand, pulling it free from Ada's face, shoving Seda backward with all of the strength my body can provide. To the song, *"Get your hands off of her,"* I stand with Ada to my side—a woman ten years older than me, but who now seems younger in mind and spirit.

"Who the Hell do you think you are, putting your hand on me, Seda says. *"Bitch I will take an axe and sink it into the middle of your skull!"*

But when the warrior's blood flows, it prepares her for battle, the pain of the dagger blade, the glint of a sword, the flow and trickling of blood, the screams of a war cry, or the cry of agony and pain.

"Touch us again, and I swear to the Almighty God, I will make you wish you had never been born."

The bravery, the end of the world audacity of what I have to say shocks her, but not to a place of fear, which she is not capable of towards another female, especially me. Without a word, the beautiful Seda lunges at me like a white sabretooth, which raises me up on a rage buried deep, exploding to the surface of who I was before in sweetness, to create a woman of boiling red heat and hostility. For the years of pain I have suffered, for the years of

tragedy and fear, for the terror I endured in the early rising of the storm itself, for the raping she whispered into my husband's soul, I grab this beautiful woman by the neck and swing her around as I am able, being shorter than her but heavier still—slamming her into one of the nearby cages which terrifies the timid, deer like things inside, who scratch and run themselves mindlessly into the walls to get away to go anywhere, to be far away from the aura of human rage they see, the human blood that boils in violence before them. As I turn her heavily around, slamming her to the floor of the Ark, my vision is focused on the task at hand, to where I cannot see tears on my Ada's fearful expression, as she gazes onward, wondering to what fearful and gruesome end this must be. But while Seda claws at my face and hair, I am not distracted by it, focusing on my hands around her long and beautiful neck until I see the beauty in her eyes begin to fade, and the color in her skin begins to redden like the sky in a cloudy sunset. And I feel the strength in my body as it grows, as it climbs the warriors' hill without effort, to where she is now a lesser woman than I, a force inferior to mine—and I find that her strength and power has begun to fade, until I now imagine her body lifeless and thrown into the aviary, where the birds can pick at her flesh for the days that they see fit, until her eyes and her tongue are gone, and every piece of skin and muscle are pulled bloody away from the bone.

In the haze of this slow motion dream, I hear my name called, but to no affect, until I hear a sweetness in begging in my ear, the song of mercy that sings *"please Nela, in the name of God, don't do it."* And when I hear the call of mercy in the name of our Lord, it douses the heat of rage and murder in my soul, until I feel the spirits of Chaos and Discord flee, and I am returned to unblissful sanity. I sit still and strong on top of the

beautiful, choking woman, watching her cough and struggle to catch her breath in the dank, smoky wooden dark around us. I am compelled to rise up, walking to where one of the torches is lit, picking it up and strolling back over to where the woman lies in choking defeat. With one hand, I turn her over and sit on her buttocks, ripping the cloth of her garment down and away from the top of her back. *Hold her legs*, I say to Ada, who is apt to refuse. *Do as I say!* I command her, until she is firm at Seda's legs, holding them as tight as she can. Then, with the burning flame of the torchlight, I press it hard against her back in searing, until the flesh is burned to smoke, while she screams loud and long, in writhing for the curse of Eve, and the sorrow that womankind has brought into the world, and of what pain from it she must bear. In Seda's loud and fervent scream, I hear the agony of the future, the warning screamed into the annals of the new world that *mankind is evil,* and there is no hope without the mercy of God.

Jonathan Lovejoy

I do set my bow in the cloud, and it shall be a token of a covenant between me and the earth.

Genesis 9:13

Part Six

Jonathan Lovejoy

*W*arm winds of renewal beckon across the Judgment Sea. Drifting us far away from icy captivity, to where the breezes blow with the promise of summer. The skies are a deeper and richer blue than those of my childhood, I think, as if the heavens had been cleansed and made new. The raven that I saw many days ago betrayed us all, in the manner of his calling, I suppose, as I watched it fly until it was but a black speck on the horizon. But what hope of Redemption we may have had disappeared along with it, and we never saw it again. I can remember when Noah decided to send a dove, the snow white dove of my dreams, saying that this is the spirit of the Almighty God, and the last hope for redemption for all mankind. *What does the symbol of the Cross mean to you, Noah?* I had asked, when he gathered the dove in his hand. *Redemption*, he said. *And the dove is Salvation.*

But how? I say. *In what way?*

Only God knows, he had said. And I was there when he put both hands outside the Ark, and raised them to the sky. I was there when he opened his hands, and released the white dove into the summer sky. I was there, when the white dove flew. And here I am at the window of my renewal, waiting for my salvation to return in the purity of beauty and white, in the glory of his name.

And to my shock and soul's delight, I see the sign of the dove in the far and distant sea—flying towards us from parts unknown, getting closer and closer to where we are, until it disappears below where I can see. I hurry down from my place above the sea, down to the third floor window that was built into the Ark, to see the hope for my salvation, and what promise of life he may bring. And I must put my hand to my mouth, as my eyes haze over with tears, when I see the glowing green vision of an *olive leaf* plucked from a tree, held so tightly in its beak, to the chorus of weeping from every woman's voice on the Ark, and the exclaims of Thanksgiving from every man. And to the very first, I find the arms of the lovely Seda, and I hug her in weeping and sorrow of contrition, which melts what heart of ice and snow which remains in her, and I feel her body tremble under the weight of past sins forgiven, and the power of forgiveness which pours from her own spirit in epic weeping and humility.

And as the days and weeks pass into our history, we languish inside the Ark, tending to the animals in the strength of joy and happiness, and to one another in the renewed patience and tranquility of the Lord. For we know now there is nothing to do but bide our time, as Noah tells us to trust in the Lord and wait patiently.

The Ark

And in the dinner hour of the day, when the sun has gone past the horizon of the sea, we are all filled with a sudden terror, when the world we are in crashes to noisy oblivion, to where it seems everything we know is shaken and thrown about, until we are convinced that God has abandoned us to his wrath, to take up the ship in his mighty hands and rend us both splinter and board in two. But after a great moment of fear, we are settled into quiet again, gathering our wits about us, then hurrying up to our Hall of Voices, to the window room on the deck of the Ark, so that we can see to what tragedy we have befallen.

And when we arrive, in the fading light of the Evening Day, we are taken aback by the sign of his coming, by the bright and evening star, so nearby the crest of a jagged mountain peak, rising high above the Ark, into the starlight and approaching night around us. *Oh, my Lord,* Sara exclaims with open arms to the heavens—Oh, my dear Lord, she exclaims, shaking her head in disbelief, then turning to leave our observation room for the last time, never to return. Noah follows quickly behind her, as do every other soul, charged to walk away in silence, to leave me at the window of revelation, where I might worship the Lord with a heart of gladness in the strength of my salvation and my renewal.

*A*nd we watch the days come and go, as do the seasons, until the waters of the flood are abated, and the judgment of God is lifted from the Earth. And in the sunrise of a new day, we are all subject again to the power of his might, when we hear the force of a hissing sound, feeling a rushing mighty wind in the corridors of the Ark, as the door opens by the power we have come to know, and is lowered under a strength both subtle and unseen, until the door of the Ark is laid upon the rocky ground at our feet. And we stand in silence, fearful, unable to move or breathe, as our vision is affixed upward into the gathering of fluffy white clouds in the clear blue sky, and the great arc of color that rises up from the ground in

the nearby distance. From beyond a rocky hill, this band of color in beauty rises, as though painted into the air itself, rising high above us so that we must peer outside the Ark to see the top, then flowing downward to the ground afar off, as though it were at a place where we could go in thereat, and see up close where it touches the ground.

What is that, someone says.

Its his promise, says Noah. *The promise of his mercy. His forgiveness. And his love.*

And the eight of us step outside the Ark, to breathe the fresh, mountain air so crisp and cool, looking out past the mountain hill where we have come to rest, to the promise of what lies ahead, and the life that He has brought us to, and the future where it is that we must go. In the days and weeks ahead, we will open the cages and stalls and great rooms containing the life he has delivered to this new world, and we will guide them forward in a line that stretches from the Ark in these jagged mountain peaks, to somewhere in the valley far away below.

I smile knowingly at Noah, and then my husband, taking my dearest Ada by the hand, and we are the first to walk slowly down the door of the Ark to step foot on dry land. We walk a good distance away from the Ark, looking back in the spirit of Love and Humility. In awe of the beauty of the mountain peaks that rise high above the ship, and the glory of God's Promise in the band of color, that will rule over our departure from the Ark, and the line of creatures that will stretch from these mountains, to somewhere on the other side of his Creation.

The End

Jonathan Lovejoy

I dedicate this novel to thee, O Lord

I pray it is to your liking

I praise thee, O Lord, to thine glory—

For the gift thou hast bestowed

ABOUT THE AUTHOR

Jonathan Lovejoy is a graduate of the University of North Carolina at Greensboro, with a B.A. in Religious Studies. He is also a graduate of Liberty Baptist Theological Seminary at Liberty University, with an M.A. in Theological Studies. He currently lives in Winston Salem, NC.

For more info on the author's life and career, visit jonathanlovejoy.com.

www.ingramcontent.com/pod-product-compliance
Lightning Source LLC
Chambersburg PA
CBHW061315170626
46817CB00001B/189